THE KISS OF BETRAYAL

Evangeline felt suspended in time. She was aware of her heart beating furiously against Richard Clarendon's chest, of his dark eyes devouring her. She raised her eyes mutely. His mouth covered hers savagely, his tongue probing against her lips until she parted them to him.

Now she would be exposed, she thought, *as the innocent she was. Now Richard would discover she was not a widow seeking comfort, but a spy seeking to betray him and his country.*

But then as the kiss deepened and she felt Richard Clarendon's expert hands caressing her, she realized that what was being exposed was not her innocence but her passion—a passion more overpowering and perilous than she had ever dreamed . . .

And Evangeline trembled in anticipation of what discovery might come next. . . .

An Intimate Deception

An Intimate Deception

Catherine Coulter

A SIGNET BOOK

NEW AMERICAN LIBRARY

To Lörinc

NAL BOOKS ARE AVAILABLE AT QUANTITY DISCOUNTS WHEN USED
TO PROMOTE PRODUCTS OR SERVICES. FOR INFORMATION PLEASE
WRITE TO PREMIUM MARKETING DIVISION, NEW AMERICAN LIBRARY,
1633 BROADWAY, NEW YORK, NEW YORK 10019.

Copyright © 1983 by Catherine Coulter

SIGNET TRADEMARK REG. U.S. PAT. OFF. AND FOREIGN COUNTRIES
REGISTERED TRADEMARK—MARCA REGISTRADA
HECHO EN CHICAGO, U.S.A.

SIGNET, SIGNET CLASSIC, MENTOR, ONYX, PLUME, MERIDIAN
and NAL BOOKS are published by NAL PENGUIN INC.,
1633 Broadway, New York, New York 10019

First Printing, April, 1983

4 5 6 7 8 9 10 11 12

PRINTED IN THE UNITED STATES OF AMERICA

1

Evangeline laid her hairbrush on the dressing table, too tired to braid the long tresses of hair. Her maid, Margueritte, fussed with her blue velvet evening gown, smoothing out errant wrinkles with her nervous fingers and maintaining a chorus of good-natured chatter. The evening had been long and trying, largely because the Comte de Pouilly, a young nobleman from an esteemed and wealthy family, had decided with surprising conviction that Evangeline would make him the ideal wife. Even at her most distant and frigid, Evangeline had been unable to put him off. She drew a resigned sigh and turned at a light tap on her bedchamber door.

"Entrez."

Her father, Guillaume de Beauchamps, walked thoughtfully through the door, his habitually abstracted expression comfortably in place despite the late hour.

"Tu es fatiguée, ma fille?"

"Oui, Papa, très fatiguée. Margueritte, c'est assez. Laissez-nous maintenant. Margueritte, please leave us now."

Margueritte's plump fingers batted at a final wrinkle before she closed the door to the armoire.

"Bonne nuit, Mademoiselle, Monsieur." She curtsied,

1

dipping slightly from her ample waist, and retreated
from the bedchamber, humming cheerfully.

"Ah, Papa, *assieds-toi*. Sometimes I wish I could be
as bluntly happy as my dear Margueritte. Nothing troubles her. *Rien!*"

Monsieur de Beauchamps sat himself down in a faded
brocade chair of the last century, so frail that it creaked
even from his slight weight. "You did not enjoy yourself
this evening, *ma fille*. Henri plays the persistent suitor."

Evangeline shrugged pettishly. "If he would but realize that there are other things in this vast world besides
the Church, his acres, and the prospect of adding me to
his possessions, I vow I would find him more to my
liking."

"You must forgive a young man's foolishness. His
father is high in the king's favor, you know. And, my
dear child, you are nineteen years old. It is time you
took a husband. I have been too selfish."

"A commendable foundation for marriage, Papa. I
thank you, but no. He is so very un—" She ground to
an embarrassed halt, and looked away from him.

"Un-English, *ma fille?*" Monsieur de Beauchamps
regarded his daughter beneath his heavily hooded gray
eyes and felt a tug of concern, for he had spent little
time with her the past nine months since they had
returned to France in the wake of the Bourbon king,
Louis. Unlike him, she was not adjusting well to her
new life in France, or to the French.

"*Oui*, Papa." She sighed. "I would rather depart this
earth as an old maid, I think. Even Monsieur Deschamps,
and Monsieur Lafay . . . they seem so caught up in
such petty concerns and ridiculous arguments. I do not
think I like their politics, Papa." She gave a sublimely
Gaelic shrug, most unlike, he thought with a fleeting
smile, her English mother.

"There has been much change, Evangeline. The Bourbon has not behaved as he ought. Can you condemn
them for feeling betrayed by his foolishness?"

"No, of course not. At least, I shouldn't. But when they are so cursedly petty toward everyone, including their own countrymen, and mock the English, who indeed saved France, I must tell you it makes me quite angry! Ah, forgive me, Papa, I am tired, and my fatigue is making me ill-humored."

Monsieur de Beauchamps rose and walked haltingly to his daughter, his step betraying the stroke he had suffered three years before. He patted her shoulder and kissed her lightly, in his ritual manner, on both cheeks. "You are too used to the stolid English. They are, I suppose, a comforting race, if one does not mind being perpetually fatigued by their heavy meals and boring conversation."

"Now it is you who are too severe! After all, Papa," she said with an impish smile, "I am half English, a fact that you are perpetually pleased to ignore. And surely, Mama never bored anyone!"

"Why do you think I married her, *ma fille?*" He gave her a gentle smile. "Perhaps an old man should accept the fact that you are, despite his wishes, more English than French." His tone changed abruptly. "Do you wish to return to England, Evangeline? I am not a blind man, you know, and I realize that since our return you have not been happy."

She said firmly, "Papa, my place is with you. I will grow accustomed. But a French husband . . . !" She threw up her hands in mock horror.

His tentative laugh died on his lips. Both of them whirled about suddenly at the sound of a high female screech. It was Margueritte. Then came Joseph's voice, loud and argumentative.

"What the devil!" Evangeline said in English, and flew up from her chair. Monsieur de Beauchamps, his limp suddenly more pronounced, walked toward the bedchamber door. She saw his hand close about the doorknob as the sound of heavy men's boots thudded on the wooden floor of the corridor.

He backed away, and Evangeline rushed forward to stand beside him. The door was flung open and two heavily cloaked men appeared in the doorway.

"What is the meaning of this?" Monsieur de Beauchamps demanded finally, stepping in front of Evangeline. "Why have you broken into my house?"

"You are Guillaume de Beauchamps, Monsieur?"

"Yes. Now, you will tell me who you are and what you want."

The slighter of the two men slewed his eyes toward Evangeline before replying. "My name is Biron. You and your daughter will accompany us to Paris, Monsieur, immediately."

"We are under arrest?"

Biron waved a dismissing hand. "In a manner of speaking, Monsieur. I want no trouble from either you or your daughter. You will come with us peaceably, else . . ." He shrugged his slight shoulders, then nodded toward the other man. "Villiers does not like argument and can be most unpleasant if the need arises."

"But the king!" Monsieur de Beauchamps cried. "Surely he cannot have ordered this!"

"You are right, Monsieur," Biron said, a pronounced sneer on his lips.

"Then what can this mean?"

"Shut up, old man!" Villiers' voice was low and grating. "It is late and we must be in Paris by morning."

"How dare you speak to my father like that!" Evangeline cried.

"Villiers spoke hastily," Biron said, his sneer more pronounced. "We do not wish to insult such loyal royalists. We are merely your escorts. Now, Monsieur, you will accompany me whilst Villiers here remains with Mademoiselle. You will not be harmed as long as you do as you are bid."

Evangeline drew back instinctively, for Villiers had stepped toward her.

"You will not touch my daughter!" Monsieur de Beauchamps thundered, and shoved Evangeline behind him. "I will fetch her maid."

"Your daughter's maid is not available, Monsieur. Villiers will remain only to ensure that your daughter does not do anything foolish, and to perform any duties Mademoiselle cannot perform for herself. You will come with me. Villiers, we leave for Paris in half an hour, no more." He paused a moment and gave Evangeline a long, considering look. "Houchard will be pleased."

"Papa," Evangeline whispered, "what does this mean? Who is behind this?"

"*Je ne sais pas, ma fille*," Monsieur de Beauchamps said grimly, "but for the moment we must do as they say. I fear that we have no choice."

"Come," Biron said. He grasped her father's arm and prodded him from the room.

Villiers leaned back against the closed door and crossed his arms over his massive chest. He was close enough so that Evangeline could see pitted pox marks on his heavily jowled face.

"Dress yourself, Mademoiselle, and be quick about it."

For a moment, Evangeline did not move. Where were her maid, Margueritte, and Joseph? What had become of them? There was naught but silence in the house, save for her own erratic breathing. Her fingers moved hesitantly to the ribbons at the throat of her nightgown, then froze.

"Hurry, else I'll do it for you," Villiers growled. He uncrossed his arms, and Evangeline rushed toward the armoire.

She pulled out underclothes and turned her back to him while she struggled into the garments, pulling them clumsily on beneath her nightgown. The silk felt icy cold against her skin.

Villiers would have preferred to reassure the girl, to let her know he had not come to harm her, or to ravish her, but Houchard had taught him otherwise. Houchard knew the value of fear and shock, particularly late at night. "One never doubts your sincerity," he had said, "if you act the ruthless, unfeeling brute." He watched her shrug off her nightgown and fling a flimsy dark blue muslin gown over her head.

Evangeline's shoulders slumped forward. The tiny buttons at the back of the gown were beyond the reach of her fumbling fingers.

"Hold still, Mademoiselle," Villiers said. He stripped off his thick wool gloves. "Pull your hair out of the way."

He was near to cursing with vexation at the impossible little nubs when the final button slipped into its hole. His fingers wrapped about a thick tress of hair. She jerked away from him so quickly that he had not time to release her. Evangeline swallowed a cry of fear.

"It is cold, Mademoiselle. Fetch your heaviest cloak."

When Villiers led her from the room, dressed from throat to toe in her winter cloak, only fifteen minutes had passed. He shoved her lightly ahead of him. He was pleased. She had neither screamed nor fainted nor shed copious tears. He looked at the tangle of thick chestnut hair that streamed down her back. Lovely hair she had. He could still feel its silken touch against his fingers. She was tall, far taller than most women; but then, he remembered, she was half English. Yes, he thought, Houchard would be pleased.

Two carriages stood outside the Beauchamps house, the grays harnessed to them stomping at the frozen ground.

"*Non,* Monsieur." Biron's sharp voice stopped Monsieur de Beauchamps. "You will ride with Villiers. Mademoiselle will have my company."

"Papa," Evangeline whispered. Her breath whiffed back to her, white in the frigid night air.

"*Courage, ma fille,*" Monsieur de Beauchamps called to her. Villiers pressed his hand against her father's back, forcing him into the carriage. "Be still, old man."

"Leave him alone, you beast!" Evangeline screamed, and rushed toward Villiers. Biron grabbed her arm, and she struggled against him. He found that she was strong, stronger than any gently nurtured lady was supposed to be. He grabbed her elbow and twisted it behind her back.

"Enough, Mademoiselle! Calm yourself, else it will be the worse for your father!"

Finally, she stilled against him.

"That is better," he said as he shoved her into the carriage. Biron smiled into the darkness. He was delighted at her show of loyalty toward her father. She had become a little savage when he was threatened. Biron slapped his arms briskly against the cold, and tossed Evangeline a thick fur rug.

Evangeline stared into the darkness toward the house. She thought she saw Margueritte and Joseph peering through a front window. Thank God they had not been harmed. Soon, the Beauchamps house and its naked-branched elm trees receded into the distance. Evangeline lowered her head, scarce aware when the carriages rolled through the village of Vauchamps, past Père Armand's small cottage that lay nestled between the ancient stone church and the graveyard.

There had been no letters of arrest, no official uniforms. Nothing save these two villains. She raised her face to Biron. "We go to Paris," she began.

"*Oui.*"

"Why, Monsieur? Will you not at least tell me why you broke into our house?"

Biron gave her a long, considering look and, almost imperceptibly, shook his head. "You will find out in due time, Mademoiselle. Suffice it to say that it is the Emperor who has need of you."

Evangeline blinked several times. "The Emperor! Yours is a miserable jest, Monsieur. Napoleon is safely held on Elba. My father and I serve the Bourbons."

"We will see, Mademoiselle. You will now hold your tongue."

Evangeline sat back and closed her eyes. Biron's words meant nothing to her. This was like a nightmare, made worse because it made no sense. But there had to be a reason. She considered questioning Biron further, but his eyes were closed and his long, thin face set. She hoped for the moment only that her father had a rug to warm him. He had become so frail during the winter.

Gray streaks of dawn were lighting the early morning sky when the carriages rolled into the still-sleeping city, the horses streaming with sweat. Evangeline saw the Seine to her left and the formidable Notre Dame in the distance.

"Excuse me, Mademoiselle," Biron said. He leaned over and pulled down the black shades over the carriage windows. The carriage rumbled on for some fifteen more minutes, turning now and again. Evangeline guessed their direction to be west, but she could not be certain. She felt fatigue begin to draw at her eyelids, and forced herself to sit upright and study Biron's face in the dim carriage light. He did not have Villiers' heavy, brutish features, and he was young, not above thirty. His thick, black hair hung over his forehead, nearly touching his brows. He looked really quite ordinary, and not like a man to be feared. Whatever could he have meant about Napoleon? Surely he could not have escaped from Elba. And even if he had, there was no place for him, particularly in France. She thought of her father's words, spoken to her in private. He had decried the foppery and appalling ignorance of Louis, but he was the true king. The royal blood of centuries flowed through veins, fat and overweeningly foolish though he was.

Evangeline leaned her head back against the worn leather squabs. She had been presented to Louis the preceding spring when he had made his triumphal entry into Paris, her father a minor appendage to his impressive retenue. His return to France had signaled theirs. Evangeline would never forget the joy on her father's face when he had received the news at their modest home in Somerset, near Sutton Montis.

"We go home, *ma fille*," he had said joyously. "Finally we go home."

Since Mama had died the year before, her elegant and stubborn English Mama, Evangeline had felt cut adrift, surrounded by acquaintances who did not touch her. Even if there had been enough money for her to be presented in London society, she would not have wished it. It had all seemed frivolous and useless. She thought, upon reflection, that even if she had wanted to remain in England, it would have made no difference, for Papa had made up his mind. "You are but eighteen, child," he had said. "Your husband will now be of the French aristocracy, not one of these prosy, boring Englishmen who put me to sleep with their sluggish minds." She had not gainsaid him and she would have accompanied him to faraway India had that been his wish. He was all the family she had left.

In Papa's mind, all had been as it should again, to be returned to his homeland seemingly all that he desired. If he was disappointed upon their return to France, he had not let on to Evangeline. As to their vaunted position in the aristocracy, Evangeline, who was possessed of all the French common sense her Papa seemed to lack, saw readily enough that money was every bit as important as the blueness of one's blood. They had left the Paris of Louis and returned to Vauchamps, to live in a small house near the once great château that had belonged to Grandfather.

It seemed, upon inquiry, that a rich bourgeois banker now owned the château. Louis was content to leave matters as they were. And Papa, well, he was content to be home once again.

"Wake up, Mademoiselle. We have arrived."

Evangeline blinked away her memories and sat up.

Biron raised the black shades, and dull gray morning light flooded the carriage. Evangeline peered out the window, but had no idea where in Paris they were. The horses came to a halt in front of a tall stone building that looked as bleak as the winter day. It stood on a narrow street, covered with melting snow that ran in black rivulets into the gutters. There were few people about, and all of them, she realized, were men, dressed soberly, heavy scarves about their throats to protect them from the stiff winter wind.

She had scarce time to look about, for Biron prodded her forward. She saw the other carriage pull up some distance behind, and though Biron pushed her toward the narrow front door, she resisted until she saw her father, looking tired and drawn, step down.

"Papa!" she called.

He looked up and smiled at her. His white hair was disheveled and his slender shoulders were hunched forward in fatigue. His fine gray eyes, so lively with intelligence, looked worried and questioning.

"He will be taken care of, Mademoiselle," Biron said, his voice softening slightly.

"If any harm comes to him, I will kill you."

Biron's head snapped back and he stared at her. Her voice was calm, deadly calm, and he was surprised to feel gooseflesh rise on his arms. He heard himself give a nervous laugh. Because she made him doubt himself, he tightened his grip on her arm until he knew that he was causing her pain.

No royal palace this, Evangeline thought, looking around her. Roughly clad men milled about the long, wide, dim-lit corridor inside the vast building. They were all armed, and to Evangeline's eyes, they looked uncaring and hard. She heard low, muted whispers among them as she passed.

"Is this place a prison?"

"No, merely a place where men of like principles have come together."

"If they have principles such as you have demonstrated, Monsieur, we must cry for the future of France."

"You have a sharp tongue, Mademoiselle."

"At least, Monsieur, it is an honest one."

Biron looked at her profile. He knew that she must be frightened, but she looked haughtily proud, even arrogant. For a moment, he felt familiar hatred for her and all her kind pulse through his veins. They had once rid France of her kind and would do so again. Houchard would break her; Houchard could break the Pope himself.

They came to the end of the long, windowless corridor. Biron nodded to a man who stood at attention beside a set of double doors. The man turned and rapped lightly.

"*Entrez.*"

The man opened the door and Biron, his anger at her still sharp, pushed her roughly inside.

Evangeline found herself in a dingy room, long and narrow, filled with dark, old-fashioned furniture of the last century. Windows, small and square, were set high on the outside wall, crusted with years of grime. At the end of the room stood a large mahogany desk, a fine piece that contrasted starkly with the other furniture, neat stacks of paper, maps, and books piled on its polished surface. As she approached, she saw a man move from the shadows to stand beside the desk, a man who reminded Evangeline of a Spanish priest she had seen in a painting about the *autos-da-fé* in the fifteenth century, a man who knew he held power and accepted it as a mission from God. His face was thin to the point of gauntness. Despite the current fashion, he wore a pointed beard that elongated his face even more. She met his eyes, dark and wide-set, and they held her. They were expressionless, holding no surprise or question, yet she could see intelligence in them, and purpose. He was dressed soberly, like any of the countless functionaries who inhabited Paris. He bowed politely toward her.

"Mademoiselle de Beauchamps."

His voice was deeply resonant, strangely compelling. She nodded.

His eyes flickered toward Biron. "You have done well. Monsieur is safely with us?"

"*Oui.*"

"You may leave us now, Jules. Mademoiselle and I have much to discuss."

Evangeline saw Biron nod respectfully to Houchard and quietly leave the room. The door grated loudly shut behind her.

"My name is Gaspard Houchard, Mademoiselle. *Asseyez-vous, s'il vous plaît.*"

Evangeline remained standing. "What have you done with my father?"

"Your father is quite safe, Mademoiselle. He is at this moment undoubtedly resting after your fatiguing journey."

She looked at him, anger rising in her at his calmly dismissing reply. "Monsieur, you will forgive my stupidity. Your ruffians broke into our house, forced us to come in the dead of night to Paris, and now, you speak in riddles, after, I daresay, you have spent the night soundly sleeping in your bed."

Monsieur Houchard's thin mouth parted into a pained smile. "I was told that you carry your father's intelligence. You have thus far not disappointed me. I trust also that you are endowed with reason, Mademoiselle. You are fatigued. I will allow you to rest after I have satisfied myself that you understand fully what is expected of you."

"I was raised, as you undoubtedly know, Monsieur, in England. The French always prate that it is the English who speak in laborious circles. You are proving that that is not at all the case."

Monsieur Houchard did not again smile. "Very well, Mademoiselle. Let me make myself quite plain. You have been brought here for a purpose. You will do exactly as I tell you, else your father will suffer the fate of many of his royalist friends and be guillotined as a traitor."

"You are mad, Monsieur! There is nothing I could possibly do for you. Perhaps your brutish spies misinformed you. It must be someone else you wish. As to my father, his fault as I perceive from your henchman, Biron, is that of wishing to live quietly in his homeland."

Monsieur Houchard sat back in his chair. He pursed his thin lips thoughtfully as he gazed at the girl in front of him. Though he deplored her arrogance, she was showing courage beyond her years, and he gave her credit for the strength she obviously possessed. And she was undeniably lovely. It appeared that she was everything he had hoped for.

"*Non*, Mademoiselle. My spies did not misinform me. You are Evangeline de Beauchamps, only child of Guillaume de Beauchamps. Your mother was Louise Sellington, eldest daughter of the Baron Torrville. Your father's elder brother was the Marquis de Crécy, a greedy, rapacious nobleman who escaped the guillotine and fled to England with your father, a king's ransom worth of jewels in his possession. His daughter, Marissa, married the Marquis of Arysdale——"

Evangeline raised a haughty brow. "Really, Monsieur, your knowledge of my family is most edifying. As to my uncle, his supposed rapaciousness is your own twisted notion. If you have a point, I pray that you will soon make it."

"You begin to try my patience, Mademoiselle," Houchard said in a cold voice. "You will sit down and keep your mouth tightly closed, else I will have Biron stuff a dirty cloth in it."

It was the indifferent, detached tone of his voice that made Evangeline believe him. She tried to still the twist of fear he made her feel. "Very well, Monsieur," she said, and sat on the edge of the chair. She winced at the slight grin of satisfaction about his mouth.

"Marissa, your lovely first cousin, as I said, wed the Marquis of Arysdale. She gave him one son, then died two and a half years ago. The Marquis is now the Duke of Portsmouth, a powerful and quite wealthy English peer. And you, my dear Mademoiselle, are related to the duke."

Evangeline raised wide, uncomprehending eyes to Monsieur Houchard's face. "I do not understand. What you have said is true. But I have not seen the duke since his marriage to my cousin some six years ago."

"I intend that you will see him again, very soon. But I move too swiftly. Perhaps you have guessed, Mademoiselle, that this place—" he waved a thin arm about him—"is not known to the Bourbon. We work for the Emperor, the rightful ruler of France."

Evangeline repeated dully what she had said to Biron. "Napoleon is on Elba, Monsieur. Hopefully, he will rot there. My father and I returned to France only when we knew it would be safe from that Corsican monster."

"You tempt me to cut your throat, Mademoiselle." He saw her draw instinctively back in her chair and moderated his voice, pleased. "I do not particularly care what you think of Napoleon. It is really unimportant. I will tell you, since it makes no difference, that he is at this moment near France. He will be in residence very shortly in the Tuileries and that buffoon, Louis, will remove his worthless carcass from France for the last time."

"That is not possible! You rant nonsense, Monsieur! France has suffered too much under that madman's rule! Never would the French allow him to return!"

He gave her a thin smile, one filled with contempt at her naiveté.

"There are many men, men in extraordinarily high places, who have worked to put the Emperor back on his throne. And you, my proud lady, have you any great love for that fool, Louis? Has he not in the past brief months turned France into a gutter ruled by rapacious aristocrats and gluttonous churchmen, whose only purpose is to ravage the land? Has he shown any love for the French, for the glory and honor of France?"

"He is an old man, Monsieur, foolish and given to flattery. But he is France's rightful ruler! At least he does not seek to slaughter the sons of his country on foreign soil to feed his unending lust for power! Not only did Napoleon ravish France, Monsieur, he ravished all of Europe!"

Monsieur Houchard gave a growl of laughter, but his voice when he finally spoke was hard and devoid of emotion. "I marvel at the ignorant prattle of your kind. And I think I hear the insufferably hypocritical dogma of the English aristocracy. Suffice it to say that our Emperor will once again rule Europe, and this time he will not fail. No, spare me more of your political zeal, Mademoiselle. I care not what you think. Let us return to your purpose."

Evangeline shook her head. "As you will, Monsieur. You said that I would see the duke again. I do not understand why you would possibly want that."

Monsieur Houchard tapped his long fingers together and began to recite what seemed to Evangeline like a prepared speech. "The duke's ancestral estate is, of course, near Portsmouth. It is called Chesleigh Castle, and is of considerable antiquity. It commands a vast holding of land as well as a long stretch of secluded private beach. This will be your setting; now to your purpose. We have an Englishman in the English Ministry, placed high enough so that he has access to much of the information we need to judge the intentions of the English. His name is John Edgerton, Sir John Edgerton." At her look of shock, he smiled. "Ah, yes, you know him, do you not, Mademoiselle? You displeased him it would seem, rejected his quite honorable advances two years ago. It was he who suggested that you would be ideal for our purpose. But I digress. Sir John Edgerton has worked in the past for Napoleon, used his power to aid the Emperor. However, on two occasions he was very nearly found out and destroyed. It seems that one of his couriers was greedy and laid himself open to a bribe. His throat was slit barely in time. The other man turned out to be a patriot, one of those damnable martyrs to whom life means nothing.

"In any case, Sir John is now justifiably concerned. He will continue to be useful to us only if he can be assured his troubles will not be repeated. In short, Mademoiselle, he wants someone who is uncorruptible, someone who cannot be bribed, someone who would die before betraying him. He believes that you will be ideal. I see that you still do not understand. Your brain is fogged with fear for your father and with fatigue. I will allow you to rest in but a few minutes. But now, attend me closely. With the return of our Emperor, the movement of vital information in and out of England is critical to our cause.

"The duke's private beach would be suspected by no one, since the duke himself is above suspicion. Nor, Mademoiselle, would a close relation of the duke's merit any undue scrutiny. You will first return to England. Then, Mademoiselle, you will install yourself in the duke's home, become a valued and trusted member of his household, and carefully follow the instructions that Sir John and I will provide you."

Evangeline looked at him stupidly. Sir John Edgerton a spy! The quiet, elegant gentleman whom she had regarded as something akin to an uncle. It was true that he had asked her father's permission to pay her his addresses, but her father had believed him much too old for a girl of seventeen. She raised wary eyes to Monsieur Houchard's face.

"But Sir John is so very English. I cannot believe that he would willingly be a traitor to his country."

"Nonetheless, it is true. And you, my dear Mademoiselle, will work for him."

"You want me to be a spy? To help my enemies carry their information in and out of England?"

"Your position is far more important than that. You will be the go-between. You will examine the men's papers and verify that they are who they claim to be. Further, when our agents land on the duke's very private beach, you will be their only link to Edgerton. In return, I will protect your father from those who would wish his neck severed from his body."

"You are mad, Monsieur, quite mad! It is impossible! It is doubtful that the duke would even remember me. If you have investigated my family so thoroughly, you must know that there was some sort of falling out between my uncle and the old duke. I have not seen the present duke since the day he wed my cousin."

Monsieur Houchard rose slowly from his chair, hovering over his desk like a gaunt black vulture, a beast of prey. "I am not mad, Mademoiselle, not in the least. I have a mission to accomplish, and you will obey me. Now, to be exact, you have not seen the present duke since you were thirteen years of age."

A rough image of Richard Clarendon came to her mind's eye, an image that was six years old. She remembered an extraordinarily handsome man who had been amusing and even kind to her, an ungainly child as tall as Marissa, and painfully thin. She mustered contempt into her voice. "You know that I would do anything to protect my father, Monsieur. However, I am not, like you, blinded by fanaticism. Your plot is insane. It cannot work. Would you kill my father and me because of the failure of such an outrageous scheme?"

Monsieur Houchard was smiling. "Allow me to continue, Mademoiselle. It is likely that you have been protected from the present duke's reputation. He is what the English call a Corinthian. More than that, he is very fond of women. I was delighted to find you as lovely as my reports said. A poor, indigent relation, and a beautiful woman, he will not turn away from Chesleigh.

To comply with English propriety, you will not present yourself as a young unmarried lady, but rather as a widow. Thus, there will be no need for a meddlesome chaperone. You are a poor widow, Madame de la Valette, to be exact. Your charming husband, Henri Naigeon, did, in fact, exist. However, he lost his head and his life in a duel over a lady. The past I have created for you is quite acceptable, *je vous assure*. If there is ever any suspicion about you, rest assured that you will not be undone. *Our* truth about you and who you are will be verified immediately. I would add finally that if you are not to the duke's liking, he is still an Englishman. His English honor would forbid him to behave shabbily toward you, a kinswoman."

Evangeline felt the color drain from her face. She had underestimated him. She was to be his cat's paw, the duke her dupe.

"Papa."

"You will see your father before you set sail for England, not before. Never forget that he is a weak old man. It would be wise for you not to tell him what you will be doing. Remember, Mademoiselle, it is the life of a loved one in the balance, not an abstract patriotic principle."

Evangeline ran her tongue over dry lips. "How will I know that you will keep him safe once I am in England?"

"I trust you know your sire's hand. My men will bring you letters from him."

"I do not trust you."

"I am a man with a mission, with obligations, Mademoiselle. It would give me no pleasure to send a rotting old man's soul to his maker. Now, we have much work to do and little time. I require your answer, Mademoiselle."

Evangeline looked up at him with dulled eyes. "I do not see that I have any choice."

"You are right, of course. To ease your conscience,

Mademoiselle, know always that you are saving your father's life by doing exactly as you're told."

Slowly, she nodded. She closed her eyes against the sight of him, standing behind his functionary's desk, his eyes glittering and a thin, pleased smile on his lips.

2

Richard Chesleigh St. John Clarendon, the Duke of Portsmouth, tooled his matched bays up the serpentine gravel drive of his ancestral home, Chesleigh Castle, and brought them to a steaming halt in front of the wide stone portico. He sniffed the tangy salt air and gazed upward for an instant at the squawking sea birds that flew overhead before he jumped gracefully down from his curricle and tossed the reins to his tiger, Juniper.

"Stable 'em," he said, his tone curt. "We'll not be going out again today." He was brought up short by a sudden hacking cough from his tiger and turned abruptly to face him. "What the devil ails you, Juniper?" He thwacked his flushed tiger between his narrow shoulder blades.

"Thank you, your grace," Juniper managed at last, wiping his watery eyes with the sleeve of his crimson livery coat.

"Well?"

Juniper knew quite well what ailed him, but his master was in a black mood, and he only said, " 'Tis just a touch of the influenza, your grace." He looked hopefully up at the duke, a giant of a man whose health was every bit as hardy as his physique suggested. Spending an afternoon in an open curricle was an exhilarating experience for the master, in spite of the damp air and howling wind from the Channel that chilled Juniper to the marrow of his thin bones.

The duke frowned down at him a moment, his dark eyes narrowed, and turned when the great oak front doors were flung open by his white-haired butler.

"Send Murdock out here, Bassick!"

Scarce an instant passed before a tall red-headed footman, impressive in his crimson and gold livery, appeared at the duke's side.

"Take care of the horses, Murdock." As the footman relieved Juniper of the reins, the duke said, "To bed with you, Juniper. And next time, man, don't be such a bloody martyr!"

"Yes, your grace." Juniper thought to add, his tone apologetic, "No, your grace, I'll not be a martyr again." He should not have been so precise in his answer, for he fell into another paroxysm of coughing.

"Go see Mrs. Needle, and that's an order, Juniper."

The thought of that wispy-haired old lady treating him like a mewling sick cat made the tiger square his shoulders and essay a feeble protest. But the duke cut him off.

"She won't destroy your manhood, Juniper." A gleam of amusement lit his eyes and he said, his tone less curt, "I am given to understand that my old nurse now praises the restorative powers of spicy French mustard and mulled wine. Which of these ingredients is destined for your chest, I am not precisely certain."

The duke's tone, though less severe, was as good as a command, and Juniper drew a resigned breath, his gaze traveling fleetingly toward the second floor of the north wing of the castle. He fancied he could already smell the noxious odors that emanated from her herbal laboratory. He wished now that he had said something to his master, for the two-hour ride to and from Grimsby

Hall, the home of his grace's great-aunt, had sent the influenza right to his chest and left him feeling as wobbly as a new foal.

The duke grinned after his tiger's retreating figure, and strode up the deeply indented stone steps, nodding briefly toward Bassick. He did not wait for his butler to assist him out of his greatcoat and gloves, but continued in without a backward glance, his hessians clacking loudly on the marble entrance floor.

"Your grace!"

The duke's black brows snapped together. He knew he was not being particularly amiable, but he wanted to be alone, without the bother of the tender ministrations of a staff of servants whose numbers seemed to swell with each passing year. He turned slightly and waved a dismissing hand toward the old man who had been at Chesleigh Castle since before the duke was born. "No, Bassick, I have no wish to hear anything. And if you please, keep everyone out of the library. I do not wish to be disturbed."

"But your grace . . ."

The duke felt a sudden stab of apprehension. "Is Lord Edmund all right?"

"Certainly, your grace. His lordship spent his afternoon on his pony. He is now enjoying his dinner with Ellen, in the nursery."

"Excellent. Then say no more! If Cook is beating the scullery maid, tend to it yourself!"

The duke turned on his heel, his tan greatcoat swirling about his ankles, and strode the length of the entrance hall, past the medieval tapestries that hung like thick curtains over the ancient stone walls. He left Bassick with his mouth unbecomingly open, half-formed words still on his tongue, a look of perturbation in his rheumy eyes.

Enough was enough, the duke thought. Two hours spent with his great-aunt Eudora, in one of her rare twits, a martyred sick tiger, and now . . . he pulled up short, a sudden pain in his foot.

"Damnation," he muttered under his breath, and heaved his large frame into a heavy mahogany Tudor chair that sat beneath the portrait of a bewigged ancestor of the seventeenth century. He tugged off his hessian, found the offending pebble, and tossed it aside.

He rubbed the sole of his foot, then rose, ignoring the footman who stood quietly by, awaiting any request he might make. He tucked the hessian under his arm and opened the library doors.

The Chesleigh library was the present duke's favorite room. It was a dark chamber, its walls lined with inset bookshelves, its windows covered with rich maroon velvet curtains. There was a fire flaming in the cavernous grate, and a single branch of candles lit against the coming night. It was a masculine, very comforting room to the duke, and he felt himself begin to relax. He stripped off his gloves and greatcoat and tossed them over the back of a dark blue brocade chair, then sat down and tugged on his boot. As this was a chore that he rarely performed by himself, he found himself cursing at his own ineptness.

A low, throaty laugh came to his astonished ears. He looked up quickly to see a woman standing to the side of the fireplace, in the shadows, swathed from head to foot in a voluminous cape.

"I suppose I should offer to help you," the female said in an amused voice, but she did not move.

The duke rose swiftly to his feet, taken aback by this intrusion into his privacy.

"Who the devil are you? How did you get in here?"

For a long moment the woman did not reply, and anger replaced surprise in his voice.

"Bassick's head will roll for this! The servants' entrance is in the north wing! If you have any wish to keep your position, you will use it in the future."

"I beg your pardon?" came a surprised inquiry.

Because the duke's mood was as black as the scowl on his face, he said with the peremptory hauteur of a medieval seigneur, "Out of here now, wench, and send me that blighted butler of mine."

"I have never before been called a wench. Are you usually so rude, your grace?" She waited, her breath suspended, praying she hadn't misjudged him.

A discordant note struck in the duke's mind. To his well-tuned ear, the female's voice was well-bred, with an occasional trace of a French accent. But she had made the mistake of raising his hackles with her impertinence, beyond the control of his frayed nerves.

"Rude!" He advanced toward the motionless female. "You tempt me, *wench*, to take a birch rod to you!"

"I think, your grace, that you much mistake the matter." She turned to face him, and deliberately drew back the hood of her cape. The duke drew up short. He wasn't quite certain what he had expected, but the young lady who faced him, her chin held arrogantly high, fit no image he would have conjured up. He stared at her flawless white skin, high cheek bones, and proud, straight nose. Her every feature, even to his critical eye, was undeniably lovely. Her eyes held an impish quality, and were a deep blue, their slight almond shape somehow striking a familiar cord in his mind. Her hair was a rich chestnut with lighter wheat-colored streaks, thick and lustrous, and was pulled back from her face into a chignon at the nape of her neck. Errant curling strands of hair escaped from the knot and framed her face. As he stared at her, her wide mouth slowly curved into a half questioning smile.

"I trust you are through with your examination, your grace. I am beginning to feel like a slave on the block." If his scrutiny and roughness of manner ruffled her, she gave no sign.

"I think," the duke said slowly, his manner less intimidating, "that it is time for you to tell me exactly who you are, and what it is you are doing in my library."

His eyes still searched her face, as if, she thought, he was trying to place her in his memory. She found that she was gazing at him almost as closely as he at her. He had changed not one whit from her child's image of him; he still seemed as large and overpowering now as he had six years before. His dark features were more finely honed now, she thought fancifully, etched into a more harsh perfection.

When he had strode into the room, one boot tucked under his arm, Evangeline had given herself over to momentary amusement, despite her trepidation. Even his unexpected rancor had not overly upset her. But his abrupt gentling left her suddenly uncertain, her confidence plummeting. To her surprise, her voice emerged from her throat cold and challenging. "You do not recognize me?"

"There is something about your eyes," he said. His thoughtful frown turned into a frozen smile at her impertinence, and he added in a calculated, mocking drawl, "You are too old to be a by-blow, so is it possible that you are the wronged mother? Did we perhaps bed together some dark night?"

Evangeline sucked in her breath and stared at him. Unconsciously, her hands fisted about her cloak and drew the material more closely about her. She saw mockery in his dark eyes and knew that he had resumed the role of the arrogant nobleman, intent on taking her to task. As his assessing gaze flitted over her caped form, she drew herself up, forcing herself to say calmly, "No, we did not bed together, your grace. If we had, you would have been classed as a molester of children."

The annoyed frown returned to knit his brows. Had this impertinent chit no shame?

"Are you not overly warm?" He saw her hesitate perceptibly and grinned, again at his ease. "I have never been addicted to rape, ma'am. Whatever virtue you still possess is quite safe with me, I assure you."

"Yes," she agreed affably after a moment. "It would be most ungallant of you to do such a thing in your ducal estate." With deft, graceful movements, she untied the strings of her heavy wool cloak and slipped it from her shoulders. "Before you . . . examine me further, your grace, let me tell you that it is very rude of you to accord such treatment to your cousin."

"Cousin! The devil!"

"Well, not precisely. Actually, I am your cousin-in-law. Marissa was my father's niece."

He stared at her, studying her face for a likeness to Marissa. The thick brows that arched delicately over her lilting blue eyes—there was a likeness there.

"Your name, Mademoiselle?"

"De la Valette, your grace."

"My wife's family was Beauchamps."

"As mine is also. De la Valette is my husband's name."

"Ah . . . Madame. I trust you will forgive my inhospitable greeting, but I am unused to finding ladies alone in my library. Will you not sit down?"

Evangeline inclined her head in assent and eased herself into a large wing chair near to the fireplace. She smoothed the outmoded dove-gray gown about her, a gown that attested to the fact that although she was a noblewoman, she had fallen on hard times.

"I am surrounded by faithful retainers, Madame. Would you be so kind as to tell me how you managed to be in my library without my being informed of your presence?"

"I arrived but a few moments before you, your grace. Your butler was kind enough not to make me wait in the entrance hall. I was very cold, you see, and he did not wish me to be uncomfortable."

"I trust you are sufficiently comfortable now, Madame. Would you care for tea?"

"No, thank you, your grace." She eyed him warily, for his moods seemed to change like quicksilver. She had no inkling what he thought of her.

"Will I also have the pleasure of meeting your husband?" He disposed his large frame upon a settee across from her.

"I am a widow."

"You are quite young to be a widow, Madame."

"And you, your grace, are quite young to be a widower." The words slipped smoothly from her mouth, and to her own ears, she sounded perfectly at her ease.

"Thirty is not so very young," he said. "I daresay you have not yet attained your twentieth birthday."

"True, but I am nearly twenty." She lowered her eyes, not wishing for the moment to meet his piercing gaze. "I was married when I was quite young, younger, in fact, than was Marissa when she wed with you."

"Have you children?"

"No, your grace. And, I might add, I still feel like a prisoner in the dock."

"Forgive me, Madame," he said, but she guessed that he was not at all sorry. "I assume that I met you some six years ago when Marissa and I were married."

"Yes. I have not seen you or Marissa since that time," she added unnecessarily.

"Is your father likewise in England?"

"No," she said without hesitation. "As you know, Mama died some three years ago and Papa just recently . . . in Paris."

The duke raised an incredulous brow. "I find that quite odd, Madame," he said softly.

Evangeline forced her features into blankness. "Odd, your grace?"

The duke sat back in his chair, balanced his elbows on the padded arms, and tapped his fingertips thoughtfully together.

"Your father, as well as Marissa's, was an émigré, as you well know. He hated Napoleon. That he would ever consent to return to a France under the Corsican's thumb I find difficult to credit."

Evangeline breathed more easily, for her response was a straightforward one. "We returned to France only last spring, your grace, when Louis regained his throne. Papa saw no reason at that time to inform you of his plans, as he had no further ties to your family or to you. He was not well, and wished more than anything to see France again before he died. Although Louis did not see to the return of my uncle's estates, it mattered not."

"Did your husband die in England, Madame?"

A faint blush stole unbidden to Evangeline's cheeks. "He did, your grace. He was, like my family, an émigré." She sought to distract him. "I have never seen my cousin, Edmund, your grace. Mama was quite ill throughout those years and I could not leave her. Also, I believe, there was some sort of falling out with your family, and such visits, had they been possible, were discouraged."

She saw a flash of anger in the duke's eyes. "I don't suppose, Madame, that your father or your uncle told you the reason for our . . . falling out."

She shook her head. "I should like to know, your grace, for I was very fond of Marissa and missed her sorely."

The duke looked away from her for a moment, then said dismissively, "Perhaps some day you will know. If your father did not tell you, it is not my place to do so. As for your cousin and my son, he is a winsome little scamp, five years old now."

At the mention of his son, the duke's voice softened and pride lit his eyes, but only briefly. He sat forward in his chair and asked her abruptly, "Perhaps, Madame, you will tell me now what service I may perform for you, in addition, of course, to your most understandable request to see your cousin. I do find myself lamentably curious about another matter. Why is it that you did not write to tell me that you wished to see Edmund? Had I but known, you would have been spared an . . . uncertain welcome."

Suddenly she looked to him very alone and vulnerable. "If you would know the truth, your grace, I was afraid to write to you."

"I did not believe my reputation extended to being an inhospitable bounder. Did your father turn you so against me, Madame?"

Her hand fluttered in denial. "No," she said.

"I see."

He had become the formally distant nobleman again, and her well-rehearsed words seemed to lie leaden on her tongue. She knew that she must have time alone, to assess him anew. She rose to her feet. He quickly followed suit and she found herself staring at his snowy white cravat. Evangeline had always thought of herself as a lanky, graceless maypole. As she raised her eyes to his face, she felt suddenly quite small, an ineffectual wisp, unequal to her task.

"I am hungry!" she blurted out.

"A situation that is easily remedied. Where is your maid, Madame?"

She squared her shoulders. "I do not have a maid."

His dark eyes narrowed. "Are you telling me that you traveled from France alone, with no protection?"

She thrust up her chin, having decided it would better suit her purpose than to burst into tears.

"I am not a helpless young girl, your grace, and am perfectly able to take care of myself. Besides," she added, her voice taut, "I had only enough funds for myself."

For the first time, the duke took close note of her clothing. The gown was of good material, though frayed and somewhat outmoded.

"Very well," he said only. "Allow me, Madame, to ring for Mrs. Dickinson, my housekeeper. Have you any luggage?"

He already regarded her as an indigent relation, she thought, come to plead for his noble bounty. Nonetheless, it rankled. "I have one valise, your grace."

Her voice was defensive and the duke said nothing. He did not yet know what she expected of him, but it was apparent to him that she was alone in the world, and without funds. The thought of spending his evening quite alone with a comforting decanter of brandy at his elbow had become a frivolous fancy. He could not very well dismiss her to her room with a dinner tray.

He moved to pull at the bell cord. Suddenly, he growled, "Damnation!"

"I beg your pardon?"

"The proprieties, Madame. My mother is in London."

Evangeline shrugged her shoulders with forced indifference. "I cannot see that it much matters, your grace. After all, I am a widow, a mature woman, beyond the need for such observances. And I am also your cousin——"

"Cousin-in-law."

"Yes, to be sure. Nonetheless, relatives are a different matter entirely."

The corners of his sensual mouth lifted in a rueful grin. Obviously, his cousin-in-law had no notion of his reputation. He became aware of a tense set to her mouth and an anxious narrowing of her eyes, and forebore to probe the matter further.

"Doubtless you are right, Madame. One of your advanced years need not be concerned about such things."

Following a light tap upon the door, a diminutive woman entered, her black bombazine skirts rustling loudly in the silence of the room. The thick key ring about her thin waist bespoke her station.

"Mrs. Dickinson," the duke said, "this is Madame de la Valette, my . . . cousin, come to pay us a visit. Unfortunately, Madame's luggage and, tragically, her maid were both lost in a Channel storm."

"I—I have one valise," Evangeline said, doing her

best to cloak her surprise at the fluent tale he had just spun for his housekeeper's ears.

"Ah, yes, one valise was saved from the storm. Please show Madame to the duchess's bedchamber."

Mrs. Dickinson's guileless round eyes did not blink at the duke's tale. She turned pitying eyes upon Evangeline. "How very terrible for you, Madame! But now you are safe! If you will please follow me, I will try to make you comfortable."

The duke lowered amused eyes from Evangeline's face, and consulted his watch. "Mrs. Dickinson, please attend my cousin. Madame, we will dine in an hour, if that pleases you."

"Certainly, your grace," Evangeline managed. She felt giddy with relief. He was behaving toward her, at least for the moment, just as Houchard had predicted. She proffered him a slight curtsy and turned to follow Mrs. Dickinson's swishing skirts from the room.

The duke turned from the door and walked slowly to the fireplace. He gazed down thoughtfully into the glowing embers and conjured up the image of a thirteen-year-old girl, tall for her age, he remembered now, taller than her older cousin Marissa. He vaguely recalled thinking her oddly mature for her years, her thin shoulders proudly set, and her dark eyes wide and serious when they rested upon his face. Six years later now, her eyes held an anxious appeal, though she had tried to cloak it, an appeal that as her kinsman he could not dismiss. He turned away from the fireplace and shrugged his shoulders. If she wished to remain in England, as he supposed, he would provide her sufficient support and turn her over to his mother. She appeared well-bred and intelligent, and properly gowned, she would do herself, and him, credit.

Although he did not wish it, another lady came to his mind. He felt no particular anger at Sabrina now. It had come as a shock to him to realize that Sabrina had fallen in love with another man, but in all fairness, she had done the right thing in marrying Phillip Mercerault. Being honest with himself, he knew that he had not loved her, merely desired her, that his was not a wounded heart, only wounded vanity. He dismissed her from his thoughts, something it was becoming easier to do, and left the library, his destination his young son's nursery.

"Your grace!"

The duke turned to his butler, whose evident agitation brought a smile to his lips. "Don't concern yourself, Bassick. It is not your fault that I refused to listen to you. I thank you for seeing to my cousin. Incidentally, how did she arrive?"

"In a hired gig, your grace, from Portsmouth. After I realized that she was related to your grace, I paid the driver," he added in the most expressionless of voices. "She seemed a most pleasant young lady, if you'll allow me to say so, your grace."

"You did the right thing, of course. As to her pleasantness . . ." he shrugged his broad shoulders and turned away, as if dismissing her from his mind. Actually, the duke thought, mounting the stairs, she did indeed seem a most unusual young woman, and he began to think himself a bounder for having treated her so roughly. She had not resorted to tears even when he had mocked her virtue, and she had a ready wit and was unafraid to speak her mind.

When the duke reached the landing, he turned into the east wing corridor, oblivious of the muted chatter of his servants and the scores of portraits that graced the walls of the vast hallway. What a rabbit warren of a house, he thought, as he walked the some hundred feet to the nursery suite. As his hand turned the knob to the nursery door, he smiled, hearing his son's high childish laughter.

"Papa! Ellen has set my table like yours! I am now to begin my third course. She, of course, is my butler."

The duke felt a certain sense of well-being whenever

he entered the Chesleigh nursery. It held many fond memories for him, as, he suspected, it had for many generations of his family. He strode across the long, carpeted expanse toward his son's dining table that Ellen had pushed into a place of honor in front of the fireplace. Edmund had risen from his small chair, his eyes, as light as his father's were dark, shining with excitement.

"Your grace," Ellen murmured.

The duke nodded kindly toward her, a shy local girl he knew loved Lord Edmund perhaps more than had his own mother. He carefully perched himself on the edge of the table. "Very impressive," he agreed easily, taking in the covered dishes set grandly around his son's plate. "Bassick tells me that you rode your pony this afternoon."

Lord Edmund raised his light blue eyes to his father's face. "Yes, sir. Grimms and I explored the beach. We built a castle with turrets and a moat." He added seriously, "I don't think Pansy much cares for all the sand and the water. She was snorting and pawing, until I had to tell her to keep quiet. Grimms said I should always be firm, but kind, particularly to my horses."

The duke squatted down to his son's eye level. "Sound advice, young scoundrel. Now, my lad, before you retire for the night, let me tell you that we have a guest whom you will meet on the morrow."

"Lord Southwold, sir?" Lord Edmund inquired respectfully. "I like him, you know," he added in a confiding manner, "better than the other gentlemen who visit Chesleigh."

The duke shook his head. "No, our guest is a lady, a very pleasant lady."

Lord Edmund looked resigned. "A lady," he repeated, too young to hide his disappointment. He muttered, "She'll want to pat me on the head and try to look interested in me. It's all a sham!"

"No she won't," the duke said coolly, "and I'll thank you not to be unbecomingly impertinent."

Lord Edmund, abashed, looked dolefully down at his shoes. "I will be honored to make her acquaintance, sir."

"Endeavor not to forget your honor on the morrow. Now, Edmund, you will allow Ellen to serve you your last course, give you a much-needed bath, and tuck you up." He ruffled his son's dark curls and rose.

"Lord Edmund's cousin, Madame de la Valette, is here from France," he said to Ellen. "I know I can count on you to make him presentable. I imagine that she will wish to see him some time during the morning."

"Yes, your grace." Ellen bobbed a curtsy and watched the duke pat his young son's shoulder, bid him an affectionate good night, and stride from the nursery.

"How very delicious! Your Cook shows genius with veal." Evangeline sat back in her chair with a sated sigh and wiped her fingers on a napkin.

"Thank you. Bassick, please convey Madame's compliments to Cook. Would you care for a sherry?"

Evangeline nodded assent. When the delicate crystal goblet was filled, the duke dismissed Bassick.

Their conversation during dinner had been limited to the most mundane of topics, namely the unseasonably warm weather in the south of England, the duke having no intention of providing the two footmen and his butler with any choice bits of information.

Evangeline, who understood this quite well, found herself wishing now that they had remained. She gazed from beneath her lashes toward the duke, who sat at the head of the long table in a high-backed chair that seemed suited for royalty. His mood during dinner had been perfectly satisfactory, that of a coolly friendly host, not overly interested in either his dinner or in his guest. She had changed into her only gown fit for evening wear, a high-waisted dark gray muslin that was stark in its simplicity. His formal black satin evening attire made her feel the perfect dowd by comparison. She chided herself at her misplaced vanity, for she appeared exactly as she was supposed to.

"Do you find your room satisfactory?"

She answered in an equally cool, polite voice, "It is quite lovely, your grace. It was Marissa's room?"

"Yes. She did not much care for Chesleigh Castle, except that room, which she used to inform me was her only sanctuary from the dampness of the sea."

Although he spoke in an expressionless voice, Evangeline sensed that Marissa was not a comfortable subject for him, and made haste to turn the conversation away from her cousin. "Do you spend much time here, your grace?"

"Not an excessive amount. I rather prefer London and all its diverse attractions."

Evangeline wondered what an excessive amount of time meant to the duke. Houchard had told her that the duke divided his time nearly equally between London and Chesleigh. Houchard had been most adamant that she was to remain at Chesleigh until she received further instructions. She said, "I, myself, am not like you, your grace. I fear I am much addicted to the country and to the sea." She added on a wistful note, "Chesleigh Castle is more beautiful than I had ever imagined. It is written of in all the guide books as one of the most noble and stately residences in all of England. Not Blenheim, to be sure, but nonetheless."

"Blenheim is a tasteless heap of stone, of no particular style and no antiquity. It has no pride of ancestry in its walls, no sense of permanence. Warwick Castle, now, is quite another matter. One can feel centuries of human misery and triumph within its walls. Unfortunately, my ancestors had not the famous Warwick's wherewithal." The duke paused and cast Evangeline a rueful grin. "Forgive me for boring you, Madame. When

I am not being a useless fribble, my attention sometimes turns to history, and occasionally to politics."

"I had not guessed that of you," she said.

"Do not, I pray, sound so very incredulous. In all
truth, I suppose I most often do precisely what pleases
me at the moment." He added, a self-mocking smile on
his lips, "Much of what pleases me is not fit conversation for a lady's ears. But I digress lamentably. Now,
Madame, if you would be so kind as to tell me how I
may serve you."

Evangeline lowered her eyes for a moment to the
dark gold liquid in her goblet. A lump formed in her
throat and she quickly swallowed. She had, after all, no
choice. "I have no money, your grace!"

"A fact that is quite evident."

"I do not wish to . . . importune you. Indeed, I can
imagine nothing more repugnant than having one's indigent relations camping on one's door!"

"But you are indigent, and you are here."

"Yes, but it is not my intention to hang on your
shoulder."

He smiled at her peculiar expression.

"Sleeve, Madame."

Evangeline blinked at him. "Sleeve, your grace?"

"Yes, Madame. You have no wish to hang on it."

"Ah, *oui.*" She smiled fleetingly, reminded that her
English still lapsed on occasion during moments of stress
or anger. One of his dark brows remained quirked and
she hastened to say, "Although I was born and raised in
England, only French was spoken in our household. I
fear Papa always believed that English was an inelegant
tongue. Sometimes I forget myself."

"Particularly when you are feeling anxious?"

She fanned her hands in front of her, momentarily
surprised that he understood so readily. "Yes, I suppose so." She drew a deep breath and took the plunge.
"I wish to stay here, at Chesleigh, for a while. I am
quite prepared to work for my keep. I am well edu-

cated and wish to offer you my services as a temporary governess to my cousin."

A dark brow winged upward again. "What? A young lady who has no wish to join the social scene in London? Please, Madame, there is no earthly reason for noble protestations. I doubt not that my mother would be delighted to introduce you into the *beau monde*. With your French blood, and your undeniably lovely face and figure, I predict your instant success. I am not at all tight-fisted, Madame, and will provide you sufficient dowry to support a suitable second alliance."

It had never occurred to her that he would be so wretchedly generous. She had, at all cost, to stay at Chesleigh. She finally muttered, "I am half English, I told you."

"Of course. Forgive me."

"And I do not wish to go to London."

He smiled cynically, and a black brow arched upward. She said sharply, "I do not understand your skepticism, your grace. I have told you what it is I wish, yet you pretend to disbelieve me."

"Were you widowed so recently that good taste forbids gaiety? If that is your reason for wishing isolation, I must applaud your nobility."

"I was widowed over a year ago, your grace. I have satisfied my social obligations. I wish only for peace and rest."

He regarded her for some moments in thoughtful silence. "You must have been most attached to your husband."

"No!—I mean yes, of course! He was a great man."

"And a poor one, evidently."

Evangeline said smoothly, "No, only I am left penniless because I did not bear him an heir. His English lands were all entailed and his younger brother is now master."

He regarded her with some astonishment. "Forgive

me, Madame, for prying, but I find it difficult to credit that this new master tossed out his brother's widow."

She heard disbelief in his voice and assumed a taut, embarrassed expression. "No, it was not his desire. He wanted me for his . . . mistress. I could not abide his intentions and thus returned to my father. After he died in Paris, I came here."

"I see," he said mildly, sensitive to her embarrassment. "Exactly who was your husband, Madame?"

"Le Comte de la Valette, Henri Naigeon, by name."

The duke fell silent again, his impassive face giving no clue to his thoughts. He said suddenly, "And what is your name? I cannot continue to call you Madame, or Cousin."

"Evangeline."

"Since we are related, do you mind if I call you by your given name?"

"No, your grace."

"Thank you, Evangeline. And my name is Richard."

She nodded, for she really could not refuse. She should have been relieved that he had so quickly accepted her, but instead she felt ashamed.

"What if I had not been here when you arrived? Had been in London or in the north?"

She shrugged helplessly. "I suppose I would have begged your butler to allow me to remain until you returned."

"You appear to place great faith in my complaisance. But it is a moot point. If it is truly your wish to remain at Chesleigh, in the company of my son, I suppose it would be ill-natured and unreasonable of me to disallow it. You will not, of course, be treated like a governess. Indeed, I will expect you to be mistress at Chesleigh when I am not here."

Evangeline raised startled eyes to his face, and tried to hide her surprise. "It is very kind of you, your grace, but——"

"Richard."

"Very well, it is most kind of you, as I said, but I would never presume to such a degree on our kinship!"

"The fact remains that you were my wife's first cousin, and thus a welcomed guest in my house. Would you prefer an airless room in the attic? Really, Evangeline, your protestations do me little compliment."

"Forgive me," she said stiffly, and turned her face away.

"Consider yourself forgiven, this time. No, don't pucker up at me again. Having my lovely cousin in residence at Chesleigh cannot but puff up my consequence. Once you have settled in, I will bring my mother here to meet you. The propriety of your living here, without proper chaperone, is another matter upon which my mother is well versed. We cannot have your reputation sullied by being here with me. Perhaps my mother should come to Chesleigh."

"You forget, your grace, that I have already been married. There is nothing to . . . sully."

He smiled mirthlessly. "Given that you are half French, I find that opinion extraordinarily naive. Where, Madame, is your touted French common sense? Surely you plan to wed again some time in the future. Let me assure you that the gentleman of your choice will be much concerned."

"I have no intention of marrying . . . again." Before he could put his incredulous frown into words, she hastened to add, "I venture that her grace would not particularly appreciate being hauled willy-nilly from London to meet an indigent relation!"

He was gazing at her thoughtfully. "Perhaps you are right. In a month or so, after Edmund has driven you quite distracted, you will pay a visit to London." He saw her start.

"You have no liking for London?"

"I have never been to London, save once when I was a child. I told you, sir, that I prefer the country and the sea."

"We shall see," he said. He drew his watch from his waistcoat pocket and consulted it. "It grows late. I prefer to believe that your . . . uncertain humor results from fatigue."

"Just because I have no liking for *your* kind of life, your grace, you believe me ill-natured!" She bit her lower lip at her hasty words, and quickly dropped her eyes to the tablecloth.

"I am merely offering you an altogether reasonable explanation, my dear, to spare you from further offending your host."

Evangeline mumbled an apology under her breath, and made to rise.

"Before you retire, let me inquire exactly what you believe my kind of life to be?"

He spoke in the most impassive of tones, but to Evangeline's sensitive ears, his voice held a challenge. He was pushing her, she realized, because it amused him to bandy words with her, a pastime, she imagined, in which he excelled.

She said quietly, easing back into her chair, "I believe you to be a man of the world, a man who can have most anything he wishes with but a snap of his fingers, a man, in short, who, because of his wealth, rank, and personal attributes, can indulge himself in any pursuit he fancies."

"In conclusion, not a very estimable man."

"I will always believe you an estimable man, your grace. I think you have a good deal of kindness. Indeed, how could I ever believe otherwise?" She rose and an impish smile lit her eyes. "After all, have you not allowed a poor cousin-in-law to invade your stronghold and cut up your peace?"

Richard eyed her with some astonishment before he gave her an answering smile. "Just so, Madame. I trust you will not regret your return to England . . . or your visit to Chesleigh."

"I must not regret it, your grace," she said. She

turned quickly on her heel and walked from the dining room before he could accompany her.

Her choice of words perplexed him. Although her English seemed perfectly fluent, perhaps she had had some difficulty in expressing the nuances of her thought properly. He removed himself to the library, having decided to postpone his return to London, at least for a week, until he was certain that she and Edmund rubbed along well together.

3

Evangeline slept fitfully, and started awake to what still seemed a fantastic dream of unreal cloth. She reminded herself that the duke, for the moment, had accepted her, had welcomed her as a member of the Chesleigh household. Houchard's drama was set irrevocably into motion and there was nothing she could do to prevent his characters, herself included, from playing out their roles.

She turned at the sound of slow, heavy steps outside her bedchamber door, and quickly pinched her cheeks to bring color to her face. She patted the severe chignon at the nape of her neck and forced her voice to lightness at a light tap on the door. "Enter," she called.

An old woman shuffled into the room, her face the texture of fine parchment paper, her back hunched forward with age. Her sparse white hair was pulled into a skinny bun, revealing patches of white scalp. Her eyes were brightly assessing as they rested intently upon Evangeline.

"Yes?" Evangeline asked uncertainly.

"So ye be her dead grace's cousin," the old woman said in a soft, sing-song voice.

"Yes," Evangeline said, wondering if she had not newly escaped from Bedlam.

"Aye, ye've something of the look of her in yer eyes. Dark blue like the sea in a tempest. But her grace had no strength in her jaw . . . aye, a weak jaw she had, and her chin quivered when things did not suit her exactly. Spoiled she was, petulant and demanding one minute, a charming, winsome child the next."

"Mrs. Needle!"

Evangeline turned reluctantly toward Mrs. Dickinson, who stood in the open doorway, her usually placid expression dashed away by embarrassed alarm.

"Now, Mrs. Needle, you mustn't make Madame uncomfortable with your chatter."

The old woman paid no heed to Mrs. Dickinson, her ancient, wise eyes still resting on Evangeline's face. "Ye'll come to the north wing, Madame. I'll wager yer only memories of yer cousin are from yer child's mind. But ye've come home, just as I hoped ye would. We'll talk, child, aye, there's much we have to speak about."

"Now, Mrs. Needle," Mrs. Dickinson expostulated weakly.

"Mind yer simple tongue, Lucy! Ye're forever acting the halfwit and treating me in the same way. Forget not," she continued in a curiously gentle voice, turning back to Evangeline. "Come to the north wing. There is much more to ye than I had imagined."

With those curious words, she turned slowly and trailed from the room, muttering under her breath as she went.

" 'Tis Mrs. Needle, Madame," Mrs. Dickinson provided unnecessarily. "Pay her no heed, she's old and grown peculiar, if you know what I mean."

"Who is she?"

"She was his grace's nurse, and nurse to his grace's father, the old duke. His grace will not hear of removing her from Chesleigh, and indulges her every whim. She even has an herbal laboratory that gives off the most offensive of odors! She normally stays in the north tower. It's most odd that she sought you out." Mrs. Dickinson shrugged, her face once again resuming its placid expression. "It's unlikely that she'll bother you again."

Mrs. Dickinson, having disposed of Mrs. Needle to her satisfaction, walked briskly forward, her black bombazine skirts rustling loudly. "You're already dressed, Madame! I had not expected you to rise so very early. How very unhappy you must be to have lost your luggage and your maid! Poor woman . . . such a tragedy!"

"Oh . . . oh yes, it was a great loss. I shall miss poor . . . Millie dreadfully. She was old, so very old, and quite ill. Perhaps it was for the best, for the ending was quick and merciful."

"Well, you mustn't fret, my lady," Mrs. Dickinson said in a soothing voice. "His grace has asked me to find a suitable girl to attend you. I think Mrs. Miller's niece will suit you just fine. Emma's a bright girl and quick to learn. I will have her fetched here today."

Evangeline wanted to protest the undeserved luxury of a maid, but she knew that it would appear odd to do so in Mrs. Dickinson's eyes. She swallowed and said in an expressionless voice, "That is very kind of his grace."

"If you would care to follow me now, Madame. His grace is already in the breakfast parlor, awaiting your presence. He has told Bassick that he will not be leaving for London today." She beamed her pleasure. "Now we shall have him here for at least another week, I am informed."

Evangeline started. Another week. She had felt relieved that the duke was to leave, that she would have time to accustom herself to life at Chesleigh without his disturbing presence. She had found it difficult yesterday to play her role with him, to parry his inquiries with rehearsed replies, always wondering how he would react when her tongue betrayed her into naturalness. His moods changed so quickly, from mocking arrogance to polite formality, that she could scarce keep pace with him, or with herself.

Mrs. Dickinson's chatter continued as she led Evangeline down the long, carpeted corridor in the west wing to the wide curved staircase that rose in ancient dignity to the upper floors. She followed Mrs. Dickinson across the vast entrance hall, past the library and the formal dining room. They entered a small, charming room flooded with morning light through wide windows framed with pale yellow curtains.

"How lovely!" she exclaimed.

"Thank you."

Evangeline drew in her breath, despite herself. The duke had lowered his newspaper and was smiling at her from the head of a small table. He wore a buff riding habit, exquisitely tailored to emphasize the hard, graceful lines of his body.

"Is something wrong, Madame?"

She flushed, realizing that she had been staring at him. Unwittingly, she remembered how she had envied Marissa six years ago, lucky Marissa who had secured the duke's hand. But Marissa had not been so very lucky. Dead when she was but twenty-three, in childbirth that took the life of her tiny infant as well as her own.

"Of course nothing is wrong! I was but thinking that you look splendid."

He gave her a roguish grin. "You are blessed with French candor, I see. I thank you for the compliment. Come and sit down. Cook has prepared a breakfast that will have us feeling fat as geldings."

He motioned to the place setting to his right and Evangeline slipped into the chair held by a footman. She must mind her tongue, she thought. Although he was no doubt quite used to being flattered and admired by ladies, she could not let him see her in that light. She remembered Houchard's graphic discussions of the duke's likes and dislikes, and felt herself flush slightly.

He must see her as nothing more than a penniless widow here to take care of his son. The footman served their breakfast and left the morning room after a dismissing nod from the duke.

Having never cared for the hearty English breakfasts, Evangeline stared down in some dismay at a plate piled with scrambled eggs, kidneys, and thin slices of baked ham. She reached instinctively for a piece of toast and began to spread it with thick butter.

"You did not rest well."

Evangeline looked up from her toast. "You are wrong, your grace. How could one not be perfectly content in such a beautiful room and a comfortable bed?"

"I cannot answer that. I merely note the strain about your eyes."

"It is the . . . newness, I suppose."

"And the tragic loss of your maid and luggage in the Channel storm."

She chuckled despite herself. "What a marvelous clanker! I had to embroider upon the tragic event somewhat with Mrs. Dickinson. But it seems that no one will dare disbelieve you, much less gainsay your word."

"You least of all, I trust."

"It would be most foolish of me to do so, since it seems that your servants will now show me ample respect, despite my being a ragtag female with naught to her name."

"Just so," he said easily, forking down a bite of thick sirloin. "You must eat more than that. Not only do you insult Cook, you do a disservice to yourself."

"I beg your pardon?"

"You are tall, Madame, and at the moment, far too thin, save for your——" He broke off abruptly, but not before Evangeline saw that his eyes had been upon her bosom.

"Save for what, your grace?" she inquired with deceptive innocence, hoping to put him out of countenance for his impropriety.

"Save for your fingers. I have never before observed such stumpy fingers. It is your French blood, no doubt."

"Stumpy fingers! You know very well that . . ." His dark eyes were laughing at her and she thrust up her chin. To call him untruthful would be to confess her own mock innocence in taking him to task. She had been correct in her assessment of him—he very much liked to bait her, and others as well, no doubt. Very well, she would give him as best as she could.

"I do not believe eating more will remedy that problem, your grace."

"Likely not. I will simply have to be tolerant of your physical flaws."

She opened her mouth, but her quickness of wit seemed to have deserted her.

"Do you enjoy crossing verbal swords, Madame?"

"Evangeline," she snapped. "Madame makes me feel like an old woman."

"A lovely name, but a mouthful. I shall contrive to come up with something more suitable. Something shorter, with unique character."

"You are not Adam!" She bit her cheek for her unruly tongue.

"The lady's mind runs on wheels! You are already turning Cheslcigh into a garden of paradise and me into . . ." He paused a moment, looking thoughtful. "My memory is sometimes lamentable, but I seem to recall that Eve did not care for floral adornment. I wonder what Adam had to say about such immodesty in his mate."

"I have no interest in, or knowledge of such matters," she said in a discouraging thin voice.

"Ah," he said, much enjoying himself. "I wonder what your husband would say about your regrettable lack of interest and knowledge."

She paled, and her half-eaten slice of toast fell from her suddenly nerveless fingers to her plate.

"Forgive me, Evangeline. I did not mean to recall memories that are perhaps not pleasant to you."

"You presume, your grace. My memories are not your concern. I told you yesterday that . . . Henri was a great man. He was also a sensitive man, not given to causing embarrassment to others."

"An effective set-down. We will leave your sensitive husband to his eternal rest. Now, Madame . . . Evangeline, if you are sufficiently fortified, I will take you to meet Edmund."

Lord Edmund had apparently just finished his own breakfast, for they found him pained to be having the remains washed from his hands and face.

"Good morning, Edmund," the duke said, stepping momentarily in front of Evangeline.

"Your grace," Ellen said as she curtsied, dropping Edmund's hand.

"Papa! Ellen told me that the lady . . ." His young face flushed as he peered around his father's large body and saw Evangeline standing quietly by the open door.

"This is the lady, Papa?" he essayed, quickly drawing himself up to his full height.

"Yes, my boy, this is your cousin, Evangeline. She has come all the way from France to pay you a visit."

Edmund's blue eyes widened, and he regarded her with a child's candid scrutiny. "You do look like a cousin," he allowed finally. He proffered her a deep bow. "Welcome, Cousin Evaline, to Chesleigh."

One of the duke's black brows rose a good inch. "Very creditably done, Edmund. I am pleased."

Ellen said, "He insisted that we practice, your grace. His honor depended upon it."

"Your pronunciation needs some refinement, Edmund, but that problem I have already solved. You may call her Eve, if that is all right with you, Madame."

"Of course you may call me Eve, Edmund," she said, ignoring the wicked twinkle in the duke's eyes. "And thank you for your very grown-up welcome." She dropped to her knees and opened her arms to him before remembering that small boys had no use for such displays. She quickly recovered and stretched out her hand to him.

Edmund tentatively placed his fingertips on her palm. "Do you look much like my Mama? I don't remember her, you see."

"No, not really. Your Mama was a beautiful lady, like an angel. You have somewhat the look of her." She quickly saw that this did not find favor with Lord Edmund, and hastened to add, "But I can see that you will be a great, handsome man like your father."

"Was Mama short? I have no wish to be short when I grow up."

"Somewhat, but I think you have no reason to worry. Look at your feet, Edmund. What massive feet! Your body will have to grow, just to keep up. And you have long fingers, not the least bit stumpy! Ah yes, I see a giant of a man in the making!"

Edmund beamed. "I am glad you are here and not Lord Southwold, even if he always brings me a present," he added wistfully.

"You greedy little beggar!" the duke said. "You will make your cousin think that you are shamefully deprived."

"But I did bring you a present, Edmund. I hope that you will like it." Evangeline withdrew a small wrapped box from the pocket of her gown and handed it to her cousin.

The duke gave her a surprised, pleased look. His lips curled in amusement as his son enthusiastically ripped away the paper.

Lord Edmund gave a gasp of delight as he drew out a carved wooden pistol, so finely constructed with wires and weights that the hammer cocked and the trigger could be pulled.

"Even the barrel is hollow, Papa! Now I can duel!" He clasped the pistol in one small hand and aimed it at

Ellen. "Will you pretend you're a bandit, Ellen? Papa, when will you take me to the target range?"

"When you have thanked your cousin, and promised not to torment Ellen."

Lord Edmund gave Evangeline another very proper bow. "Thank you, ma'am. Lord Southwold never gave me such a present!"

"Most moving," his grace said dryly. "Now, young man, if Ellen is finished with you, I suggest that you and I give your . . . Eve, a tour of the castle grounds."

"Can we ride, Papa?"

"If Eve does not mind."

Evangeline had never before witnessed so pitiful a pleading look as emanated from Edmund's blue eyes. She smiled and tousled his black curls. "I would prefer riding above all else."

Rising, she said softly to the duke, "I fear, sir, that I do not own a riding habit. My lost luggage, you know . . ."

"Just so. Go to your room, I will send Mrs. Dickinson to you."

Not above half an hour later, Evangeline made her way down the wide ornately-carved staircase clad in an elegant royal blue riding habit, a plumed riding hat set jauntily over her chestnut hair. She had been held in surprise when she had reached her room to see Mrs. Dickinson brushing the skirt of an exquisite riding habit that had, the housekeeper informed her, belonged to Marissa.

"I—I don't understand," Evangeline had stammered.

Mrs. Dickinson had beamed. "His grace ordered it altered for you, Madame, early this morning. Unfortunately, we've had only enough time to let down the skirt."

Indeed, the skirt had been lengthened a good five inches to accommodate Evangeline's height. She was feeling rather overwhelmed, not only by the duke's generosity, but also by the speed at which he had acted, when she met him in the entrance hall.

His eyes swept over her, and he nodded in approval.

"It is most kind of you, your grace, to lend——" Her shy attempt was cut off with a negligent wave of the duke's hand.

"You are most welcome, Madame. The habit becomes you, though I see that more seams need to be adjusted."

Evangeline was thinking the same thing herself, for the jacket would not meet over her breasts. "It is most improper of you to notice, your grace."

"Incidently, I am lending you nothing. The riding habit as well as Marissa's other gowns now belong to you."

"You are too kind, your grace! I really cannot——"

"Of course you can. It cannot but enhance my consequence to have you appropriately gowned. Now, Edmund, if you will cease tugging at my leg, we will be off."

"Yes, Cousin Eve, the horses are waiting!" Edmund bounded through the front doors, held wide by a complacently smiling Bassick. Evangeline shook her head ruefully and followed father and son out of the castle.

The Chesleigh stables stood in splendid isolation near the east wing of the castle. A faint aroma of freshly cut hay assailed Evangeline's nostrils and she inhaled deeply. She stood for a long moment staring toward the Channel, some three hundred yards beyond the rugged promontory upon which the castle was built. The water was a deep blue, calm save for the frothy whitecaps that formed as the waves rolled to the beach, out of her sight. For the moment, as she gazed out over the water, she felt almost carefree, as if nothing could touch her here.

"You cannot see France, Evangeline, even on the clearest of days. If you like, we can take my yacht to the Isle of Wight. I own a small estate near Ventnor. It will provide you with an exquisite prospect."

She shook her head and smiled. "I have no desire to see France, your grace. My homesickness was always for England."

The duke's attention was captured by a tall, bearded man, dressed in homespuns, not in the duke's crimson and gold livery. He tugged respectfully at a shock of graying hair that fell over his forehead.

"Good day, yer grace. Yer stallion's in a waggish temper, and needs a good gallop. I thought Biscuit would do the lady. Lord Edmund's pony is ready."

"I'll go talk to Tommy, Papa!" Edmund cried, and at his father's absent nod, scurried toward a thin boy who stood next to a fat, sleek Shetland pony.

"Biscuit," the duke said, turning to Evangeline, "is a steady, rather plodding old hack that will not cause you a moment's worry. She is the only horse in my stable that Marissa would ride. I do not know your skill. Would you prefer a horse with more spirit?"

Evangeline was on the point of saying that the most plodding horse in his stable would suit her admirably, when another stable hand emerged into the courtyard, leading a great black stallion, who snorted and tossed his proud head with every step.

"That is Emperor. He is Mameluke-trained and is blessed with a most exuberant spirit." Evangeline imagined Biscuit plodding along beside that marvelous specimen and without further thought, quickly said, "Most certainly I would prefer a more spirited horse, one that can best yours in a race, your grace!"

He laughed. "Trevlin, fetch Dorkus for Madame."

Dorkus proved to be a velvety bay mare whose soft brown eyes held a good deal of mischief, Evangeline quickly decided. She had not ridden since she and her father had returned to France, and she sent a silent plea heavenward that her modicum of skill had not totally deserted her. The duke cupped his hands and tossed her into the saddle. Evangeline held Dorkus's reins tightly, guessing that the mare would do her best to lay her low, if given the chance.

The duke led the small cavalcade down the lime-bordered drive toward the homewood that lay to the north of the castle. He skirted the forest and headed east, paralleling the coast, and pointed out the various tenant farms as they passed the neatly patchworked fields.

"Papa," Edmund cried, "let's go down to the beach. I want to show Cousin Eve my boat."

Evangeline gave a start, and Dorkus, her reins suddenly slackened, snorted and snapped up her head. It took her a moment to bring the mare back under control. She knew that she had to become familiar with the cove and the surrounding terrain, and the small cave that Houchard had told her about. It brought her back to a bitter reality. "Yes," she said to the duke, "I would like to see the beach, and Edmund's boat."

The incline to the beach was slight, the path well trodden. Evangeline turned in her saddle and looked back at the castle, judging its distance. It was a half a mile, no more, she decided, and the terrain was not overly hazardous.

Chesleigh's private stretch of beach was, Evangeline knew, blessed with a curved inlet surrounded by hearty trees and steep cliffs. It was indeed a very private spot, Evangeline soon saw, well hidden from the path above.

Before Evangeline had a chance to swing off Dorkus's back, the duke encircled her waist and lifted her easily down. For an instant, she felt the strength of him, his large hands nearly spanning her waist. She felt a trifle breathless when he released her, and wondered at herself. If he felt her reaction, he made no sign, merely turned to Edmund, who was scurrying across the coarse beach sand toward a small sloop anchored at the end of a long wooden plank.

"Take care, Edmund! I have no desire to take a swim!" He turned back to Evangeline, who was carefully scrutinizing the cove and the surrounding steep cliffs.

"Well, Madame? You appear to take great interest in the sea."

Evangeline started suddenly, for she had been too obvious, too interested, and launched instantly into speech. "Of course. As I told you, I much enjoy the sea. And just smell the air, and the sound of the waves, it is so very invigorating . . . it makes one feel alive!"

Richard cocked a black brow at her. "Your enthusiasm leads me to wonder if you are a changeling. If I remember aright, your esteemed uncle detested the smell of the sea. As did Marissa."

"You mistake the matter, your grace. My uncle was afraid of the sea, for he nearly drowned when he was a boy. Perhaps he gave his fear to Marissa."

"Oh no, you're wide of the mark there. Marissa's main objection was that the nasty salt spray made her hair curl into tight little ringlets."

"You forget, your grace, that Marissa was my first cousin," Evangeline said in a stiff voice.

"I will contrive to remember, Madame, that I am to treat everyone who has passed to the hereafter as a saint, miraculously cleansed of all faults and vanities."

"I did not mean to sound like a . . . prig. It is just that——" She drew to an abrupt halt, and pursed her lips, for she saw that he was laughing at her.

"No, not a prig, merely an overly sensitive girl who has, I wager, despite her French blood and her marriage, been too much sheltered."

"Hardly a girl, your grace!"

"Very true. An overly sensitive matron, in short."

"You are being quite provoking! I am not *that* old!"

The duke did not reply, his attention turned to Edmund, who had climbed into his small sloop and was lurching from port to starboard, delighting in making the boat heel wildly.

"Excuse me, Madame, but it seems I must rescue my

son. My valet, Bunyon, would give me a raking down if I returned with my hessians soused with salt water."

He turned on his heel and strode to the wooden dock toward Edmund. Evangeline's eyes followed him, a smile on her lips at his amusing banter. She caught herself and forced her attention and her thoughts back to her surroundings. She scanned the cliffs for a sign of the cave Houchard had told her about.

She slewed about at a shout of laughter, and her mouth curved reluctantly into a grin. The duke held Edmund high above his head, threatening, she imagined, to toss his recalcitrant son into the water. He lowered Edmund and tucked him under one arm, like a small, wriggling package.

"I think the little beggar is half fish," the duke said as he set Edmund on his sturdy legs. He looked down at Evangeline, his dark eyes twinkling outrageously, but said to his son, "Have patience, Edmund. We will leave your cousin in a ditch somewhere and come back for a swim. Unless, of course, she would like to join us."

"But Papa," Edmund said in disgust, "we never wear anything when we swim. Ladies do not like to bathe naked."

"He is quite young," the duke said in a bland voice.

"I think, Edmund," Evangeline said, avoiding the duke's eyes, "that I should much enjoy swimming, but only if the weather continues so warm. I have no wish to freeze to death. It is your father who will have to be left in a ditch."

"And I had thought to be bored for the next week," the duke remarked as he tossed her into the saddle.

"All of us must occasionally admit to being in error, your grace."

4

That afternoon, Evangeline was introduced to her maid, Emma, a slight, gentle-looking girl of some sixteen years.

"I remember this gown," Emma said in her soft voice, her hands caressing a gossamer yellow silk gown. "Her grace wore it on Christmas morning, three years ago. She gave me my Christmas present herself—a sewing box. So very lovely she was. Such a pity that she was taken so soon."

"Did you do sewing for her grace?"

"Oh, no, I did not have enough skill. She thought that I could do the mending for the servants." Emma raised questioning eyes to Evangeline. "I promise to be most careful, Madame."

Evangeline smiled. "I believe you will do quite nicely, Emma. As you can see, her grace and I were of a very different size. I am the maypole of the family."

Emma said with a briskness that belied her gentle countenance, "When I am finished, the gowns will look as if they were made especially for you."

"Even the bosom?"

"Even the bosom," Emma said firmly, her eyes twinkling.

Evangeline left Emma over an hour later, her fitting completed. She had done a gay pirouette in front of the mirror, clutching the yellow silk gown against her, laughing in her pleasure. Evangeline suddenly caught herself, for she realized with a start that she was indulging in vanity. She wanted the duke to notice her, to see his eyes light up in approval again. She was thinking of the duke as would a lady with nothing more on her mind than flirtation.

She forced her thoughts to Edmund, for that young lad had as yet no notion that his cousin Eve was to be his governess. But she found herself wondering about the curious old woman, Mrs. Needle. She supposed that she was a bit batty, but certainly harmless, and likely would tell her more about Marissa, the duke, and life at Chesleigh.

Evangeline made her way to the north wing. Unusual odors assailed her nostrils and her nose twitched as she climbed the winding stone steps to Mrs. Needle's room. She rapped lightly on the old oak door and heard a gentle voice tell her to enter.

Mrs. Needle did not look at all surprised to see her. "Welcome, Madame, I was hoping you would come to see me. Come in, and I'll give ye a nice cup of herbal tea."

Evangeline nodded, and followed the slight old woman into one of the oddest rooms she had ever seen. The room was much larger than she had expected, and divided by fine silk screens into a sitting area, a sleeping area set in an alcove, and what Evangeline guessed to be Mrs. Needle's herbal laboratory. There were rows of tables upon which stood an assortment of labeled bottles, containers of what she assumed were dried herbs, and pots set upon small braziers, emitting strong, but not unpleasant smells.

Mrs. Needle pointed an arthritic finger toward a worn crimson brocade settee, and Evangeline sat down.

"It was kind of you to invite me to your room, ma'am. It is most unusual. Have you skill as a physician?"

Mrs. Needle poured the herbal tea from a delicate china pot into two small cups and handed one to Evangeline. "No, Madame," she said, carefully easing herself into a high-backed chair across from Evangeline. "But I fancy that I have more knowledge than many of the charlatans who hold claim to that title."

As Evangeline sipped at the strong tea, pleasantly surprised by its piquant flavor, Mrs. Needle gazed at her silently for some moments.

"Forgive me for being blunt, Madame, but it seems to me that ye don't want to be here," she said at last, her voice soft and lilting, "but Chesleigh is where ye belong, I think."

Evangeline started. "I do not know what you mean," she said warily.

"Ye seem unsettled, as if ye're afraid of something. Ye know, her grace talked about ye, Madame. It was fond of ye she was, and she was saddened that she would not see ye again, so long as her father felt the way he did."

Evangeline said, "I do not know the reason for the falling out between my family and the duke's, Mrs. Needle. Perhaps you can enlighten me. You see, I also missed my cousin, and Lord Edmund."

Mrs. Needle sipped noisily at her tea before setting the cup upon a small table at her side.

"Her father sever the connection? Not likely, Madame, no, not at all likely. Far be it from him to willingly close off the till when his pockets were to let!"

"You are making no sense, Mrs. Needle. Marissa's father was an honorable gentleman, and a man of some means."

"Ye'll believe what ye wish, m'lady. It is not my place to tell ye truths ye have no wish to hear."

"I hope I am not so close-minded as to not want to hear a truth!" As the old woman merely regarded her in tolerant silence, Evangeline made to rise, not enjoying being treated like a stubborn child.

"Ye're impetuous, just as she was, but ye've known a very different life. Yer English mother was the saving of ye, child. She gave ye balance, curbed yer willful ways. Ye're proud, but not so proud that ye'd lose sight of what is right."

Evangeline nearly fell back onto the settee, her eyes fixed on Mrs. Needle's face. "How could you know about my mother? Indeed, what can you possible know of my character? You never met me until yesterday!"

"I know people, child. And of course her grace spoke of yer family. It's true of many people that their character shines in their eyes. You are one of those, Madame. But I sense something else about ye. If I did not think it impossible, I would say that ye feel not only fear about something, but also remorse."

Evangeline started forward at Mrs. Needle's words, though they had been wrapped in the gentlest of tones. She said quickly, with impatience, "You are saying nonsensical things, Mrs. Needle, and you are guessing at things you have no notion of!"

"I upset ye, child, forgive me."

Evangeline forced herself to calm. "I—I am sorry, but you are making me uncomfortable. I suppose it is all because of my new surroundings."

Mrs. Needle cocked her head, her eyes intent on Evangeline's face. "Aye, and there's his grace. He was a lad more impetuous than I think ye were, so wild that the old duke knew not which way to turn. He pushed the lad into marriage to tame him." Mrs. Needle shrugged her narrow shoulders. "At least he was blessed with Lord Edmund."

"I cannot believe you, Mrs. Needle. The duke's marriage to my cousin was a love match. I was told that it was by those I trust."

"Aye, the duke wanted her, as he's wanted many women. Ye were so young at the time, Madame, and like I told ye yesterday, ye've only memories from a child's mind. All yer truths are from the mouths of those who spoke to ye as a child."

"Well, I am no longer a child, and I pray you will grant me some sense. After all, I have been married."

The faded old eyes closed for a moment. "Aye," she said softly. "Loyalties are sometimes such dreadful burdens. They tear and rend us, even blind us if we let them."

Evangeline rose and shook her head, bewildered, and more shaken than she wanted to admit to herself. Was she so very obvious that one could just look at her and tell that all was not well? "I do not understand you. You know well that I am a . . . poor relation, here to be governess to Lord Edmund. That is all, I assure you. I thank you for the tea, Mrs. Needle. I must go now."

The old woman's soft voice stopped her at the door. "If ye wish to speak of anything, Madame, I am always here. One always needs a friend."

"I thank you, Mrs. Needle," Evangeline said finally. "Friendship is not something to be offered lightly or accepted lightly. You are very kind. Good day, ma'am."

Evangeline allowed Emma to dress her hair high atop her head with two heavy curls falling over her bare shoulders. She looked at herself in the long mirror, aware that Emma was standing behind her, awaiting her reaction. She smiled tremulously at her image. The yellow silk gown, high-waisted, and cut low over her breasts, fell in soft folds to the floor. Emma had removed the adorning flounce.

"You look magnificent, Madame," Emma said, her pleasure in her own handiwork sounding clear in her voice.

"Thank you, Emma. You are a wonder." She made her way down the staircase to the Crimson Salon where the duke was awaiting her for dinner.

She drew up short as Bassick moved to open the door

to the vast salon. The sound of a high tinkling laugh reached her ears nearly at the same moment as she became aware of an elegant young lady who was laughing up at the duke, her slender fingers resting lightly on his black sleeve. She saw another lady from the corner of her eye, a lady of older years, seated near the fireplace, two gentlemen standing behind her.

"Madame de la Valette," Bassick intoned.

The young lady dropped her hand and turned, her head cocked questioningly.

"Do come in, Madame," the duke said easily, walking toward her. His dark eyes warmed as he gazed at her, and she looked down at the toes of her yellow kid slippers, Marissa's slippers that pinched her toes, a flush rising on her cheeks.

"I would like you to meet my great-aunt, Lady Eudora Pemberly, and her goddaughter, Miss Felicia Storleigh. The gentleman with the overblown cravat that will choke him before the night is out, is Lord Pettigrew. And Sir John Edgerton, a dapper gentleman who fancies himself as great an arbitrator of fashion as the departed Brummel. Ladies, gentlemen, my cousin, Madame Evangeline de la Valette, recently arrived from Paris."

But Evengeline was not listening. She was staring, open-mouthed, at John Edgerton.

"An introduction is not necessary, Richard," John Edgerton said smoothly, stepping forward. "I have known Madame de la Valette since she was a girl with tumbled hair and rumpled skirts." He bowed deeply, took her lifeless hand in his, and lightly kissed her palm. "It is a pleasure to see old friends, Evangeline. I hope you are well. May I say that you are looking beautiful."

She saw the duke gazing at them with some surprise. "Yes, it is a pleasure and . . . unexpected, sir," she forced herself to say. Her eyes met his but she read nothing in them save simple pleasure at seeing her.

"I am monopolizing you, my dear. I beg pardon,

Lady Pemberly, but I have not seen Madame for some two years."

Evangeline forced herself to turn and make her curtsy to Lady Pemberly. Her how do y'dos were barely above a whisper.

"So you are Marissa's first cousin," Lady Pemberly said, examining her closely. "There is no great resemblance." Her tone left it uncertain who had been determined lacking in the comparison.

Evangeline squared her shoulders and replied in a distant voice, "That is true, ma'am. But then again, I am half English."

Lady Pemberly's painted face froze, and then, under Evangeline's fascinated gaze, slowly relaxed into lines of humor. Her green eyes, sly fox eyes, Evangeline thought, glinted. "Well, my girl, I'll say one thing for you—you're no mealy-mouthed chit! Come here, Felicia, and make your greeting! You've cast sheep's eyes long enough at poor Richard."

"Godmama, you know that his grace detests sheep! I beg you not to cast me in so low a light!" Before anyone could reply to this bit of fluff, Felicia dipped a credible curtsy to Evangeline.

"A pleasure, ma'am. I hope you will forgive our intrusion, but Godmama insisted that we come to dinner. And as Lord Pettigrew and Sir John were paying us a visit, she volunteered their escort for the evening. His grace, of course, is in an agony of delight at our presence. He has most nobly assured us that he adores surprises!"

"Your tongue runs on well-oiled wheels, child. You'll give Madame an odd notion of your character, in addition to making Richard cover his ears. My lord," she continued, turning to Lord Pettigrew, "methinks you have turned to stone. Have you nothing to say for yourself?"

Lord Pettigrew, who Evangeline had thought at first glance to be nothing more than one of those foppish

English gentlemen that her Papa so despised, surprised her by saying in a deep voice filled with kind humor, "With the lot of you about, my lady, it is difficult to fit in a word. Madame, I am delighted to meet you. I only hope that you, like Richard, adore surprises." He turned to John Edgerton. "You scoundrel, you gave no hint that you and Madame were already acquainted!"

"Gentlemen occasionally know when to keep their mouths shut, Drew," Lady Pemberly said, "particularly when it involves a lady."

"A lesson to be learned," John Edgerton said gently.

Evangeline forced a smile to her lips and said to Lord Pettigrew, "You have brought me so many unexpected surprises that I must think carefully before I thank you."

"Oh pooh, Godmama, his grace is far too polite to ever do such a thing! Isn't that so, your grace?"

"What the devil are you talking about, Felicia?" the duke drawled, forcing himself to turn his attention to her. He had been surprised to learn that John Edgerton had known Evangeline, and had found himself musing about what she had been like as a young girl of seventeen.

"Godmama said you would cover your ears if I did not control my tongue."

"It is ever a pleasure to look at you, Felicia," the duke said. "As to the rest, well, I must leave such judgment in better hands."

"Ah, you are ever a scold, your grace! I am trying so very hard to be a grown-up lady! You know my come-out is in just two months."

"Then shut your mouth and at least look the lady," Lady Pemberly said.

"Don't mind them, Madame," Lord Pettigrew said with soft, wry humor, seeing Evangeline blink. "Felicia is indestructible, you know, and much enjoys the twitting. I only hope that you are not overly fond of conversing. If you are, I fear that you are in for an exhausting evening. John and I find ourselves reduced to sign language, for we can't get a word in edgewise."

"I, fortunately, my lord, am an avid listener. I expect to find myself well entertained."

"You an avid listener, Madame?" the duke asked her. "I had not believed it of you."

"Why the sardonic tone, Richard?" Sir John said. "Did you lose a wager or something?"

Lady Pemberly snorted. "More than likely, John, it was a lost wager over a filly—of the two-legged variety."

The duke raised a supercilious eyebrow. "My dear ma'am, I sincerely doubt there is a man in the kingdom who would wager against me on such an occurrence."

Lord Pettigrew laughed heartily. "He's got you there, ma'am! I for one certainly would not!"

"Nor would I," John Edgerton said, smiling blandly. "I have learned to bow to the force majeure. Do you not agree, Evangeline, that it is sometimes best?"

Evangeline, aware that the duke was looking at her, said lightly, "Indeed, sir." She continued, turning her eyes to the duke, "I think, your grace, that you are beginning to sound like a conceited coxcomb. Surely there must be some lady who would not find you to her liking."

She had expected him to give her a set-down, but to her surprise, he did not. He smiled, a self-mocking smile. "There was such a lady, Madame."

Lady Pemberly said severely, "Come, Richard, do not fall into a fit of the doldrums! Sabrina Eversleigh did just as she ought. Only your pride was bruised, my boy, not your heart."

Lord Pettigrew looked distressed, and even Miss Storleigh appeared at a loss for words and fell to fretting with her reticule.

"Just so, my lady," the duke said softly. "A lady of my acquaintance, Madame," he said to Evangeline, "who is now comfortably wedded to a good friend of mine." He continued in an expressionless voice, "I was just telling my great-aunt that her sources of information are alarmingly rapid. You only arrived yesterday, and here she is, camping on my doorstep."

Evangeline was not at all surprised. It was likely, she thought, that John Edgerton was responsible. She looked toward the duke, wishing she could apologize to him. She had meant only to tease him. She had never considered that he could have been involved with another lady, much less been so recently entangled. She made haste to follow the duke's lead and change the topic. "I cannot imagine why my arrival could cause such interest, my lady," she said, a hint of challenge in her voice as her eyes flitted to John Edgerton's face.

"I could hazzard a guess," the duke said acidly.

Lady Pemberly rose from her chair to a majestic height, and shook out her stiff satin skirt. "You are being disagreeable, Richard, a character flaw you inherited, I daresay, from my niece. I trust that Bassick has seen to laying four more settings. I, for one, am ready for my dinner."

She turned to bend a penetrating look at Evangeline. "Richard tells me that you wish to remain at Chesleigh as Edmund's governess. I was expecting a faded, mousish girl with a tepid temperament and no pretense to beauty. You are not what I expected."

"Ah, my dear great-aunt, you did not behold her yesterday. Being at Chesleigh for just one day has wrought a great change."

"Your grace, Godmama is quite right," said Miss Storleigh. "You are behaving abominably! Poor Madame does not know what to make of us."

"Miss Storleigh," Evangeline said with a grin, "I believe that I have stepped into Bedlam! I look to you for support."

"Support!" Lady Pemberly snorted. "That's an uncertain commodity from Miss Loose Lips! I only brought her and not one of the other charming young ladies of my acquaintance so that Richard could not accuse me of matchmaking, in that disagreeable way of his."

Miss Storleigh said pertly, swinging her brown eyes toward the duke, "What would you say if his grace found me quite to his liking, Godmama?"

"I would say, you little twit, that Madame would be quite correct in her assessment—the lot of us would be ready for Bedlam! Now, Richard, I am prepared to be quite conciliating. Not another word shall pass my lips about your black behavior of recent weeks—all because of . . . well, never you mind! I do think the girl showed uncommon good sense to prefer the Viscount Derencourt to you, but I shall say nothing more about it."

The duke's expression was sardonic. "You show great restraint, my lady."

Evangeline said quickly, seeing that Lady Pemberly looked ready to take up her cudgels again, "Let me ring for Bassick. I vow I am famished!"

"No, allow me," Lord Pettigrew said. It seemed to Evangeline that all eyes were fastened on the ridiculous bell cord, all eyes save John Edgerton's. The duke raised a staying hand, walked to the gold tasseled cord, and gave it a ferocious tug.

The duke turned and said blandly, "Great-Aunt, will you take my arm? Perhaps I can contrive to have you trip on the way to the dining room."

"Rude boy," Lady Pemberly said in high good humor. "If you managed that, lad, you would have me camping here for a good three months!"

"Oh my God!" the duke said, appalled.

"Felicia," Lord Pettigrew said, moving quickly to that young lady's side, "my arm requires your attention."

"It appears that you are to put up with me, Madame," John Edgerton said softly. "May I have the pleasure of escorting you to dinner?"

Evangeline nodded, not meeting his eyes. She felt fear, raw and ugly within her, and it pulled her remorselessly back to that night in Paris. He walked slowly and they lagged behind Lord Pettigrew and Miss Storleigh. "It has been a long time, Evangeline. I always knew that you would grow into a beautiful woman. You do not disappoint me. But my gallant words find no favor, do they?"

"You are a lowly cur, sir," she hissed between her teeth. "You were supposedly my father's friend."

"And yours, my dear, until you rebuffed me. I have forgiven you, I suppose, for you were so very young and skittish. Have you never wondered what your life would have been like had you accepted me as your husband?"

She shook her head and stared stonily ahead of her.

"Well, it is now a moot point, I believe. We are at last together in an equally important venture. You are now well-placed, just as I foresaw. I see Richard looking back, so I must make haste. You will meet me tomorrow night at the cove at nine o'clock. There is much for us to discuss. Do not fail me, Evangeline, in anything. You could not bear the cost. Now smile, my lovely widow, and play the charming hostess."

Somehow her lips curved upward into a travesty of a smile. She said nothing more until they reached the dining room. As a footman held her chair for her, it seemed to her finally that her silence must be noticed, and she spoke to Miss Storleigh in an unnaturally high voice. "Tell me, do you live with your godmama?"

Lord Pettigrew swallowed a laugh.

"Good heavens no! She would have my tongue tied within a week if I did. She says she can only stand me in very limited doses, like some unpleasant medicine! No, I live with my mama in Pluckley. She's a widow, Madame, but not young and beautiful like you. She is so very quiet that people are constantly surprised to learn I am her daughter. Now, Papa——"

"An infinitesimal dose would be more like it," the duke said. "Eat your soup, Felicia, and give us all a moment's respite."

Lord Pettigrew laughed, reached over and patted Felicia's hand. "The soup is really quite exceptional," he said. His eyes, Evangeline saw, rested warmly on her upturned, impish face.

"Well, John," the duke said after some moments, "this is indeed a surprise. I hadn't expected to see you out of London at this time of year."

"He said that if I deserved a rest in the country, then he certainly did too," Lord Pettigrew said. "We shall be returning to London in a couple of days, Richard."

Miss Storleigh maintained a lively flow of chatter during the first course, and Evangeline's silence was fortunately not remarked. She learned over the course of braised pheasant and veal in thick cream sauce that Lord Pettigrew was a friend of long standing, who, Miss Storleigh sunnily informed her, had known her since she had been in leading strings, and had always treated her as would an indulgent uncle. Lord Pettigrew seemed so aghast at that statement that the duke saw fit to remind Miss Storleigh that the indulgent uncle had not yet attained his twenty-eighth year.

"His grace is quite right, Miss Storleigh," Evangeline slipped in. "It is the duke who more accurately fits that role. After all, he is all of thirty years old."

Miss Storleigh's eyes grew bright with mischief, and she wagged her fork at Evangeline. "Do not say so, Madame! Richard is the handsomest gentleman in all of England! Just imagine how dashing he would have looked as a gallant knight, his sword drawn——"

"You are making me ill, Felicia," the duke interposed, "as well as everyone else. Eat your dinner before I spill green asparagus all over my tablecloth."

"As if Richard needs an empty-headed chit right out of the schoolroom to extol his male beauty," Lady Pemberly said acidly. "It's a wonder to me that he hasn't become quite bored with all this silly female attention."

"I would say rather," Evangeline said, "that he has come to expect it as his just due."

"Don't be impertinent, Madame, else I might be tempted to extoll your . . . stumpy fingers in public."

Evangeline flushed, and dropped her eyes to her plate, only to see her full breasts blossoming above the lace ruching of her bodice. She raised her face to see John Edgerton gazing at her, an oddly assessing expression in his brown eyes.

"Really, Richard," Miss Storleigh scolded, "Madame's fingers are not at all stumpy. It is too bad of you to say such a thing."

Lord Pettigrew, seemingly recovered, turned indulgent eyes toward Miss Storleigh. "Richard only jests, Felicia, as Madame well knows."

"Yes, I know," Evangeline said lamely. She could hardy pay attention to the lively chatter. She looked at John Edgerton again, and a frisson raised gooseflesh on her arms. He was a traitor to England, and she, his accomplice.

Lady Pemberly said in a peevish voice to no one in particular as her dessert of Chantilly cream was unobtrusively placed in front of her by an expressionless footman, "I fear I shall go to my grave before I find a proper gentleman to marry my goddaughter, unless I can find one who has the good fortune to be deaf."

"Allow me to join the search," the duke said, robbing his words of offense by winking broadly at Felicia.

Miss Storleigh sighed and sat back in her chair. "It is so mortifying, Madame. I am just turned eighteen, indeed, I am to go to London for my come-out in two weeks. Godmama thinks I will end up on the shelf."

"Nonsense," Evangeline said stoutly. "You have the liveliest, sunniest disposition imaginable and are, I will add, quite pretty. You will have the gentlemen flocking to your door."

"They will quickly unflock," Lady Pemberly said, her tone sour.

"Perhaps Drew and John can induce their friends in the Ministry to send Felicia to Vienna to join Lord Castlereagh," the duke said. "I would trust her to keep the avaricious kings and petty princes from cutting up Europe to their own advantage."

Evangeline quickly lowered the spoonful of Chantilly cream back to her plate. She waited until the general laughter had subsided, then asked Lord Pettigrew, "You are part of the Ministry, my lord?"

"Yes, as my father was before me." He rubbed his thumb along the line of his jaw. "What worries me is that damned Corsican. I had thought that once on Elba he would have faded out of mind and into the history books, but I fear that he grows stronger even as we talk."

"I share your concern," John Edgerton said. "I myself never believed that it was a wise decision to imprison Napoleon on Elba."

"If only Louis were not such a bloody fool!" the duke said, unaware that Evangeline's face was as white as her bosom. "It has reached my ears that the French are turning against him. What do your informants say, John?"

"They feel that soon the Emperor will be strong enough to leave Elba and return to France," John Edgerton said quietly. "It remains to be seen what the French will do when and if he returns."

"You have informants, sir?" Evangeline asked.

"Every government must have a network of trustworthy people to provide needed information, Madame."

"Indeed," the duke said. "It is an occupation as old and honored as——"

"Just so," Drew said quickly, giving Felicia a sideways glance.

"I do not think *honored* is particularly the apt word, your grace," Evangeline said.

"Whatever else it is, it is a necessary function," Drew said, "and not a very suitable topic for dinner. I know, Madame, that even though you are half French, you have no love for Napoleon. I have no wish to distress you."

"And you are safe in England," the duke added, "no matter what happens."

"How can anyone be truly safe so long as there are men who support that monster?"

"Oh la, Madame," Miss Storleigh said, "leave the gentlemen to worry about such unpleasant things! Drew will see to it that we are not murdered in our beds."

Lady Pemberly said, as if on cue, "In your case, Felicia, perhaps I can convince Drew to be lax in his duties."

The gentlemen did not remain in the dining room over their port, Lady Pemberly having decided that she did not wish to spend the night at Chesleigh.

"You are convinced, Great-Aunt," the duke said ironically, "that Madame will not strangle Edmund?"

"I am convinced of many things," Lady Pemberly said obliquely, and swept majestically into the entrance hall. "Come, Felicia, don't dawdle! Drew, do help the girl with her wrap, else we'll never be on our way! John, you might as well make yourself useful by aiding Drew. Madame, I shall doubtless see you again. Don't let Edmund run you ragged."

"I much enjoyed meeting you, Madame," Lord Pettigrew said, forcing Evangeline's eyes to his face. "Shall I see you in London?"

"No, my lord. I have no desire for the social press."

"I will yet convince her otherwise, Drew," the duke said. "Oh my God," he said suddenly, in mock horror. "Don't tell me that you will be prisoner in the carriage all the way back to Grimsby Hall!"

"I fear it is to be my fate."

"And mine as well, Richard," John Edgerton said. He turned to Evangeline. "Again, it is a pleasure to renew our acquaintance. Perhaps we can all play a part in changing your mind. London, like the country, has its diversions."

"Indeed," Evangeline said.

"You needn't be so unflattering, Richard," Miss Storleigh said, harking back as she tapped her fingertips on his sleeve. "I have much to discuss with Drew. Unlike you, he finds me fascinating. Is that not true, my lord?"

"Of course, Felicia. I find I never have to worry about uncomfortable pauses when I am with you."

"Prettily said, Drew," Lady Pemberly said, and sailed majestically out the front doors.

After much fussing with rugs and hot bricks, Lady Pemberly was ready to depart, and with an imperious wave of her cane to the driver, the ancient carriage rolled away from Chesleigh. Evangeline watched with the duke from the wide portico until the carriage disappeared from their view.

"Will you join me in a glass of sherry before retiring?"

Evangeline wanted nothing more than to be alone, but she knew it would be churlish to refuse.

"I should like that, your grace," she said, forcing a smile.

Once in the library, the duke walked to the sideboard, poured her a glass, and handed it to her. "To your transformation. I did not have the opportunity to tell you, but you look charming tonight. Marissa's gowns do you justice."

"Thank you, your grace. You are most kind."

He waved away her words. "What do you think of my great-aunt Eudora and that minx Felicia?"

"I think they were both quite charming and so very . . . unexpected. Lord Pettigrew was also quite pleasant."

"You have no kind words for John Edgerton?"

Evangeline was silent for a moment. "It is pleasant to see old friends again, particularly after such a long time."

"He appears to know you well," the duke said. He sipped his sherry.

Evangeline wondered at his interest, but since she saw no reason to lie to him, she said quietly, "If you would know the truth, I was taken aback to see him so unexpectedly. He and my father were friends and he spent a good deal of time in Somerset, where he has a summer home. He asked my father if he could pay me his addresses, and my father refused because of the difference in our ages. I was not even seventeen at the time. I had not seen him again until this evening."

"He seemed rather pleased to see you. He has never married, you know."

Although his tone was cool, Evangeline saw that his dark eyes were intent upon her face. She said, "I have never cared for Mr. Edgerton, but since he is your friend, as well as Lord Pettigrew's, I suppose that I will meet him from time to time. I assure you, your grace, that I will be civil." She added in a low voice, "I only hope that he will not wish to continue where he ended over two years ago."

"I see no particular reason for you to worry," the duke said. "Edgerton is a gentleman, and would not seek to importune you with unwelcome attention. Besides, you are under my protection."

"Of course, you are quite right," she said in a toneless voice. "There is no need to concern yourself, your grace." She saw that he would say more and hastened to ask, "You have known Lord Pettigrew long? He seems quite nice, rather unsuited to his profession."

Richard nodded. "All my life. Drew chose to labor for England, following in his father's rather ponderous footsteps. He owns a country house near my great-aunt Eudora's." He paused a moment, aware of a strained look in her eyes, and wondered if all the talk of Napoleon at dinner had upset her. "If it is Bonaparte that disturbs you, Madame, I assure you that there is nothing for you to fear. You are quite safe here."

"No, no," she said quickly. She did not want to think about what she felt.

"I am *fatiguée*—tired," she managed, wanting only to get away from him and escape to her room.

"Your lapse into French tells me as much," he said lightly. "I hope you will sleep better tonight."

"Yes, I am certain that I shall. Good night, your grace," she said with a taut smile.

Evangeline bounded upright and jerked away the covers. She dashed her hand across her damp forehead and pushed her hair away from her face. She was trembling violently, though the room was cozily warm. She squirmed back under the covers, pulled them to her chin, and gazed up at the dark ceiling. Her dream had been so real that she could still hear Houchard's voice. "You are innocent for your nineteen years, Mademoiselle. See that it does not endanger your common sense."

She lay staring wide-eyed, unable to keep the images from her mind. Evangeline felt tears sting the back of her eyes, but she did not give over to a bout of weeping. It would solve naught.

She rose from her bed and draped her wool dressing gown over her cotton nightgown. She wriggled her feet into slippers and padded from her room, her destination the Chesleigh kitchen, in the east wing. She raised her single candle high in front of her as she trod soundlessly down the carpeted corridor to the staircase.

The vast house was eerily quiet, but Evangeline felt no trepidation. Lying in her bed bound to that terrible dream was far more frightening. She suddenly smiled at herself. A glass of warm milk. Always her mother's solution to any upset, her answer to any nightmare.

Evangeline drew up suddenly as the great front doors flew open. She felt a prickle of fear before she recognized the duke. He kicked the doors closed with the heel of his boot and strode into the entrance hall, his step none too steady. She stepped from the shadows, her lone candle held tightly in her hand.

"Your grace?"

His head whipped up, and for a long moment, he simply stared at her. He ran his hand through his disheveled hair, muttered an oath under his breath, and barked, "What the devil are you doing here?"

"I believe that I live here, your grace," she said, a tentative smile on her lips. "I'm sorry to have startled you. I was going to the kitchen for a glass of milk."

A look of acute nausea crossed his face.

"Allow me to offer you something more comforting than milk, Madame. Would you care to join me for a moment in the library—for a glass of brandy?" Without waiting for her response, he strode to her and took the candle from her hand. "You can tell me why on earth you're even awake at this ungodly hour."

She realized that he was drunk, and stood uncertain, wondering what she should do. "Perhaps I should just . . ." she began, only to realize that he would likely leave her and take her candle. "Very well, your grace."

She followed in his wake into the library and watched him fling off his greatcoat and gloves and throw himself into a chair before the fireplace.

He was silent for many moments, and she walked quietly to him and gently touched her hand to his shoulder.

The duke, foxed though he was, was not completely under the hatches. He slewed about in his chair and closed his fingers over her wrist. "Forgive my inattention, Evangeline." He grinned crookedly up at her. "I forgot that you were waiting for your brandy."

"Oh no," she said. "I really would prefer a glass of milk. I had a nightmare, you see."

He seemed unaware that his grip had tightened about her wrist and she winced. "I would that you not break it, your grace."

Her hand was dropped. "Forgive me again, Madame." His voice was only slightly slurred. He turned penetrating, dark eyes up to her face. "Do you often have nightmares?"

"Of course not," she said quickly, shaking her head. "And you, your grace, why are you coming home so very late?"

"I do not need to justify anything I choose to do, Madame," he growled in a harsh voice through the brandy haze.

She dropped to her knees beside his chair and looked up into his flushed face. "I am sorry. It is just that I was worried about you."

"I have no need for another mother." Suddenly his eyes narrowed as he took in her appearance. She realized with an uncomfortable start that her hair hung loose down her back, several tresses falling free over her shoulder.

He reached out his hand and lightly wrapped a mass of thick hair about his long fingers. "Why did you come in here with me, Evangeline?" he asked, his voice strangely thick.

"I feared that you would take my candle and leave me in the dark."

"So the pleasure of my company had nothing to do with it. Are you always so forthright?"

"I meant no insult, your grace."

He leaned toward her, and his fingertips lightly traced the line of her jaw. He tugged at the mass of hair wrapped about his fingers to bring her face closer.

Evangeline could think of nothing to say, and for a long moment, closed her eyes. She knew that she should pull away, but her body did not obey her.

"Your hair is exquisite," she heard him murmur. She opened her eyes to see him gently rubbing a thick tress against his cheek. A fleeting look of anger or pain, she could not be certain which, darkened his eyes.

"Richard?" She closed her fingers tentatively over his hand. "I do not wish to see you unhappy. Is it the lady . . . who wed another man?"

He pulled his eyes away from her and stared into the fireplace, though he did not release her hair. "Sabrina," he said softly. He gave a deep, self-mocking laugh. "It makes no matter! I am by no means a broken man, my dear, merely a vastly conceited one who has never before had his will gainsaid. The lady in question, Sabrina Eversleigh, did me the honor of falling in love with a viscount before she rejected my suit. I believe that her husband, as great a rakehell as I, did her the service of finally returning her regard. It is just as well. I did not love her, Evangeline. I sometimes believe that such an emotion is quite beyond my ken. But I wanted her."

Evangeline remained very still, her eyes fastened upon his face. She knew that he would regret his words on the morrow when he was once again sober and in full command of himself. She should have left him, stopped him from speaking further, but something held her still.

"Why are you so questioning, Madame? You were married, you know what it means when a man wants a woman."

Inadvertently, she shook her head.

"Then allow me to enlighten you, my lady." He lowered his head and she felt his warm breath at her temple. She felt his hand stroke her throat, and when his lips lightly touched hers, she felt a tremor of unexpected pleasure. His mouth grew more demanding and she felt his tongue gently probe at her lips. She parted her own and arched toward him, as if by her body's instruction. Tentatively, she clasped her hands about his shoulders, drawing him closer to her. He released her mouth and rained gentle, caressing kisses upon her eyes, her cheeks, the tip of her nose. His fingers moved gently downward to caress her breasts through her cotton nightgown, and she cried out softly into his mouth, her mind begging him to let her go. But his fingers lightly closed over her. She pulled back, awash with embarrassment, for a man had never touched her there before.

"I—I am sorry, your grace!" she gasped, trying to calm her ragged breath. "I did not mean to . . ."

"No, it is I who am sorry, Evangeline," he said gently, pulling himself up. "I would not have dishonored you. I would never be that drunk."

She stared up at him, mute.

"You are a beautiful, responsive woman, Evangeline. Your husband was a very fortunate man to have possessed you."

She flushed her embarrassment, and shook her head. "I know nothing of such things, your grace."

Richard stared down at her bowed head. He had felt her tentative passion, and wondered whether he would have caught himself in his drunken state, if she had not. It was likely that she had not been with a man since her husband's death, and was obviously vulnerable. But her simple words struck a discordant note in his mind. If her husband had been a selfish, stupid man who had cared only for his own pleasure, why had she responded with such passion toward him?

He stood up quickly, pulling Evangeline to her feet with him.

"I pray you will forgive me, Evangeline. Such a thing will not occur again, as long as you are living under my roof. Please do not take me into dislike or fear. I would not hurt you."

"I know. There is nothing to forgive, your grace."

He gently set her away from him, for he felt desire twist in his groin. "You must go to bed, Evangeline. It is very late."

She stared at him silently for a long moment, then said in a curiously sad voice, "I could never fear or dislike you. That would have to fall to you. But you are right, it must not happen again. Good night, your grace." She picked up her candle with a trembling hand and walked quickly from the library, quietly closing the door behind her.

Richard dashed the back of his hand over his befuddled brow, and stared balefully at a full decanter of brandy on the sideboard. He turned and kicked the dead embers in the fireplace with the toe of his boot, and watched the cold ashes flutter lightly upward. What a stupid way to have spent the night, he thought, disgusted at himself, drinking himself into oblivion and for no particularly good reason.

When he gained his bedchamber, a vast, beamed room that was as glum as his mood, he found to his relief that his valet, Bunyon, had already taken himself to bed. The last thing he wanted at three in the morning was a bear-jawing from that severe individual.

He lay in his bed wondering at himself and about Evangeline, her eager yet uncertain attempt at returning his passion, the breathless moan of desire that had escaped her lips, innocently, naturally. Even as he tried to convince himself that this night must be forgotten, he felt again the soft roundness of her breast in his hand, the urgent arching of her young body against him. It was just as well, he thought, that he was returning to London at the end of the week. He found her company too tempting, her beauty too disturbing. He would put distance and time between them to clear his mind of her. It was what he wanted.

5

Evangeline trailed downstairs the following morning, even more awash with embarrassment than she had been in her bedchamber after she left the duke. Her response to him, though it seemed quite natural even now, still shocked her. How often during the past two years her father had chided her about her aloofness, her complete lack of interest in the young men, both English and French, who had found their way to the Beauchamps' door. "But Papa," she had protested, "they are so very nice and so very boring! Or they are ridiculously possessive, like Henri!" "They are young, *ma fille*, and inexperienced," he had said with a sorrowful shake of his white head. "Boys become men, just as girls become women." But Evangeline knew it was not their youth. She had met older gentlemen, men of the world, and not one of them had touched her head or her heart, not one had ever made her want to feel passion, or even to laugh or quarrel. She remembered yet again the duke's strength, and the gentleness of his caressing hand upon her breast. She reminded herself that he had been foxed, that if he had not imbibed so much brandy, he would never have allowed himself to behave toward her as he had.

She had agreed with him that it must not happen again, although her reasons were quite different from his. Nothing could change the fact that she was here dishonestly, that she was, in fact, betraying him, just as Edgerton and Houchard were using her.

She shrugged her shoulders dolefully. In all likelihood, he had dismissed her from his mind the moment she had left him. He was, after all, a man who took it for granted that every lady of his acquaintance would willingly shave off her eyebrows for the privilege of securing his regard, if for but one evening.

When she reached the breakfast room, she flushed in embarrassed anticipation. She discovered that the duke was not there, much to her relief. He was likely still abed, she thought, sleeping off the surfeit of brandy he had consumed. She reached out for a slice of toast, only to find a plate of *croissants* in front of her plate.

"Good morning, Madame," Mrs. Dickinson said placidly. "I see you have noticed the croxants. Cook hopes they're to your liking, she not being French and all."

"It is most kind of Cook, Mrs. Dickinson. Please convey my thanks to her."

"I shall, of course. But it was the duke's suggestion. His grace said you don't care for hearty English breakfasts and as he did not want you to fade away, he believed the croxants to be just the thing."

"They are delicious," Evangeline said, biting on a warm, flakey roll.

Mrs. Dickinson beamed. "Is there anything else you require?"

"Do you know when his grace will be breakfasting, Mrs. Dickinson?"

"He already has, Madame, at least an hour ago. He is now riding with Lord Edmund, I believe."

Evangeline heaved a sigh of relief that she did not as yet have to face the duke. And there would be no governessing for the morning.

She was thinking how to spend her new-found time

when a knot of anxiety formed in her stomach at the thought that she was to meet John Edgerton that night. Although Houchard had told her something of the private beach and the hidden cave, she had not seen the cave the day before. She knew she should search it out now. There was too much at stake to risk being late for her meeting.

She changed into a serviceable old gown and a stout pair of walking shoes and walked briskly from the castle. Tangy salt air greeted her, and a light breeze ruffled her hair. It was a glorious, warm day, quite a surprise for the first of March, so warm in fact that by the time she reached the cove, her gown clung uncomfortably to her back.

When she reached the beach, she shaded her eyes with her hand and gazed southward. The seaward side of the cliff jutted out nearly to the water's edge, its cragged face shadowed in the morning sun. She made her way quickly toward it through the coarse sand. She saw the cave only when she was nearly upon it; overhung with scraggly bushes that protected it from all but the most inquisitive eyes.

She bowed her head as she entered and shivered at the sudden damp chill. She groped her way inside until her eyes grew accustomed to the darkness. It was long and narrow, extending some twenty-five feet into the cliff. She pulled up short, realizing suddenly that the ground was wet beneath her feet. She reached up and ran her fingers along the stone walls, slimy with sea moss, to a level well above her head. At high tide the sea no doubt filled the cave.

She retraced her steps to the mouth of the cave and stood quietly for a moment, lifting her face upward to the warm sun. She was on the point of leaving when she saw the duke, waist-high in water, carrying Edmund upon his shoulders, some thirty feet up the beach. She quickly drew back into the dim entrance in alarm. She considered staying safely in the cave until the duke and Edmund had left the beach, but she saw that the tide was rising quickly, and she would likely get a good soaking. It was, after all, not at all suspicious that she should be exploring. She resolutely lowered her head and emerged once again from the cave, but her unruly eyes would not remain fastened to her toes. She had never before seen a naked man. The muscles of his broad back rippled as he lifted Edmund high above his head and tossed him forward into the water. She heard Edmund's shriek of delight and saw a tangle of arms and legs. When the duke stood again, Edmund was clinging to his father's back, his arms wrapped about his neck. He set off toward deeper water with sure, swift strokes.

Before the duke could turn toward shore, she walked to the shade of an overhanging bush, and stepped behind it, out of sight. She watched as he swiveled about in the water, back toward shore. He stepped down in waist-high water, the gentle waves lapping about him, raised Edmund again to his shoulders, and strode forward, his curling black hair falling in boyish disarray over his forehead.

Though her face reddened, she did not lower her eyes. Her pulse began to race. There was nothing else remotely boyish about him. His chest was broad and covered with a tangle of black hair that narrowed over his muscled belly, then bushed out below. She had never thought that a man could look so exquisite. Her eyes dropped to his thick muscled thighs, and to his manhood, and she swallowed in surprise. She wondered what it would feel like to touch him, and her tentative knowledge of what occurred between men and women left her strangely breathless.

"Papa! Papa!" she heard Edmund shout. "There's Cousin Eve!" He was waving wildly toward her hiding place. "She's here to watch us swim!" Drat Edmund anyway for having such sharp eyes! Since she couldn't very well hide, she picked up her skirts and dashed past the cave away from them, only to realize that the cliff curved in sharply toward the water, cutting off her escape.

"I see her, Edmund!" she heard the duke shout. "Indeed, I believe we have been providing her a swimming exhibition for some time now!"

Evangeline stopped in her tracks and whirled about. He had known she was there, all along he had known! He stood ankle-deep in the water and made no move whatsoever to cover himself. Her unruly eyes did not leave him, and she heard him laugh.

"Fetch me a towel, Edmund. Perhaps your Cousin Eve would care to join us, scamp."

He finally took the large fluffy towel his son brought to him and began to dry himself. "You might as well join us, Madame," he called to her, lazy amusement in his voice.

"Ladies can't swim, Papa," Edmund said with conviction. "Not like you can."

"Then perhaps," the duke said easily, as Evangeline did not speak, "she would like me to give her lessons."

"I swim quite well, your grace!" Evangeline said in a haughty but unnaturally high voice. Had the man no modesty?

"I thought perhaps you would," he agreed with a wolfish grin. He began to walk toward her, the towel wrapped about his waist, and she saw devilment in his dark eyes. "Get dressed, Edmund," he said over his shoulder, "whilst I speak to your cousin."

"I was out walking!"

"Of course you were, Evangeline. I trust you have found all the . . . scenery to your liking."

"You seem to be quite sure that I have," she snapped at him. She thought he would continue to mock her, laugh at her, but to her discomfort, his dark eyes searched her face, his expression thoughtful.

"You must go back to the castle, Evangeline," he said, his voice suddenly gentle. "I will endeavor that

Edmund not shout to the world that his cousin watched him swim with his father."

"I—that is, I shall your grace." She turned on her heel and struggled back up the cliff without a backward glance.

"You're unseemly quiet, my lady," Emma said to Evangeline in a shy voice as she brushed her hair and pushed a hair pin into its proper place.

"I am homesick, I expect," Evangeline said, not meeting her maid's eyes.

"It is such a pity that his grace will leave soon. Chesleigh is so much gayer when he is here, at least that's what Cook and Mrs. Dickinson say."

"You are likely right," Evangeline said, staring vacantly into the mirror as she shook out her skirt. The elegant dark green gown was cut simply with no adorning flounces, its high neck exquisitely hemmed with Valenciennes lace. Marissa had always had exquisite taste. *Even Monsieur Houchard had known that.* "You will not have to wear your rags long, Mademoiselle," he had said. "The proud duke would not allow it." The memory of Marissa's wedding day came to her mind as she stared at the dress—Marissa, dressed in her white bridal clothes, laughing in her soft, enticing way.

"The gown is lovely, Emma," Evangeline said. "You're an accomplished needlewoman."

Evangeline flushed with embarrassment when she saw the duke standing at the bottom of the stairway, watching her descent.

"Will you join me for luncheon, Madame?" he asked in a bored, polite voice.

"Yes, your grace," she said only.

It was not until after the duke had dismissed the footman that he said, "Do come out of the boughs, Evangeline. I had no wish to put you to the blush, as I believed I might after this morning, and, of course . . .

last night. There are a multitude of alert eyes at Chesleigh, you know. Did you enjoy your walk?"

"It was rather warm today for a walk."

"Agreed, which was why I allowed Edmund to talk me into a swim."

"Do you swim often?" she asked, hoping for a neutral topic.

"Whenever I am in residence here, yes. If the mild weather holds, you can expect to find me in the cove at about the same time every morning."

"I did not go to the cove to find you swimming, your grace!"

"I know. Incidentally, I saw you stepping out of the cave. Do have a care if you visit it again, especially at high tide. When I was a boy, I was foolish enough to hide there from my tutor, and got a good soaking for my efforts."

She smiled, trying to picture him as he must have looked at Edmund's age. "I shall be careful. I noticed that the cave walls were damp even at the very back. When the tide is high, it fills the cave?"

"Indeed it does."

"I shall be quite careful," she said, and lowered her eyes to her plate. She knew that he was regarding her and felt impelled to say something, anything. "I was simply exploring! It was so warm, I thought to wade in the sea."

"Forgive me for disturbing your solitude." His voice was filled with amusement at her inept effort at explanation, and Evangeline stood up and looked down at him. "It would be quite small of me, your grace, to wish to forego such an . . . educational experience!"

"Surely, Madame, I did not provide you with an excess of new . . . knowledge."

Her eyes widened at him. She had blundered. "No, of course you did not! It is just that I was not precise in my choice of words."

"Odd," he said lazily, sitting back in his chair and

crossing his arms over his chest. "I was of the opinion, formed of course after an admittedly short acquaintance, that you are usually quite precise in your conversation."

"You are being quite provoking," she said, turning to leave him.

"I am also of the opinion that you much enjoy crossing swords with me, Madame. Why are you running away?"

She turned in her tracks and snapped, "I have never run away from anyone, your grace! As to crossing swords with you, I will admit that you are not a dullard, as I have found most Englishmen to be."

The duke nodded agreeably. "Since you spent your years in the country in Somerset, I am not surprised at your prejudice. Red-faced squires and provincial locals smelling of the stables would cause anyone's wit to grow rusty with disuse. Was your husband such a man?"

"Of course not! He was French!"

"Ah. Allow me then to describe him, as you have so politely described Englishmen. He was short, quite dark, was undoubtedly possessed of an oily kind of charm, and did not bathe every day."

Evangeline flushed. The man she had picked to describe as her husband was Henri, the Comte de Pouilly, the young Frenchman who had been enamored of her, who happened to fit the duke's description quite nicely. "He did bathe often!" she snapped. She suddenly remembered that Henri was much addicted to the cologne bottle. "At least I think he did," she added, without thinking.

"You *think* he did? Really, Evangeline, if you had half the curiosity for your husband that you have shown for me in just two days, I cannot imagine that you would have any doubts at all on the subject."

For a long moment, she simply stared at him. "I—that is, Henri was . . . very modest!"

"He sounds like a . . ." Richard stopped, seeing that

Evangeline was quite red in the face. He wasn't certain why he was drawing her, save that he couldn't seem to resist. He rose and looked down into her stormy blue eyes. "I am off to Portsmouth to see a new hunter. Is there anything I can bring you?"

She shook her head. "No, I thank you. You have provided me with quite enough. I am hopeful Lord Edmund will show more pleasure in my company."

"I wish you luck, Madame. Incidentally, when I return, I would like to go riding. Will you join me?"

Evangeline was silent for a moment. She knew that she could hardly avoid being with him, if he wished it. "Yes," she said, "I should like that."

"But why do I have to learn all the letters?" Edmund squirmed about and cast her a put-upon look. He was a bright child, precocious in his speech, and possessed of an abundance of restless energy.

"You must learn your letters so that you can read and write." She quickly saw that he was not convinced. "I thought, Edmund, that you wished to be like your father," she added coolly.

"I am like my father," Edmund announced.

"Your father knows how to read and write."

He eyed her suspiciously, and Evangeline, certain that she was violating every precept of governessing, resorted to bribery. "If you learn your letters, Edmund, I promise you that after your father returns to London, I shall swim with you mornings that are warm enough. Indeed, I shall teach you how to swim . . . as well as your father."

"You are big enough," he observed.

"And strong as an ox." Forgive me, Miss Blackader, Evangeline said silently to her former governess, who now resided in splendid isolation in a cottage near Manchester.

"A is for anchor, like on a ship," Evangeline began,

her finger over Edmund's, tracing the letter on the page.

Evangeline was amazed when she chanced to look up at the clock at how quickly the time had passed. She gave Edmund a quick hug, for he had proudly written out his name. She glanced up to see the nursery door open and a tall, gauntly thin man dressed in unremitting black step into the room. She had seen him several times in the past two days, but had not met him.

"Bunyon!"

Edmund bounded from his chair, his letters forgotten.

Only the veriest hint of a smile rose on the man's thin face. "Forgive my intrusion, ma'am," he said, walking with Edmund toward the small table. "His grace suggested that I relieve you of your duties before Lord Edmund runs you ragged. I am Bunyon, you know, his grace's valet."

"I can now write, Bunyon!" Edmund wrapped his short arms about the valet's thin leg and gave it a tug.

Unlike the other Chesleigh servants, Bunyon did not appear to be overly gratified by the Heir's attention. Indeed, he paid Edmund no heed, his brown eyes fastened on Evangeline.

Evangeline smiled and rose from her chair. "At least I have gotten him through the alphabet. And he can indeed write his name." She tousled Edmund's black curls. "Would you like to show Bunyon how much you have learned?"

"Most impressive, Lord Edmund," Bunyon said, peering down at the large blocked letters.

"I would like to play now, if you please, Cousin Eve," Edmund said.

"I know," Evangeline said, suddenly contrite. "I fear I have held you too long." She continued to Bunyon, "I have not often been with children before, you see, save, of course, when I was younger. I must learn more than he does, I think."

"Bosh," Bunyon said. "It is his grace who has need to learn."

Evangeline blinked.

"Now, Lord Edmund, you must take your nap. Then we shall talk about playing."

Edmund began to wail his protest, but Bunyon merely lowered his bushy eyebrows. Edmund hemmed and hawed, but seemed to know it would gain him naught. "Very well," he said at last.

"I shall tuck Lord Edmund in his bed, ma'am. He has a way of cozening Ellen that is shameful."

The duke rode at a leisurely pace back to Chesleigh, a satisfied smile on his bronze face. He had purchased the hunter he wanted, and at a price that suited him. Indeed, he thought, he had been uncharacteristically tight-fisted, as was his father's habit. When he turned Emperor into the stable yard, he saw Evangeline standing next to Trevlin, in serious conversation. His eyes crinkled in amusement, for she spoke very expressively, her hands leaving no doubt of her meaning.

"Dorkus, Madame?"

She smiled at him ruefully. "I do wish to try, Trevlin. Bring her out. I shall endeavor to keep her at a slow pace."

"Tommy exercised her this morning, Madame. I doubt she'll give you any trouble today."

"Your timing is exquisite, Evangeline," the duke said, drawing Emperor to a halt. "But if you wish to race, it will have to be another day, for Emperor is fagged."

"Perhaps you could ride Biscuit," Evangeline suggested with a bland smile.

"Up with you, you smart-mouthed chit."

Dorkus seemed in an amiable mood when they set out, not at all inclined to do away with her rider. The duke led them southward along a narrow road overlooking the sea. Richard was in the midst of telling her of the hunter he had purchased when a loud horn blast sounded from an oncoming mail coach. "Pull over, Evangeline," the duke said, guiding Emperor down a slight incline off the road.

Evangeline tugged at Dorkus's reins just as the rumbling coach pulled around a bend in the road. The driver sounded the horn once again, and Dorkus, taking exception to the pounding horses' hooves and the raucous horn, reared up on her hind legs as the coach lurched past them, ripping the reins from Evangeline's hands.

Evangeline gave a cry of surprise and went flying off Dorkus's back to land on her bottom by the side of the road. For a moment she simply sat there, querying her body for any hurt.

"Are you all right?" the duke shouted, vaulting from Emperor's back.

" 'Tis just my dignity that is bruised," Evangeline said ruefully, rubbing her bottom.

"A bit more than that, I think," the duke said, holding out his hand to her.

Evangeline let him pull her up and dusted off her skirt. "What a very lowering thing to have happen!"

"You are a mess, Madame," he said, grinning at her.

"It is unkind of you to be so agreeable! At least I am a live mess."

She touched a shaking hand to her tangled hair, and began to smooth it back from her forehead.

He laughed. "A woman's vanity. If all else fails to fluster her, remind her she is not the picture of perfection." He reached into his waistcoat pocket and pulled out a handkerchief to mop her face.

"That dratted coach flung dust and dirt all over me."

"Why did you not simply pull Dorkus to the side of the road as I told you to?"

Evangeline did not feel up to dissimulation. "I have been found out," she said on a sigh.

He cocked his head at her, his eyes questioning.

"I should have taken Biscuit."

"Why? What on earth are you mumbling about? It was not your head you hit, was it, Evangeline?"

Her head snapped up. "I am not mumbling. It was stupid, I suppose. I have not ridden in some time, but I did not want you to think me not up to snuff, so I took Dorkus instead of Biscuit."

"Are you telling me," he said, "that you rode a horse you were not certain you could handle?"

She nodded, feeling more abysmal by the moment.

"Not only were you foolish, Madame, you also insult me. Do you believe me such a coxcomb?"

Evangeline turned away from him and he heard her sigh deeply. "I have behaved quite badly, it seems. Please forgive me."

"I think I distrust you when you act the woebegone martyr. Enough, my girl. It is time to go home."

Although Evangeline eyed Dorkus dubiously, she allowed the duke to toss her into the saddle.

"You have no need to worry, I will stay at your side. Men are good for something, after all."

"They are also bad for many things," she said in a stony voice.

He gazed at her profile sharply. "Would you care to explain?"

She shook her head, not turning to face him.

He wanted to push her for an answer, but restrained himself, realizing that it was probably her husband she was referring to. She was so young, and although she had been married, she seemed at times like this very innocent, her flashes of temper and her ready wit sitting oddly on her shoulders.

"Bunyon has been taking me to task," the duke said over dinner that evening.

"I can't imagine anyone taking you to task, even Bunyon."

He gave her a crooked grin. "You believe me so very aloof, Madame, so very formidable?"

"Yes," she replied simply. "Do you not remember your behavior toward me when you found me in your library?"

He frowned into his glass of wine. "I was in a black mood that day. You surprised me."

"Still . . ."

He could have let the matter drop, but chose, perversely, to draw her. "How a man treats a woman in his own library has little to do with his valet. Each has their role, hers being to serve the gentlemen tea, and keep her tongue safely in her mouth."

To his admirably concealed pleasure, she flung her napkin on the table and turned on him. "You bumptious ass! I would wager that I know far more about *manly* subjects than you do, you who live the life of a frivolous hedonist, concerned with only his own pleasures!"

"Really, Madame," he said mildly, "you must watch your language. Not only is it unbecoming of you to call me an ass——"

"Bumptious ass!"

"Ah yes, bumptious ass." He continued imperturbably, "It is also highly improper for you to admit knowing about such things as hedonists. As to my pleasures, perhaps you should meet the ladies of my . . . acquaintance. I have never been concerned with my own pleasure more than with theirs."

"I have no wish to hear about your mistresses, your grace!"

"But, Madame, 'twas you who introduced the topic," he said in innocent surprise. "I was but explaining myself."

"Still, I have no interest in hearing you tout your prowess. I begin to think you woefully conceited, your grace."

"Doubtless you are right." He saw that she was flushed, whether in anger or in embarrassment, he was not certain, and elected to return to less trying topics. "As I said before you so unfairly attacked me, Bunyon roundly chided me this afternoon."

She ceased tapping her fingertips on the table. "About what?"

"For leaving you alone here with Edmund."

She felt a knot of anxiety begin to form in her stomach, next to the delicious pheasant pie. "I don't understand," she said.

"Bunyon thinks Edmund is old enough to accompany me to London, and old enough for a male tutor. He thinks you are too kind and too young to have my spoiled son in your charge."

She was caught in sudden panic. "But if you take Edmund, there is no reason for me to stay at Chesleigh."

"Quite true. Thus, the both of you will come to London with me tomorrow."

"No!"

He arched a thick, black brow upward. "I beg your pardon?"

Dear God, she could not accompany him to London! She was to meet John Edgerton in but two hours, and he had told her explicitly she was to stay at Chesleigh. She threw herself into frenzied speech. "I . . . that is, you know I have no wish to go to London! Please, your grace, allow me to stay here. I can handle Edmund, I promise you! I realize that I have much to learn about teaching children, but I will not fail you." She drew to a shaking halt, aware that he was regarding her closely.

"I do not understand what you are saying, Evangeline," he said softly.

"Please . . . I beg you. There is nothing to understand. Please, your grace, grant me this."

Richard felt himself strangely pulled. He had not expected such a reaction from her. Indeed, he had believed her initial refusal to go to London the result of her embarrassment at thrusting herself, an impecunious, unknown relation, upon his mother. He had actually felt pleased at his decision, for he realized that despite his thinking of the night before, he did want to take her to London, to show her the sights and introduce her to his mother. He was not at all certain of his intentions toward her, save that he did not want her to stay by herself at Chesleigh, her only companion his young son. And, he realized with a wry smile at himself, he disliked having his wishes crossed.

"I would worry about you," he said finally. "No," he added firmly, "I cannot allow it."

Evangeline rose slowly and pressed her palms flat on the table. She was desperate. She had already pleaded with him and he had not changed his mind. She drew a deep breath and said in a cold voice, "If you will not allow me to remain at Chesleigh, then I must leave. I will not go to London."

"You are being pig-headed, Madame!" he growled. "You will do exactly as I tell you, and that's an end to it! Now, sit down and finish your dinner."

Evangeline stood rigid. "You cannot give me your imperious orders, your grace! I am not one of your servants, though I am, at present, dependent upon you for my keep." She forced herself to turn away, her bearing haughty. "I bid you good-bye, your grace."

He bounded from his chair, toppling it over in his haste. "Dammit, Evangeline, you take one step and I swear I will take a birch rod to you!"

She shot him a contemptuous look. "You may take your paltry orders and threats, your grace, and hie yourself to the devil!" She turned on her heel and swept majestically toward the door.

The duke took three long strides and whirled her none too gently about to face him. Evangeline struggled against him, but he tightened his grip and shook her. "You little fool, you will go nowhere!"

He saw the pulse beating wildly in the hollow of her throat and eased his hold of her. His eyes dropped lower to her heaving breasts, and he felt a surge of desire for her. He pulled her roughly against him, and cupped her chin in his hand, forcing her to look up at him.

Evangeline felt suspended in time. She was aware of her heart beating furiously against his chest, of his dark eyes devouring her. She raised her eyes mutely. His mouth covered hers savagely, his tongue probing against her lips until she parted them to him. She felt his fury leave him, and only his fierce desire remained.

She held herself stiff, suddenly frightened of his passion, and uncertain of what she herself was feeling under the pressure of his mouth. She shivered when his hands stroked her hips, cupping her against him, his manhood pressed against her through the thin material of her gown. She felt an ache build in her belly.

He pressed her back against his arm and his mouth trailed kisses over her throat and downward to her breasts. She was scarce aware that her hands had tightened about his shoulders, her back arched against his arm. When he deftly freed her breasts from her bodice, her fear at his invasion made her draw back. But he did not release her and she felt his mouth lightly tease her nipple. He is making me feel passion, she thought hazily, he is making me want him.

His mouth suddenly left her and he clasped her tightly against him, burying his face in her hair. She could feel him trying to control his wild desire, to calm his ragged breathing. *What are you doing?* she screamed at herself, appalled. She had encouraged him, eager to understand the passion he aroused in her, giddy in her desire to know more of him. She was betraying him, and she was encouraging him to betray himself. She thought of her father as she had last seen him in the cold, gray light of dawn, his face drawn, his eyes bewildered. She must stop him, stop herself. She pulled away from him and he let her go. She drew herself up straight, her fingers fumbling to jerk the bodice of her gown back over her breasts.

She sought to drive him away from her, protect them

both from any feeling they had for each other. "I think, your grace," she said in a cold, deliberate voice, "that you have been too long away from your mistresses. Perhaps that is why you wish me to go to London— there is no lady currently seeing to your pleasure. Is it that you see me as only a defenseless woman, without protection, a woman who is therefore yours for the taking?"

He drew back from her as if she had struck him. The glaze of desire was gone from his eyes and she saw rage slowly building in their depths. She felt ill, but knew that she could not back down now, no matter what the outcome. She wondered, stiffening, if he would strike her.

He said finally, in a voice so soft and deadly calm that she strained to hear him, "Some women are teasing bitches, whores at heart. Marissa taught me much, Madame. And you, her cousin, are no different. You can stay at Chesleigh if you wish. I will expect reports from you, as Edmund's governess, as to his progress. I bid you good night and good-bye."

He turned away from her, as if he found her presence loathsome, and strode from the room without a backward glance. Evangeline stood motionless, staring at the slammed door.

6

Evangeline pulled her cloak more closely about her and walked swiftly toward the cove, only a sliver of white moon guiding her way. When she reached the cave, she stood for a moment at its mouth on the beach, gazing over the water and listening to the muted rumble of the waves lapping against the shore. The waves rose like silvery scallops in the faint moonlight, and dissolved gracefully as they met the shore before her.

She looked back into the yawning black cavern and felt a nearly overwhelming desire to run, to hide as far away from here as she could manage. But she felt her way to a rock near the cave entrance, sat down, and waited. It was really to begin now and there was nothing she could do to prevent it. If only her father had not insisted upon returning to France! She shook her head at the thought. She could not change the past, and John Edgerton controlled the future. Evangeline tried not to dwell upon what she was doing, but whenever she closed that door in her mind, Richard Clarendon entered, his dark eyes smoldering in fury, his voice cold and taunting.

After he had slammed out of the dining room, she had heard him shout for his curricle. She pictured his matched bays galloping even now away from Chesleigh. He hated her now and she had goaded him to it. "Marissa taught me much, Madame."

She shivered. She wished she could forget the stunned look of surprise in his eyes when she had turned on him. She wondered, tears stinging her eyes, if he felt any of the pain that gnawed at her.

"Good evening, Evangeline. Unlike most women, you are punctual. That is good."

She whirled about and stared at John Edgerton, silhouetted in moonlight against the mouth of the cave.

She said in a bitter whisper, "On this occasion, I had no choice in the matter."

"You are quite right. Had you been late, I might have wondered about your . . . intentions. It is a pleasure to see you again, my dear, though I would have preferred a different setting. But I digress. The next time you have occasion to visit the cave, bring a lantern."

She watched silently as he set his lantern upon the cave floor and knelt to light it. He straightened toward her, his face eerily shadowed in its dim light. "You will give a signal in twenty minutes." He gazed at her intently. "You are afraid, Evangeline. You are fortunate; it will keep you from making any dangerous mistakes."

"What signal? . . . I don't understand."

He stepped suddenly toward her and she stumbled back away from him. He gave a low laugh. "I have no nefarious purpose in mind, my dear. I will explain what it is you are to do, and then you shall meet some men at the dock. I will remain here to watch you."

"So you are to be protected and unseen, and I am to deal by myself with these . . . spies."

"Your fear has made you wily, Evangeline, but it is not to your advantage. You will learn more by listening than by talking. Tonight, you will perform a traitorous act against England, a single act, but one that will serve its purpose. There will be no turning back."

"Do you forget that Houchard holds my father?"

"Of course not, and never, I trust, will you forget it. Life is sweet, Evangeline. I trust you will remember that."

Evangeline was trembling. "You are English!" she spat at him. "And yet you willingly betray your country?"

He smiled at her and stepped closer to the lantern. "You speak about things you don't understand. All of us make choices, Evangeline, and mine are leading me, and Europe, to our destiny. But enough. I would not expect a woman to comprehend."

"You are despicable!"

"You will mind your tongue, Evangeline. I have not the time to argue with you. What we do here tonight is very serious business, not an occasion for banter. You are probably wondering what will be expected of you. Your duties will be varied, but none of them will place you in any particular danger. Your primary function will be to serve as a checkpoint. No one will be sent to me unless you have first verified that they are who they purport to be."

He drew a folded piece of paper from his cloak pocket and handed it to her. "All messages that you receive will be in code, this code. Only you, I, and Houchard know it. You will meet whomever you are instructed to, Evangeline, and you will examine their papers carefully. You will never clear a man until you have ensured that his instructions are authentic. Then, you will write your initials at the bottom of each page to prove that you have verified the message. It is for my protection as well as for Houchard. You and I have further protection. No one will know either your name or mine. You will be known as the Eagle, and I, the Lynx, *le loup-cervier*. Now you will study the code."

Evangeline moved close to the lantern and sank to her knees. The code was a formula for substituting numbers for letters.

"You will note," John Edgerton said, pointing over

her shoulder, "that the vowels have a separate code. You will be able to practice what you have learned in a few moments."

She looked up at him. "What if a man carries a message that is not authentic?"

"It is quite simple. If you distrust the man carrying a message to me, you will send him to this address in London." He handed her a small visiting card. "I do not expect an English spy, but one cannot be too careful. I trust you to be quite certain that you are dealing with a Bonapartist, for if you make an error, purposefully or not, I assure you it will be your last."

Evangeline ran her tongue over her dry lips, and held up the card. "Who is at this address?"

"An associate of mine. You needn't know his name. Suffice it to say that he carries out distasteful duties for me from time to time."

"You mean that he will kill anyone I send to him."

"He will do what is warranted. After tonight, we will meet only in . . . social settings. Don't look so aghast, my dear. I am highly respected and invited everywhere. Now, here is my card. Those men whom you clear, you will send there."

"My father! Houchard promised me a letter from him."

"You will have your letter when the boat arrives, rest assured. Along with instructions for your next assignment."

"Will I be expected to remain at Chesleigh?"

"Ah, you pine already for the social whirl in London. And the duke's charming company, I'll wager."

She quickly lowered her face so he would not see her eyes. "He has already asked me to accompany him to London."

"I trust you have put him off. You will remain here for the time being. I will inform you when you may journey to London. Incidentally, you gave a fine performance last evening. I congratulate you on your composure."

"You misjudge me," Evangeline said, rising to face him. "I have discovered that I have not the talent to hide my feelings. Indeed, I have been here but a few days, and already I believe I am suspected. Mrs. Needle is a harmless old woman, but nonetheless, she has guessed that something is troubling me. If I am so very transparent, I cannot be of much use to you or Houchard."

"Who is this old woman?"

Evangeline shook her head impatiently. "It does not matter. It is just that she seemed so easily to see through me. Others might do the same just as easily."

"I trust for your sake, and your father's, that you will learn your trade quickly. Women seem to have a talent for it. You are no different." He looked thoughtful for a long moment. "The duke, he suspects nothing? He has behaved just as Houchard and I predicted?"

Evangeline nodded numbly.

"I thought he would. You are a beautiful woman, Evangeline, and the duke, though he is a frivolous Corinthian, does hold to his stiff-necked English honor. I would say you have undervalued your talents as an actress. Is the duke not already taken with you?"

"No," Evangeline said, "he is not."

"No matter. You will do what you must to ensure that he does not cause us any problems." John Edgerton withdrew his watch and consulted it. "It is time. Attend carefully."

He pulled a handkerchief from his pocket, covered the lantern, and carried it to the mouth of the cave. Suddenly, in the distance, Evangeline saw a brief flicker of light, followed shortly by another.

He whipped off the handkerchief and raised the lantern high for some seconds. "You will always receive a double signal," he said quietly. "You have only to return it with a single, steady light, long enough for the men to get their bearings. They will row in and debark at the dock. You will meet them there." John Edgerton again lowered the lantern and covered it with his handkerchief.

Evangeline pointed to the encroaching water, now but ten feet from the cave entrance. "At high tide, the cave is flooded."

"Merely an inconvenience. I will ensure that my men approach the cove only at low tide. They will never draw near in any case unless you yourself give the signal."

He raised a quieting hand. "Listen."

Evangeline strained forward, waiting. Within minutes, she heard the soft, rhythmic sound of oars dipping through the water.

"You will now walk to the dock. Remember, my dear Eagle, that you are one of us. You will greet the men, and bring their packet of instructions back to me. We will read the code together tonight."

Evangeline nodded, and hurried from the cave to the end of the long wooden dock. She saw Edmund's small sloop bobbing up and down at its anchor, and beyond it, through the soft night mist, a longboat. Two men, muffled to their ears in black greatcoats, stepped onto the dock, and one of them stepped forward. To Evangeline's surprise, he spoke fluent English. "All goes well. You are the Eagle?"

Evangeline merely nodded, not trusting herself to speak.

The man looked her up and down, then said in a throaty whisper, "I was told that a woman was to be our contact. You are a pleasure to behold, Mademoiselle."

"Give me your instructions, Monsieur."

The man shrugged, reached into his pocket, and withdrew a thick envelope.

She clutched the packet and stuffed it into her cloak pocket. "You will wait here, Monsieur. I will return shortly."

Back in the cave, by the lantern light, Evangeline opened the packet and withdrew the papers. There were two envelopes, one of which, John Edgerton told her, contained a letter from her father and her instructions. The other contained papers and a message in Houchard's code. She found that her hands were shaking, and her mind did not seem to obey her. She stumbled again and again over the letters.

"They will wait until you are done, Evangeline. You have reversed the letters. Try again."

It took her another fifteen minutes to verify that the message was indeed from Houchard. The papers were all letters of reference and character for Allan Dannard for the post of secretary to a Lord George Barrington in London.

"Well?" John Edgerton asked.

"They are legitimate," Evangeline said, folding them back into the packet.

John Edgerton withdrew a slender piece of charcoal from his pocket. "Write your initials in the bottom corner. Without them, they would not continue to London."

Evangline did as she was bid. At Edgerton's instruction, she returned to the dock, handed one of the men the packet, and told them the address of the Lynx. They nodded and gave a quick salute to Evangline. "*A bientôt, Mademoiselle L'Aigle.*" One of the men kissed his fingertips to his lips. "I hope to see you again under less trying circumstances."

When they had disappeared behind the rise of the cliff and the longboat was no longer in sight, John Edgerton emerged from the cave. "You did well, Evangeline. You will find your next instructions in the envelope, as I told you." He paused a moment and touched his fingers to her cheek. She drew back.

"I regret that I am the villain in this drama, but it cannot be helped. I will see you again, my dear."

Evangeline remained where she stood for some minutes. She felt cold. Edgerton had won; she was now one of them, a traitor to England. She made her way slowly up the cliff path, clutching her father's letter to her chest.

Trevlin sat back on the cushioned wooden bench in the White Goose Inn, his thirst slacked on a mug of porter. If he had thought it odd that Madame de la Valette wished to travel some five miles from Chesleigh simply to explore the tiny Norman church that sat atop the chalk cliffs, it was not his place to let on. He supposed that Madame was bored, with only young Lord Edmund and the servants to keep her company at the huge castle, and had thus taken to exploring the countryside. In the past several weeks, he had accompanied her to Landsdown, a picturesque village in the rolling hills near Southsea, and to Southhampton, to visit an abbey that had survived despite centuries of political and religious upheavals, or so she had told him. When she first arrived at Chesleigh, he had thought her a lively lady whose laughter had more than once brought a smile to his lips. But lately, she seemed more withdrawn, more quiet than before, even during their jaunts about the countryside. Trevlin crooked his finger at the barmaid, a pretty wench with a saucy tongue, to bring him another mug. The wink she gave him removed further thoughts of Madame from his mind.

Evangeline's nose wrinkled at the overpowering smell of fish as she turned off the narrow cobbled road that served as the thoroughfare in the small village of Chitterly onto a winding path that led to its ancient stone church. Although there was no one in sight, she sensed that she was being watched. She heard a sudden rustling of leaves behind her and whirled about. There was no one.

"You are being a goose, my girl!" she said aloud to calm herself. But even so, she could not keep herself from breaking into a run. By the time she reached the top of the rise and the arched oak doors of the church, she was panting and breathless. She grasped the heavy bronze ring and pushed inward, and the door opened with a loud creak. It felt cold and damp inside, for little warmth could penetrate the thick stone walls.

The church seemed empty. She walked slowly up the narrow aisleway, past the bare wooden benches, toward the vestry. She heard a soft, scraping sound and froze, afraid to move.

"You are the Eagle?"

A slight man, dressed in the coarse woolens of a fisherman, stepped out of the shadows. He was a young man without a sign of a beard on his smooth cheeks.

"Yes," she whispered. "Were you following me?"

"Nay. 'Twas my partner. He does not trust women. He would have sliced your lovely throat had you not come alone."

He was trying to frighten her, and he was succeeding. "I am alone," she croaked. "Give me your packet."

He drew a dirty envelope from the waistband of his trousers and handed it to her. Evangeline sat down on one of the wooden benches and spread the single sheet of paper on her lap. She raised her eyes. "Are you this man, Conan DeWitt?"

"Nay, it is my partner. He is the gentleman, not I."

"Bring him to me. I must see him."

He looked undecided. "Conan told me to meet with you."

"Nevertheless, he must come in. If he refuses, I cannot do anything further." Buried in the coded message from Houchard was the description of Conan De-Witt, a man tall and fair, with a mole on his left cheek, near his eye.

"Very well," he said finally, "but there better be good reason!"

He slipped out of the church and returned some minutes later accompanied by a tall man dressed in country buckskins, swinging a cane negligently in his right hand.

Conan DeWitt stared down at the girl. She had an uncommonly lovely face, despite its pallor. "What is it you want with me, Eagle?"

"Houchard provided your description. I had to be certain that you were the man he spoke of."

He touched his fingertip to the large mole. "Are you satisfied?"

Evangeline nodded, and quickly wrote her initials on the lower corner of the paper. She handed it to DeWitt. "Have you a packet for me?"

DeWitt handed her a thin envelope. Evangeline stuffed it into her cloak pocket and rose.

"It was wise of you not to think of betrayal, Eagle. I have told Houchard that women aren't to be trusted, but he insists that you are different." He shrugged. "Women's consciences are fragile things."

"I really don't care to hear your opinions, Mr. De-Witt. I believe our business is concluded."

He merely looked at her, one fair brow arched. She quickly gave him John Edgerton's London address and turned to leave the church, but DeWitt's voice stopped her. "That man, Trevlin. Be certain that he doesn't suspect anything."

"He suspects nothing. May I suggest that you see to your own affairs and leave mine to me."

Evangeline turned on her heel and walked deliberately away from him, out of the church and into the bright sunlight.

Richard Clarendon stood at the wide, bowed windows in the drawing room of his townhouse on York Square, staring at the rivulets of rain that streaked down the glass. He held a letter from Evangeline in his hand, a governess's progress report. It was written in the most formal of styles, impersonal and lifeless.

"Something troubles you, Richard?"

He turned at the sound of his mother's voice, and shook his head. "No, 'tis merely a dismal day."

"How goes Edmund?"

"Madame de la Valette reports that he can now write a creditable sentence. Here is his effort." He handed his mother the letter. Edmund's childlike printing was scrawled beneath Evangeline's script at the bottom of the page.

"Quite a Herculean effort," the dowager duchess said. "It has been but three weeks. It appears that Madame de la Valette is making noble progress. I miss the boy, you know. I have been thinking, Richard. Edmund is no longer a baby. Soon he will need his father's guiding hand. Could he not come up to London with Marissa's cousin? I am curious to meet her, as well."

Richard eyed his mother suspiciously. Her dark eyes, so like his own, were guileless, which made him all the more wary. "Methinks," he said acidly, "that you have been talking to Bunyon. Damn the fellow for his infernal meddling! I'll box his impudent ears!"

The dowager duchess merely smiled at the duke's show of temper. He had acted strangely since his return from Chesleigh, but she knew better than to pry openly. She had believed initially that his touchy moods were still the result of his wounded male vanity. But she had dismissed her theory after witnessing his behavior a week ago at a dinner party given by the Viscount Derencourt, Phillip Mercerault, and his wife, Sabrina. The vivacious viscountess had brought a smile to his lips, but it was only his social smile. There was no longing warmth in his gaze when his eyes met hers, nothing in his friendly manner toward the viscount that gave hint of any suppressed emotion. She had verified her opinion during their carriage ride back to Clarendon House. "Sabrina looks quite content," she had essayed in an offhand voice. Richard grunted. "And Phillip appears most attentive." Richard said in a bored voice, "Yes, from what I hear, he has become the model husband." The dowager duchess continued, straining to see his face in the dim carriage light, "Lady Hardcastle informed me that the viscountess is breeding." Richard showed the first signs of interest. "Good God!" he exclaimed, "Phillip has wasted no time! It would appear that they have indeed mended all their fences."

The dowager duchess had lapsed into silence, satisfied that Sabrina no longer held a place in her son's heart. Indeed, she has scoffed silently at her concern about it. Sometimes she wondered if her son were possessed of the more tender emotions. His first marriage, forced, she knew, by his father, had held little of anything save her son's natural desire for the beautiful young Marissa. And even that had faded quickly.

"Bunyon meant no harm, Richard," she said mildly to the duke, who had not moved from his place at the window. A slight smile parted her lips again. If Richard endeavored to box his valet's ears, she had no doubt that Bunyon would respond in kind. Both of them had for years been regulars at Gentleman Jackson's boxing saloon. She gave a doleful sigh. "It has been such awful weather of late. I grow bored with inactivity. Perhaps you would consider bringing Madame de la Valette and Edmund to London, Richard. I know that you haven't wanted to before, but I own that I would find it quite amusing to have the child here."

Richard turned to face her and she was momentarily taken aback by the haggard look in his eyes. He said in a harsh voice, "As I have told you, Mother, Madame has no desire to come to London. When I informed her that I wished it, she threatened to leave."

The dowager duchess blinked. "You *informed* her, my son? From what Bunyon has told me, she is a pleasant young woman, but also possessed of a great pride. Perhaps you were too high-handed in your treatment of her."

As his only answer was a blighting stare, she continued, "What is her name, Richard? I cannot keep referring to her as Madame de la Valette."

"Evangeline," he said gruffly.

The dowager duchess rose from her chair and shook out her skirts. She was a tall woman, still possessed of a graceful, willowy figure, despite her fifty years. Her son had inherited much of his good looks from her, she knew, and she still could not gaze at him without feeling a good deal of pride. There was simply no other gentleman to match him, either in his dark good looks or his magnificent physique. She knew that he was continually plagued by hopeful young ladies, as well as by married ladies, and ladies who were not ladies at all. She wondered if he had not fallen in love because women had so eagerly thrown themselves into his arms and into his bed since he had reached the age of sixteen. Perhaps he had been even younger, she thought. Her husband had been inordinately proud of his son's sexual prowess, even though in the next breath he would decry his son's wildness. Richard had bowed to his father's wishes, married, presented the world with an heir, lost his wife, and now conducted his life in a more discreet fashion. And he was unhappy.

"You have told me that Evangeline is half English," she said, her eyes intent upon his face.

"Yes," the duke said curtly.

"Well," she said in a bright voice as she prepared to leave the room, "perhaps she will consent to join us before the Season starts."

The duke only grunted in response, and the dowager duchess, her brow puckered in a thoughtful frown, turned and walked majestically from the room.

The duke turned back to the window. He knew his mother as well as he knew himself, and she was one of the very few ladies he had ever held in affection. But at times like this, she strained his affection to its limits. Her gentle prodding would come to feel, he knew, more and more like the proverbial battering ram. Still, he thought, he had behaved callously toward her. He realized that he had, in fact, been preoccupied and withdraw in her presence since his return from Chesleigh. Damn Evangeline anyway! She had played the heartless teasing bitch with him, just as Marissa might have. Even as he thought that, he felt the same nagging doubts that had haunted him in the past weeks. It was true that he had succumbed again, had wanted her, but he had stopped himself, and she had known it. But why had she so viciously turned on him, but an instant after clinging to him? Her desire had been as great as his. He could still feel her arching her back against his arm, hear her soft moan when his mouth closed over her breast. He shook his head. It made no sense, no more sense than her ridiculous refusal to leave Chesleigh. "To hell with females!" he growled at large to the empty room.

A calculated gleam lit his eyes as he left the drawing room. He would give Bunyon his comeuppance this afternoon when he sparred with him at Gentleman Jackson's boxing saloon. Every connected punch would make him feel better, whether he or Bunyon got the worst of it.

Evangeline was surprised to see Mrs. Dickinson walking hurriedly toward the north wing, her eyes narrowed with worry.

"Is something troubling you, Mrs. Dickinson?" she asked, pulling her bedchamber door closed behind her.

"I am worried, Madame," Mrs. Dickinson said. "It is Mrs. Needle. She always eats her porridge in the servants' hall precisely at seven o'clock in the morning. No one has seen her."

"She is probably experimenting with some new potion. Let us see what she is about," Evangeline said, shortening her step to match the housekeeper's.

When they reached the turret room, Evangeline

rapped on the door and called, "Mrs. Needle, it is I, Madame de la Valette."

Evangeline heard no answer, and called again.

"Perhaps she is ill, Madame," Mrs. Dickinson said.

"Most likely she is in the home wood, gathering mushrooms, but let us check." Evangeline opened the door and stepped inside. The odor of herbs assailed her nostrils. "Mrs. Needle?"

Evangeline walked slowly about the room, Mrs. Dickinson trailing erratically behind her. Mrs. Dickinson suddenly shrieked, and Evangeline turned to see her standing frozen, her hands clasped over her bosom.

Evangeline rushed to the other side of the screen, into the small alcove that was Mrs. Needle's sleeping area. The old woman lay crumpled on her side. Evangeline knew that she was dead even before she knelt down beside her and closed her fingers over her veined wrist. There was no pulse, and her body was stiff. Mrs. Needle had been dead for many hours.

"She was an old woman," Mrs. Dickinson said in a shaking voice. "It must have been her heart."

Evangeline sat back on her heels and closed her eyes. Unbidden, the peaceful face of her mother rose in her mind, her pale lips quirked in a smile, her sightless blue eyes staring until the doctor gently lowered her lids. She had felt only shock at first at her mother's death, the stiff figure that had been her mother having seemed alien to her. Her grief had come later. "Yes," Evangeline said finally, looking up, "she was an old woman. Fetch Bassick. He will know what is to be done."

Mrs. Dickinson nodded and hurried from the room, the click-clack of her heeled shoes sounding on the stone steps.

She gazed down into Mrs. Needle's face. She seemed ancient, much older than her mother had been when she had died. She reached down and rested her palm for a brief moment against Mrs. Needle's cold cheek.

The poor old woman. She had died alone, with no one to share her passing. Her eyes fell to the open neck of Mrs. Needle's wool gown, and she saw in the hollow of her wrinkled throat two violet bruises, each the size of a man's thumb. Mrs. Needle hadn't died alone—she had been strangled!

Evangeline rocked back on her heels, numb with shock. She had told John Edgerton only of an old woman—had she even mentioned her name?—an old woman who had seemed to sense that Evangeline was not what she appeared to be. She had mentioned her only because . . . a sob tore from her throat and she covered her face in her hands. She had told Edgerton of the poor old woman, hoping to use her to frighten Edgerton into calling a halt to his madness. But instead, he must have simply ordered Mrs. Needle killed! Because of her, someone innocent had died . . . violently, uselessly.

Bassick found Evangeline rocking back and forth over Mrs. Needle's body, staring blankly down.

"Madame," he said gently, dropping his hand to her shoulder.

Evangeline drew her eyes from the old woman's face and looked up. "She is dead, Bassick," she whispered.

Bassick knelt beside her and carefully pressed the flat of his hand over Mrs. Needle's heart. He shook his head. "Yes, Madame, she is dead. Leave now and I will see to things. The doctor will be arriving shortly."

"It was not her heart, Bassick. Look." She touched her fingers to the bruises. "Someone killed her."

Bassick turned shocked eyes to Evangeline. "It cannot be! Not at Chesleigh!"

"It is true."

"But why?" he asked helplessly.

"I do not know," Evangeline said dully. "I do not know."

"It is best that we not touch her, Madame, if what you say is true. I must call the magistrate."

"Mrs. Needle was such a gentle old woman," Evangeline said, her voice a dull whisper. She rose shakily to her feet and let Bassick lead her from the room.

Mr. Edgers, the stoop-shouldered magistrate, arrived in the early afternoon. He found Madame de la Valette unnaturally withdrawn. He thought it a shame that such a sensitive young lady should have been the one to find the old woman. After duly questioning all the Chesleigh servants, he returned to the drawing room and Madame de la Valette, for there was no one else to receive him. He wished heartily that the duke were in residence. He felt uncomfortable with his young cousin.

"It makes no sense," he admitted to Evangeline.

"No, it does not," she replied in a distant voice.

"She owned nothing of value. Indeed, nothing in her rooms was even disturbed. It is a mystery, Madame, a mystery." He shook his grisled, gray head. "Perhaps it was a tinker. Those damned scoundrels still roam about, or so I've been told."

Evangeline knew without Mr. Edgers' continuing further that poor Mrs. Needle was not of sufficent importance to warrant much more of his time. Her death would remain a mystery, and soon everyone would forget.

"Yes, it is a mystery, sir," she said. "If you learn anything, you will inform me?"

"Certainly, Madame."

After Mr. Edgers had taken his leave, Evangeline rang for Bassick. "I fear," she said, "that the magistrate can do little. I will write to the duke and inform him of what has occurred." She paused a moment. "Please, Bassick, check all the locks."

Bassick saw the fear in her eyes. "Of course, Madame. His grace will be much shocked. He has always been quite fond of Mrs. Needle, and known her all of his life, you know."

"Yes, I know."

Evangeline sat at the duke's desk in the library, spread

out a single piece of stationery before her, and dipped her quill into the inkwell. How they had parted three weeks before did not seem to matter now. She needed to see him; without him, she would go mad with her guilt. "Your grace," she wrote finally, "I much regret bearing such tragic news, but Mrs. Needle has died. The cause of her death was not natural." Her quill remained poised above the paper, before she forced out the words. "Someone killed her, someone unknown. I beg you to come to Chesleigh. Your cousin—"

She scratched her name and folded the sheet.

Richard Clarendon arrived late the following morning, having driven from London in under six hours. He was tired, dirty, stunned at the manner of his old nurse's death, and tense with worry for Evangeline.

"Welcome home, your grace!" Bassick cried, so relieved to see his master that he nearly tripped over a chair in his rush to assist him out of his greatcoat.

"I came as quickly as I could, Bassick. Where is Madame?"

"In the drawing room, your grace. She is much affected and I fear that she has borne most of the burden of the funeral arrangements."

"She will bear no more," the duke said.

Evangeline turned from her post at the fireplace upon his entrance. He took one look at her drawn, white face, and strode to her, drawing her unresisting into his arms. "I am here now, Evangeline," he whispered, and lightly stroked her hair.

Evangeline had nurtured her grief to keep her apart from the pain of her guilt. At his words, rasping sobs broke from her throat and she clung to him.

"It is over now, Evangeline. It will be all right, I promise you."

But it was anything but all right. Had it not been for her, Mrs. Needle would be alive. She was racked by her guilt, and she struck her fists against his chest, wishing that she herself would be hurt. He ignored her blows and held her tightly against him. When the Chesleigh servant had brought him her letter, the anger he was still trying to cherish against her was lost to him in the shock of his old nurse's death and Evangeline's plea to him. He locked away his own grief and set himself to soothe her.

Her sobs eventually dissolved into hiccups and he loosened his hold about her. She groped for a handkerchief and began with shaking fingers to wipe her face.

"I am sorry, your grace," she whispered. "I—I am glad you have come. I have not known what to do."

"You did just as you ought. I am only sorry that you have borne all the burden." For an instant, he saw such suffering in her eyes that he was loathe to release her. "We needn't speak about it now if you don't wish to."

She shook her head and drew a deep, resolute breath. "No," she said, "you must know what happened."

The duke held a chair for her and she sank down into the soft cushions. He remained standing, resting his shoulders against the mantelpiece.

She looked at him, the man she knew she loved. She had brought death to his home. And lies, always more lies. "The magistrate, Mr. Edgers, believes it must have been some mad tinker, now disappeared from Chesleigh."

"There was nothing missing? Nothing stolen from her rooms?"

She shook her head.

"Edgers has not then discovered any possible motive for her murder?"

"There does not seem to be a motive."

"Bassick told me that you have made all the arrangements. I thank you, Evangeline." He continued, his voice suddenly abrupt in his concern for her, "You are exhausted. Why do you not rest now? I will see to whatever else needs to be done."

"No—no, I am not tired! Please, I would rather stay

with you." The thought of being by herself in her bedchamber, tormented by thoughts that would give her
no respite, made her desperate not to be alone.

The duke stared at her a moment, surprised by the
panic in her voice. He walked to her chair and laid his
hand upon her shoulder. "Of course you can stay with
me." He added after a short pause, "Death is always a
shock, but it will pass, Evangeline, the shock and the
grief."

But not the guilt, she thought silently, not the guilt.
"I thank you, your grace," she said.

Mrs. Needle was buried in the Chesleigh graveyard,
the resting place of both family and servants for more
than two centuries. Evangeline stared ahead of her at
the mound of fresh earth while the vicar lamented the
cruelty of Mrs. Needle's death, Richard's hand holding
her steady. She raised her eyes to the castle, to the
north wing where Mrs. Needle had lived. The thought
of Richard's returning to London and leaving her alone
again at Chesleigh seemed too much to bear. She wanted
more than anything to leave this place, to go to London, or anywhere that would let her forget.

Over a quiet dinner after the funeral, Evangeline
pondered silently how to convince the duke to take her
to London with him. To her grateful surprise, the duke
said over a glass of port, "You have been through a
harrowing experience, Madame. Would you care to
visit London for a while?"

She gasped her relief, and her eyes flew to his face.

He said slowly, "We have not dealt well together,
you and I. Perhaps we can remedy that away from
Chesleigh. Even though you do not care for the city,
perhaps you would not mind it for a short while."

"I would much like to go with you, your grace," she
said, so relieved that she did not care if he thought her
sudden change of heart odd.

"I am glad." He felt himself relax. He wasn't certain

why he had opened himself to another rebuff from her. He only knew that he wanted somehow to protect her, to shelter her, to make her forget what had happened. The admission surprised him.

"You still look exhausted, Evangeline. Since I wish to leave early on the morrow, I suggest that you seek your bed. Do you wish some laudanum to make you sleep?"

She rose slowly to her feet. The gentleness in his voice only worsened the guilt she felt. "No, your grace. I need nothing."

He walked over to her and touched a finger to her pale cheek. "My mother looks forward to meeting you. I thank you for changing your mind."

She felt tears well up in her eyes. "I wish you would not be so very nice!" she cried, and fled from him.

7

"Grandmama!"

The dowager duchess had scarce time to set down her embroidery before Edmund had dashed across the drawing room and clasped his arms about her knees.

"What a grand, big man you've become!" she exclaimed as she lifted him onto her lap and kissed him soundly. "How I've missed you, Edmund! Dear me, you have grown, haven't you."

"And I am as strong as an ox, Grandmama," Edmund said proudly.

"An ox, my love?"

"That's how strong Cousin Eve says she is. She is going to teach me how to swim—better than father!"

"She is, is she! I think I might have something to say about that, Edmund."

The dowager duchess looked up at the sound of her son's deep, amused voice. He stood just inside the drawing room, a striking young woman dressed in a dark blue silk gown at his side.

"Off my lap, Edmund. I am being backward in my attentions to your Cousin Eve." Edmund slithered to the thick yellow-patterned Aubusson carpet and his grandmother rose to her full stately height.

119

"Mother, this is Madame de la Valette."

The dowager duchess started slightly. It was not her son's words, but the tone of his voice—an odd mixture of pride and possessiveness. Richard stood close beside Evangeline, as if to reassure her. Good lord, the dowager duchess thought, does he think I am going to cut the girl? She quickly appraised her lovely face, her tall, regal bearing, and pinned a welcoming smile to her lips. She walked forward, puzzled to see as she approached that there was a haunted look in her blue eyes. She wondered if she was to blame, if the girl was afraid of her. She quickly set herself to disabuse her of such foolishness and said in her most charming voice, "I am so pleased to finally make your acquaintance, Madame," and extended her slender hand.

Evangeline stepped forward, curtsied, and gave the dowager's outstretched hand a firm shake. "The pleasure is mine, your grace. I trust you will forgive my unplanned visit. His grace was kind enough to include me with Edmund."

The dowager duchess found herself nodding in approval. She profoundly disliked what she called those clever modern misses, girls who, upon introduction to her, would have simpered and cooed, all the while casting half an eye toward the duke to see his reaction.

"Do not concern yourself, my dear," she said. "I have wanted you to come to London. Richard has told me much about you."

"I promise you, Evangeline," the duke said, smiling down at her, "that I have always been most guarded in my conversations about you."

"Grant me leave to doubt your word, your grace," Evangeline said wryly, turning to smile up at him.

"Do come and sit down, Madame. I will ring for tea. May I call you Evangeline? Madame sounds so very standoffish."

"Yes, of course, your grace." She turned to Richard. "Edmund is exhausted. Let me fetch Ellen."

The duke shook his head. "No, I will remove him to the nursery. I will leave you to your fate for a few moments. Come, Edmund, you can cozen your grandmother after you've had a nap and she's had time to recover from your initial visit."

"But I would like to tell her about the dueling pistol Cousin Eve gave me, Papa."

"I believe you just have," the duke said. He scooped his small son into his arms and strode to the door. He said over his shoulder, "I will give Grayson instructions for tea, Mother."

"Do sit down, Evangeline. You have had a most wearying journey, I wager, particularly if you were in the company of my lively grandson."

Evangeline merely smiled and shook her head. "Edmund is a delightful child."

The dowager duchess patted the seat beside her and Evangeline sat down and gracefully disposed her silk skirts about her. The dowager duchess took in Evangeline's figure, and was further gratified. She supposed she found Evangeline's figure so pleasing because it closely resembled her own in her youth: tall, willowy, and deep-bosomed. "Actually, Evangeline," she said after a moment, "Richard has spoken of you little, and when he was persuaded to do so, it was with a decided snarl. I gather he tried to give you orders in that medieval lord-of-the-manner tone of his. I hope you took him soundly to task for his high-handedness."

Evangeline's hands fanned a denial. "Oh no!" she exclaimed. "The duke has been all that is kind." She added with a slight smile, "Though he detests being called anything so admirable."

"No, I fancy that it would not at all be to his liking," the dowager duchess agreed. "We are much alike, Richard and I, for better or for worse. You, my dear Evangeline," she continued without a pause, "are undoubtedly picturing yourself as an encroaching mushroom. I would that you cease thinking such nonsense. Incidently, Marissa's gown becomes you."

Evangeline blinked uncertainly. "Thank you, your grace," she said, choosing the dowager's final words for comment.

"So you are teaching my scapegrace grandson to swim."

Evangeline forced a weak smile. "I suppose I must when the weather warms. I am not much of a governess, I fear. It was a bribe, you see, so that he would learn his letters."

A tall, stately man entered the room, bearing a heavy silver tea service in his black-clad arms.

"Ah, Grayson, I have been thinking longingly of you for the past ten minutes."

"Indeed, your grace," Grayson murmured, bending to set the tray down on the table in front of them.

"Grayson and I grew up together," the dowager duchess said, her dark eyes resting for a moment upon the butler's impassive countenance. "I have always thought we made an impressive pair, particularly now that our bones are brittle, our hair is graying, and our consequence is at its peak."

"Just so, your grace," Grayson said, giving a slight nod.

"Madame is looking longingly at the scones, Grayson. Please fetch a more noble plateful, and some of Cook's crescent sandwiches too."

Grayson nodded and walked with majestic nonchalence from the drawing room.

"However do he and Bassick get along?" Evangeline asked, helping herself to a scone.

The dowager duchess gave a trill of laughter. "Actually, my dear, they have never met. Richard agrees with me that we should keep the households apart. Now, Tsar Ivan—that is what I have taken to calling our butler at St. John Court, Richard's estate in the north—I have always thought him to be cut from far starchier cloth than either Grayson or Bassick. My dear, it is all

he can do not to condescend to us poor mortals! He
unbent himself sufficiently upon one occasion to inform
me that if the Conquerer had enjoyed the services of a
butler, it would doubtless have been one of his ancestors!"

Evangeline was giggling when the duke entered. He
paused a moment on the threshhold, and a smile lit his
eyes as he listened to her.

The dowager duchess waved him toward a chair. She
said gaily, "I have been telling Evangeline about the
noble Tsar Ivan, Richard."

"He is a pretentious old curmudgeon, I'll grant you
that." He added with a smile, "I gather from your
laughter, Evangeline, that my mother hasn't been too
stiff in the collar."

"You know very well that only my bones are stiff,
Richard."

"Nothing of the sort, your grace! I have been well
entertained in your absence."

"I am glad," the duke said, accepting a cup of tea
from the dowager duchess. "There has been too much
unpleasantness of late for all of us."

The dowager duchess sat forward. "Forgive me for
not asking you sooner, Richard, but have you learned
any more about Mrs. Needle's death?"

"No," the duke said. "We owe great thanks to Evangeline, for she dealt with the tragedy most ably. Edgers, you know, is completely out of his depth." He
paused for a moment, his dark eyes resting on the
heavy emerald signet ring on his left hand. "I have
taken steps to see that Chesleigh is now more carefully
guarded."

For an instant Evangeline wanted to say that there
was no need to guard Chesleigh now. But she kept her
eyes upon the Dresden china cup in her lap.

"I do thank you, Evangeline," the dowager duchess
said. "You have been most kind to my family. Now, we
will not speak of it further, for I have no wish to upset
us all anew."

"Evangeline must be tired, Mother," the duke said suddenly, his voice clipped in concern for her. "You must rest before dinner, my dear. We can dine *en famille* this evening, nothing fancy."

"Oh dear!" the dowager duchess exclaimed. "We have guests coming for dinner, Richard. It is rather late to cancel, I'm afraid."

Evangeline interposed quickly, cutting off the duke's muted curse, "Will your great-aunt be here? And Miss Storleigh?"

The dowager duchess smiled wryly. "So, you have made Eudora's vastly entertaining acquaintance! Yes, they will."

"Lord Pettigrew? And . . . Sir John Edgerton?"

"Yes, those gentlemen are also invited." The dowager duchess turned to the duke. "It appears that Drew is much in Felicia's company nowadays." She shook her head in wonderment. "It never ceases to amaze me which girl will make a man's heart flutter!"

"I hope he will not regret it if he marries the chit," the duke said. "I doubt Felicia could stop chattering even when they are——" He broke off abruptly, for his mother's cup rattled alarmingly in its saucer.

Evangeline wasn't listening. She had wrestled with the problem of getting a message to John Edgerton, to inform him of her presence in London. She forced a smile to her lips. "I should much like to come to your party, your grace, if it wouldn't disaccommodate your arrangements."

"Not at all, my dear. I should be delighted."

"At least you will rest now," the duke said, rising. His tone was peremptory, but it did not occur to Evangeline to raise any demur. She was to meet Edgerton again, and she wanted nothing more than to be alone, to cease, even for a short time, her playacting.

"I will see you later, Evangeline," the dowager duchess said. "You do look weary, my dear. Would you show her to the Crimson Room, Richard?"

The duke nodded and offered Evangeline his arm.

"Your townhouse is most elegant, your grace," she said as they mounted the circular stairs.

"Evangeline," he said abruptly, "there is really no pressing need for you to attend this evening."

"Do you think your mother would find me an intrusion? Was she merely being kind to me?"

"Don't be foolish," he said sharply. "Her feelings have nothing at all to do with what I meant."

"Then what is it you wish, your grace?"

"I wish—I do not want you to overtire yourself, that is all." He drew to a halt in front of her bedchamber.

She ventured a tentative smile. "I shall endeavor to do your bidding, your grace. Forget not that I am strong as an ox and blessed with a like constitution."

He raised his hand and touched his fingertips to her pale cheek. "Are you really so invincible, Evangeline?" She knew that he must be remembering her flailing her fists against his chest as she sobbed her grief over Mrs. Needle.

She raised her eyes to his dark face and was taken aback at the tenderness in his gaze. "You . . . you must know that I am not," she stammered. She must get a hold on herself, she told herself fiercely. She straightened and smiled at him brightly. "You are right, of course. I am tired. I will see you this evening, your grace."

When the duke returned some minutes later to the drawing room, the dowager duchess chided him gently, "You must mind your tongue, Richard. I doubt Madame de la Valette will long suffer your ordering her about in such silence. You surely wouldn't want her to rip you up in front of me."

The duke looked startled. "What the devil do you mean, Mother?"

"She is a grown woman, my son, and a widow. It seems to me that she is much used to making her own decisions, without any colorful interference from you."

"Your form your impressions much too quickly, I think," he said absently. "I find her difficult to understand."

She cocked her head at him, looking surprised and intrigued.

He smiled at her ruefully. "Do you know that she very nearly killed herself riding Dorkus? She informed me that she wanted me to think her up to snuff! She might very well have ended up in a ditch with her neck broken! My interference, as you call it, was in that particular instance most timely."

"I beg your pardon," the dowager duchess said uncertainly. "I had not guessed that she was a foolish girl."

He turned to her suddenly and smiled. "Oh no, Evangeline is not at all foolish, save . . ." He shook his head. "No, she is not foolish, merely in need of a strong hand at times."

The dowager duchess wondered if he meant it was *his* strong hand Madame de la Valette needed. She had never before seen Richard so very *caring*. He was behaving most oddly, she thought, when he turned away from her, his brow furrowed in thought, as if she were no longer in the room. She raised her half-filled cup of tepid tea and sipped it slowly. She felt as if the world had taken a new and unchartered, yet fascinating turn. She knew his reputation well; and she knew quite well that the beautiful women that had come and gone in his life had not touched him. Had her proud, cynical son finally found a woman who would hold him?

Evangeline made her way down the thickly carpeted stairs that evening and drew to an abrupt halt in the immense entrance hall. Six footmen stood at attention, all garbed in the duke's crimson and white livery. Grayson, a stark contrast in somber black, appeared to be inspecting the pristine white of their gloves. He turned as if sensing Evangeline's presence.

"Madame, the duke and her grace await you in the drawing room?"

"When are the guests due to arrive, Grayson?"

"Shortly, Madame. No one, I might add, even the Prince Regent, is often late to an affair at the Clarendon House."

"I would expect no less," she said with a wry smile.

Grayson opened the double oak doors and Evangeline preceded him into the drawing room. The duke was standing negligently against the mantelpiece, smiling at something his mother was saying. He looked magnificent in his black satin evening wear, his artfully arranged cravat so snowy white that she fancied it was cold to the touch. He gestured as he spoke and her eyes were drawn to the white lace that spilled over his large hands. How very *silly* you are, she chided herself, yet she pictured his hands touching her, strong, yet caressing and gentle.

The duke stopped in mid-sentence when he noticed Evangeline. He remarked to himself that she looked exquisite in Marissa's cream satin and lace gown, but it was the tentative, uncertain look in her eyes that made him want to stride over to her. He stopped himself, aware of his mother's speculative eyes upon him. He merely nodded toward her.

"Good evening, Evangeline. I trust you are well rested now."

"Of course, your grace." She turned and curtsied deeply to the dowager duchess.

"You look lovely, my dear. I think I shall have to keep a close watch on all the gentlemen this evening. They will likely wear their hearts on their sleeves."

Evangeline forced a smile to her lips. "I am certain that the gentlemen will have better sense and better taste, ma'am."

"I would that you cease denigrating yourself," the duke said, a mock frown on his brow.

Evangeline drew herself up at his undeserved scold.

"Would you prefer that I agreed with your grace and thus appeared unbecomingly conceited?"

"A little conceit would not tatter your character beyond all repair," he said, grinning.

The dowager duchess turned reluctantly at the sound of gay laughter coming from the entrance hall. She regretted on this particular occasion that the guests were being so punctual.

The *small* dinner party turned out to comprise no less than twenty-five guests, and Evangeline soon found herself wafting from one to the other in the dowager duchess's charming wake. Lady Pemberley greeted her affably, and Felicia, who had been tapping Lord Pettigrew's arm with her delicate ivory fan to gain his attention, turned to tell her laughingly that the duke had been sorely remiss in keeping her hidden at Chesleigh for so long.

"I had a preference for Chesleigh," Evangeline said with less ease of voice than she should have, for the duke was at her elbow.

"But no more, I see, Madame."

Evangeline started at the pensive voice of John Edgerton. "As you see, Sir John." She raised her chin and her eyes, despite herself, narrowed in ill-disguised anger on his impassive face.

Sir John bowed. "It is of course our pleasure that you have chosen to leave the country, Evangeline. I am certain that you will find much to do here in London to provide you entertainment. Perhaps we can discuss the city later this evening."

"I should like that, Sir John," Evangeline said, and turned stiffly away from him.

To Evangeline's surprise, the duke himself escorted her into the large formal dining room, and he seated her at his right hand. The place to her right was reserved for Lord George Wallis, a whiskered old gentleman who, she soon learned, had the disconcerting habit of inserting odd remarks into any conversation he chanced to hear. Opposite her sat Lady Jane Bellerman, a lovely girl dressed in pink satin and gauze, who quickly let it be known she was none too pleased at Evangeline's presence at the duke's side. John Edgerton, much to Evangeline's relief, sat near the middle of the long table, out of her sight.

She carelessly pushed her food about her plate, accepting each new course from the attentive footman with a mechanical nod of her head, and responded abstractedly to the occasional comments addressed to her by Lady Jane Bellerman and the duke. She was gazing at Grayson, who was standing like a guard behind the duke's massive high-backed chair, when she heard Lady Jane's high tinkling laughter, and saw she was looking toward her. "I beg your pardon?" she managed.

"Lady Jane is speaking to you, my dear," Lord George kindly informed her.

"I was telling the duke that you do not appear to be enjoying yourself, Madame de la Valette."

"You must forgive my inattention, Miss Bellerman. Admittedly, my thoughts were elsewhere."

"His grace tells me that you are recently arrived from France, Madame."

"But she sounds perfectly *English*, Lady Jane!" Lord George said.

Evangeline was aware that the duke was gazing at her, his wine glass held suspended in his hand. She turned her head and smiled briefly at him.

"That is true," she said to Miss Bellerman. She continued to Lord George, "I am half English, sir, and indeed was raised in England."

"I was just telling his grace," the lady continued in a low, honeyed voice, ignoring Lord George's aside, "that I had always believed the French to be a lively, amusing people, more prone than you to enjoy dinner conversation. I fear the duke will think himself and his guests slighted by your silence."

"Oh, no, my dear Lady Jane! Not at all slighted, I assure you!"

Evangeline shrugged. "I trust the duke will forgive me and turn to others who will more readily amuse him."

"Of a certainty he already has," Miss Bellerman assured her.

The duke forebore to comment, as he was busy cursing himself for having had Lady Jane placed at his left hand. He wondered now just why the devil he had done it. He gazed toward Evangeline, who sat silent with a tense set to her mouth, her hand taut as she clutched her wine glass.

"I suppose it is because of your English blood," Miss Bellerman continued sweetly, bringing the duke's wayward attention back to her, "that you are not small and dark like most of your countrymen."

"I suppose so, Miss Bellerman," Evangeline said absently.

"Still," Lady Jane pursued, "it appears that your English blood did not mix to its expected advantage. I assure you, Madame, that the rest of us feel positively *tiny* standing next to you."

Evangeline lifted her eyes wearily to Lady Jane's expectant face. Why did this particular lady, at this particular time, have to decide to spar with her for the duke's attention? And she did not even have the grace to be at all *subtle* in her wretched insults! She drew a deep breath and said coldly, "It is odd that you should say that, Miss Bellerman. I had noticed the same thing myself, although *squat* rather than *tiny* was the word that came to my mind."

Lady Jane sucked in her breath, her eyes flashing. "It is . . . unfortunate, Madame, that you are a widow. Unlike Frenchmen, Englishmen seem rarely to be drawn to ladies who have already known the married state."

The duke's reaction to this speech was one of impatience at Jane's heavy-handedness. He saw anger building in Evangeline's eyes, and for an unwanted instant, it pleased him, until he realized that Evangeline was not responding out of jealousy for him, but out of personal hurt. Good lord, he thought, appalled at himself, was he really such a conceited bounder?

He opened his mouth to put a stop to any further female warfare, when he heard Evangeline say in her coldest voice, "I do not feel any need to secure an English gentleman's regard, Miss Bellerman. I am merely a visitor to England, and am not in search of a husband. Indeed, I can imagine no more repellent an idea than that a gentleman would find me unacceptable because I am widowed. If English gentlemen are such coxcombs, then you may keep them!"

Lady Jane allowed her pursed, thin lips to resume their normal inviting pout, for she thought Evangeline's speech quite sufficient to discredit her in any gentleman's estimation. She smiled her thought toward the duke.

"I believe, Jane," the duke said in a tone that brooked no opposition, "that we have abused the topic sufficiently. I see that her grace is readying to escort the ladies from the dining room, and leave the gentlemen to their port."

Evangeline did not have to concern herself with any more barbs from Lady Jane Bellerman, for Lady Pemberly and the chattering Felicia claimed her attention once the ladies had disposed themselves in comfortable groups in the drawing room.

"Such a marvelous dinner! I vow that I can scarce breathe!"

"You shouldn't eat so much, Felicia," Lady Pemberly said, fondly eyeing her reed-slender goddaughter, "else Lord Pettigrew will look elsewhere for amusement."

Evangeline, who had eaten very little, perjured her soul. "It was a delicious dinner and I must agree with Miss Storleigh, ma'am. I am truly grateful that ladies must no longer wear those dreadful stays."

"Drew has no desire to look elsewhere for amusement, Godmama," Felicia said, harking back.

The duke, leading the gentlemen, appeared shortly thereafter, much to the delight of the ladies, who had, or so it seemed to Evangeline, fallen into desultory conversation in their absence.

Evangeline was in conversation with Lord George Wallis and his wife, Pauline, when she heard the duke's voice. "Excuse me, George, Pauline. Evangeline, you have yet to meet the Duke and Duchess of Portmaine. They have only just arrived."

As he led her across the vast room, he said quietly, "I apologize for Miss Bellerman's behavior. I hope that she did not upset you."

For an instant, Evangeline gazed at him blankly before she raised her chin and asked him coolly, "I find myself wondering, your grace, why it is that you had me seated in such close proximity to you and, of course, to the lovely Lady Jane."

"Have you really?" he aked after a brief pause. "I suppose it could be a rather interesting question." He drew her to a halt in front of a small, very lovely woman who was, Evangeline guessed, in her early thirties. She found her eyes drawn inadvertently down from the lady's lively face to a magnificent bosom that swelled in rounded splendor above several rows of soft cream-colored lace.

"Brandy, this is Madame de la Valette, my cousin. Evangeline, the Duchess of Portmaine."

"What a beautiful and unusual name," Evangeline said without thought.

The duchess smiled charmingly. "Thank you, Madame. I ask you, what else could one do with Brandella? I think I am lucky to have gotten away with so unexceptionable a name as a gentleman's drink! Ian, come here, my love."

Evangeline looked up to see a tall, massively built gentleman, nearly the size of the duke, stroll toward them. He was an older man, dark, with white wings of hair at his temples. To Evangeline, he looked quite forbidding and stern. Until he smiled. It changed his face, erasing its harshness.

"Madame likes my name, Ian," the duchess said, her lovely, amber-colored eyes twinkling up at her husband.

"I am delighted," the Duke of Portmaine said, "for indeed, there is nothing else I can find to call her."

"Och, 'tis untrue, ye wretched man! He is forever coming up with the most outlandish appellations!"

"You are from Scotland, your grace," Evangeline said, feeling for the moment at her ease.

"Aye," Brandy replied, her slender fingers on her husband's black sleeve. "Poor Ian had to scour both England and Scotland to find himself a wife."

"Little witch," the Duke of Portmaine murmured.

"How fare your children, Ian?" she heard the duke ask.

"Carmichael Hall is as close to Bedlam as you could get, as you well know, Richard. All of them are repellently healthy and in high spirits."

Evangeline saw John Edgerton from the corner of her eye gazing at her purposefully. She laid her hand lightly on the duke's sleeve. "Excuse me, your grace, but I must speak a moment to Sir John." She did not wait to see how the duke received his, but walked quickly away from the small, merry group toward Sir John.

"You are in great demand, my dear," Sir John drawled. "Imagine leaving the esteemed Duke and Duchess of Portmaine for my lowly company. Richard Clarendon treats you like quite the favorite."

"The duke is kind."

"I am, needless to say, quite surprised to see you here, my dear. I trust you have an excellent reason for leaving Chesleigh without my permission."

Evangeline spoke barely above a whisper, her voice trembling. "I came to London because I could not bear to stay at Chesleigh. You filthy murderer—you killed her! That poor old woman—you killed her!"

John Edgerton slowly pulled a snuffbox from his waist-coat pocket and, with an expert flick of this thumb and forefinger, snapped up the lacquer lid. With exquisite precision, he pinched a small quantity of the scented snuff and inhaled it. He sneezed delicately, then slowly replaced the lid.

"You refer, I gather, to the demented old lady you mentioned to me?"

"You know that I do!"

He said, his eyes limpid upon her face, "A lamentable error, I assure you. How very unusual to be holding such a conversation in the very midst of the *ton*. It is fortunate that everyone is so vocal, is it not?"

"Do not toy with me!" she hissed, her fists clenching at her sides.

"It was a *mistake*, Evangeline. My instruction to my associate was merely to investigate the information you had given me. I have dutifully punished him for his . . . presumption."

"You expect me to believe *you?* Your associate, Sir John, most likely did exactly what you bade him to do! I cannot bear it! Please, you must release me!"

"I request you, my dear, to keep your voice low! Our conversation is not exactly suited for the company, is it? I will tell you once more—the old woman's death was an accident. Now, if you are finally willing to listen to reason, I will not remonstrate with you for disobeying my orders." He paused a moment, his eyes upon his snuffbox. "It so happens that there is a small task you can perform for me whilst you are here in London."

"My God, but you are reprehensible! I cannot——"

"Evangeline, will your father's death bring back that wretched old crone?"

"Do you not understand? How can I continue all in the name of protecting my father, when you are killing innocent people?"

"Calm yourself, my dear girl. As you have probably heard from Lord Pettigrew and others, Napoleon will arrive in Paris any day now. All will be resolved soon, very soon. Then, you will be free, I promise you."

"And just *how* will it all be resolved?"

Sir John shrugged negligently. "We shall see, shall we not? Doubtless all the great generals of the Allies will be involved."

"You swear that my father will be freed? Do you swear, by your honor as a . . . gentleman that no one else will be harmed?"

Sir John threw his head back and laughed heartily, as if Evangeline had made an amusing riposte. "What a child you are! Yes, my dear, you have my word, as the Lynx, since I see that you hesitate to use the word *gentleman*."

Evangeline turned to see the duke in quiet conversation with the Duchess of Portmaine. What were they talking about? she wondered. No doubt nothing more weighty than a childhood illness that could afflict Edmund. She said dully, looking back at him, "What is it you wish me to do?"

John Edgerton smiled gently and patted her arm. "Do return my smile, Evangeline. His grace is glancing toward us."

Her lips parted in a travesty of a smile.

"I will myself bring you instructions on the morrow. Doubtless, Lord Pettigrew will pay you a morning visit. I will accompany him. Now, I do not want the duke to suspect you of dalliance. You may return to him and be all that is gracious. I bid you good night, my dear Eagle."

"Why the devil do you wish to visit the ministry?"

Evangeline raised wide, innocent eyes to the duke's face and shrugged. "I thought it might be interesting, that is all." As his look remained disbelieving, she said,

"There is no need for you to accompany me, if you do not wish to be obliging."

"When did you wish to take this exciting outing?"

"This afternoon, if it pleases you. You needn't fear that your entry will be refused. You see, I asked Lord Pettigrew this morning."

"I had intended to drive you to Richmond," he said irritably. "But likely you wouldn't have the wherewithall to find your way through their famous maze."

Evangeline rose from the dining table and looked down at him. "If you are going to be in such a foul temper, I think I would prefer Bunyon's company."

"Hold your tongue, my girl. You must know that I have little choice in the matter. Of course I will accompany you. Now where are you going?"

"To see Edmund."

He toyed with his napkin for a moment. "Do you never forget your responsibilities, Evangeline?"

She hesitated briefly. "No," she said, "I do not."

"Well, I saw Edmund this morning, and I assure you that he is driving Ellen and the other staff frantic with his antics. I am almost tempted to ship him to Carmichael Hall, to the Duke of Portmaine." He added pensively, "I suppose what he really needs is brothers and sisters."

Evangeline raised her chin and retorted sharply, "Oh, you are contemplating marriage, your grace. Miss Bellerman will be most gratified, I would imagine, or are there other ladies vying for that vaunted position?"

A devilish grin lit his face. "Yes," he drawled, "and as Miss Bellerman so kindly informed you, they are all likely to be virgins."

"You. . . ! You are a pompous English coxcomb, your grace!" She drew herself up, her hands fisted at her sides, to see that he was laughing at her.

"You really must learn more control, Evangeline," he told her kindly. Evangeline turned on her heel and slammed out of the dining room, nearly colliding with a footman.

*   *   *

Evangeline drew her cloak closely about her shoulders against the chill afternoon air, and inched away from the duke to the other side of the carriage.

"What, you are still peeved with me, Madame?" He stretched his long legs diagonally in the space she had left.

She lifted her nose in the air.

"I think you should be more . . . compliant with your employer," he suggested softly. "You would not wish to be in my bad graces, I'm sure."

"I shall not be in your employ for much longer, your grace!"

"Why is that?" he asked baldly.

Evangeline cursed her loose tongue. He much enjoyed drawing her, she knew it, yet she always seemed to succumb. "I spoke heedlessly," she said in a tight voice. "I meant nothing." She turned her eyes resolutely to the maelstrom of activity outside the carriage. The windows were only partially closed, and she could hear the loud shouts of vendors hawking their wares, amidst the clatter of other carriages and horses' hooves.

To her relief, he said nothing. She hugged her reticule to her. Inside lay a slender envelope she was to place in Lord Pettigrew's office, at John Edgerton's instruction. He had handed it to her without any further explanation when they had been alone for a few moments in the entrance hall that morning. "But why?" she had asked him. "Do you not come and go in the ministry at will?" He had merely nodded. "Just do as I have told you," he had said, and quickly turned at the sound of the duke's voice.

The duke's crested carriage drew to a halt, and Juniper's sharp face soon appeared at the window.

"I believe that we're here, your grace," he said in an incredulous voice, "at the Ministry."

"I pray you not to sound so very surprised, Juniper.

Madame de la Valette is merely ensuring that I do not pass my day frivolously."

Evangeline stepped from the carriage to face a tall, soot-darkened gray stone building, stark and uninviting, surrounded by a high, black iron fence. It seemed unnaturally quiet on the street, for there were no scrambling hawkers here to disturb the important men behind its walls. Two of his majesty's uniformed guards stood in silent scrutiny.

"At least, you can see Westminster from here," the duke said, pointing a gloved finger.

"This is delightful," Evangeline said briskly and, ignoring the duke's look of incredulity, walked with a determined step to the tall, black gate in front of the ministry.

The duke gave his name to one of the uniformed guards. It appeared that Lord Pettigrew had prepared their way, for the iron gate was quickly swung open.

"Stay with the horses, Juniper," the duke called in a weary voice.

They walked up a dozen deeply worn stone steps to the huge double doors. The guard pulled at a heavy, iron-ringed knob and much to Evangeline's surprise, bowed low to the duke.

"Lord Pettigrew's secretary will now assist you, your grace," the man said in a respectful voice.

"Does everyone toad-eat you?" Evangeline snapped behind a gloved hand.

He gave her a bewildered look. "But why would you not expect to be received with all due deference and politeness?"

"He did not have to treat you as though you were the Regent himself!"

"Oh, he didn't. He was much politer to me, I wager."

Evangeline drew up, startled. The duke's softly spoken words reverberated off the walls, like a mighty echo. She glanced about her. The main hall rose upward some four stories, wrought iron railings enclosing each of the floors. Uniformed guards stood quietly at each landing. Gentlemen of all ages, dressed in somber colors, walked purposefully through the main entrance hall, slowing only briefly when they saw Evangeline pass by.

"Ladies normally do not visit this place," the duke said smoothly after a young man, with less aplomb than the others, nearly tripped over his feet at the sight of her.

"Richard, Madame! You are exactly on time." Lord Pettigrew appeared from the far side of the entrance hall. Unlike the secretaries and clerks, he was attired in a buff coat and dark brown breeches. Despite his warm welcome, Evangeline sensed that he was harried. Doubtless he thought her request to visit the ministry a frivolous one, and was not overjoyed that she was taking his valuable time.

"Thank you, Lord Pettigrew, for allowing me to come."

"Of course, Madame." His features relaxed for a moment. "This is quite a treat for Richard, I vow."

"I wouldn't have missed such an expedition for the world," the duke said in a languid voice. "Well, Drew, do we have you for a guide, or one of your many minions?"

"The great Duke of Portsmouth escorted about by a clerk? Surely, Richard, you know that I would never stoop to such shabby treatment!"

If the duke was bored, he did a creditable job of concealing it. They were shown through stark and somber conference rooms, that reeked of stale tobacco smoke. "And I have so *longed* to see the Lord Deputy's Chamber," Evangeline murmured as Lord Pettigrew led them into that ancient, oak-timbered room that had known endless discussions about England's future.

Evangeline was all that was deferential and polite when Drew introduced her to other gentlemen. They were equally polite to her, but spoke to her in such a condescending manner that Evangeline had to bite her unruly tongue. English gentlemen were only gallant, she decided, when ladies did not venture into masculine lairs.

Evangeline was near to screaming in frustration. "Lord Pettigrew," she said finally, as he prepared to show them into yet another floor, "I would very much like to see your office if you do not mind."

For the first time, he seemed to hesitate.

"I promise you that then I will have seen my fill." She added in a coy voice, "I daresay ladies cannot be blamed for wanting to see where gentlemen like you spend their days."

"Very well, Madame," Lord Pettigrew said finally, in a good-natured voice. He added ruefully, "To the best of my knowledge, Miss Storleigh would not step foot in this mausoleum."

"There is more word of Bonaparte?" she heard the duke ask Lord Pettigrew as they walked with him to his second floor offices.

Lord Pettigrew nodded grimly. "The Corsican will be in Paris by the morrow. I have it on my best sources. Much to the Allies' chagrin, the French have flocked to him. Shout the news all over London, if you like, Richard. I think it time that Englishmen realize the danger."

Napoleon will soon be in the Tuileries, where he belongs. It was happening, just as Houchard and Edgerton had predicted. Somehow, she had nourished hope that the French would have nothing to do with Napoleon, that the French army would hastily escort him back to Elba. Houchard would have had no further use for her or her father then. She was not aware that she had weaved until she felt the duke's hand under her elbow.

"Evangeline?"

"It is the heat, your grace," she said quickly, forcing her voice to lightness. "I am all right now, I promise you."

"Heat?"

He was gazing down at her, his eyes narrowed.

"I mean . . . the cold." You are stupid, Evangeline, stupid!

She became aware that Lord Pettigrew was apologizing for the clutter that seemed to fill his large office. There were maps everywhere and piles of papers stacked atop every surface. At the back of the office stood a huge mahogany desk, and two men were leaning over it, looking at some maps.

"Gentleman," Lord Pettigrew said, "be so kind as to await me in the antechamber. I will be but another minute or two."

"Yes, my lord," the taller of the two men said. They both eyed Evangeline with impatience, as they gathered up one map and tied it with a ribbon.

She ignored them and walked nonchalantly toward the windows at the back of the office. She made a point of remarking on the view of the Thames through the uncurtained glass. She supposed that Lord Pettigrew replied in a suitable phrase, but she wasn't attending either him or the duke. She was looking from beneath her lashes at the second shelf of the bookcase on the far side of the room. It looked little used. It was there, between the third and fourth bound volumes, that John Edgerton had instructed her to leave the envelope. She stood at the window, responding to Lord Pettigrew when it was appropriate, all the while wondering how she would ever get the wretched envelope into the bookcase.

"Have you seen enough, Evangeline?" the duke asked finally.

She turned and smiled brightly, and extended her hand to Lord Pettigrew. "Yes, indeed. Thank you so much, my lord. I know that you are quite busy. I do not wish to take any more of your valuable time."

"My pleasure, Madame," Lord Pettigrew said quick-

ly, though she knew he would be glad to see them
gone.

Evangeline walked slowly to the wide doorway, and
let her glove slip unnoticed to the wooden floor. When
they reached the outer office, she said in foolish alarm,
"Oh dear! I dropped my glove. Just a moment, I shall
fetch it!"

Before Lord Pettigrew could assign one of his clerks
to the task, Evangeline had whisked back into his office. With trembling fingers, she quickly pulled the
small envelope from her reticule and slipped it between
the thick books. She returned in not above three seconds, waving the glove in her land.

"Do forgive me. It was stupid, was it not? But all is
well now." She would have continued her nonsensical
speech had not the duke shot her his most quelling
look.

"A most elevating experience," the duke said in a
sardonic voice as he escorted her back to his carriage.

"Yes, it was," Evangeline agreed brightly, not looking at him.

"I suppose now you would like to visit the Commons."

"No, what I think I would prefer is a drive to Richmond! I have a mind to show you just how quickly I can
find my way through the maze!"

8

Evangeline sat in the cushioned window seat in Edmund's nursery, gazing out anxiously into the fog-laden park across the square. She had been in London for nearly a week now, and she still did not fail to start when told there were visitors in the drawing room for fear it would be John Edgerton with yet more demands of her. The papers were full now of Bonaparte's triumphant return to Paris, the French army at his side. Wellington and Napoleon were on everyone's lips, as was the talk of war, another bloody war. She studied the paper each morning in her bedchamber when the duke had finished with it, looking for any information at all about conditions in Paris. She felt suspended in time, waiting anxiously for something to happen, yet fearing what was likely to come to pass.

She looked toward Edmund, who was kneeling by the fireplace, busy with his toy soldiers. She was spending a great deal of time with him, she knew, because it was only with him she could feel totally at her ease. She had grown quite fond of the child, indeed. Like his father, he never bored her. He would one moment be speaking most seriously to her at his lessons, and the next, he would throw his arms about her and tell her that he preferred her to Lord Southwold. That was quite an accolade.

"Eve! Wellington will kill him dead!"

"Who, Edmund?"

"Napoleon, of course. Then you can be happy again."

Evangeline rose unsteadily from the window seat and eased down to her knees beside Edmund on the thick carpet. "Whatever do you mean, love?"

Edmund did not reply immediately, his attention returning to his arrangement of the English battalion. He finally raised his large eyes to her face.

"Papa says that I mustn't pester you."

She drew him quickly against her breast, risking a rebuff at such a maudlin gesture. "You never pester me, Edmund!"

He wriggled out of her grasp. "But Papa says——"

"What does Papa say, you little urchin?"

The duke stood in the open doorway, his arms crossed over his chest. He must have stepped into the room just as Evangeline sat down beside Edmund.

Evangeline started to scramble to her feet, but the duke stayed her with an indifferent wave of his hand. "No, Evangeline, do not leave your comfortable place on my account."

He strode over to them and dropped to his knees. "Now, son, what is it that Papa says?"

"I have told Eve that Wellington will shoot Napoleon. You said that she was unhappy and I wanted to cheer her up."

The duke met Evangeline's eyes over Edmund's head. "And have you succeeded?" he asked quietly. "You must ask her."

"Your father is talking nonsense, Edmund," she quickly interposed, looking away from the duke's probing gaze, afraid that he would see too much. She tousled Edmund's curly hair. "Now, show your father how you would defeat Bonaparte."

She eased herself away from Edmund's battleground,

as father and son realigned the soldiers' positions and shifted the artillery about, to the sound of Edmund's excited chatter.

"Not a bad shot, Edmund! Aim the cannon more toward the front line. That's it. Damn, but I'll have to take care or you'll wipe out my entire battalion."

"Look, Papa, Cousin Eve's laughing. I did make her happy."

" 'Twould appear so, Edmund. Now, how would you like to go to the Pantheon Bazaar with your grandmother today?"

"Oh yes, Papa," Edmund said, nodding enthusiastically.

"Very well, then, fetch your coat. Your grandmother is awaiting you downstairs."

Evangeline remarked dryly, "Does her grace know of the treat you have just planned for her?"

"Certainly," the duke said, rising. "I had come to fetch him for that very purpose." He stretched out his hands to Evangeline, pulling her easily to her feet, and gently glided his hands up her arms until they lightly clasped her shoulders.

"You have been avoiding me, Evangeline." She felt his warm breath on her forehead and for an instant allowed herself to lean against him. The need to respond to his words brought her reason. She gave a shaky laugh and pulled away from him.

"I cannot imagine any lady avoiding you, your grace," she said. She had meant to sound light and uncaring, but she realized to her chagrin that her voice sounded strangely forlorn.

"And when you do not avoid me," he continued easily, "you engage me in verbal swordplay. Do you think it a good ploy to keep me at my distance?"

"I know nothing of swordplay, your grace," she said, looking away from him.

"Richard."

"Do you not have an engagement? Surely there are scores of ladies who must be pining for your company."

He raised his hands and gently closed them about her throat, his fingers lightly caressing her pulse. "You begin to convince me, my dear, that you want me to thrash you." His strong fingers continued to caress her, and she dropped her head, only to feel his thumbs under her chin, forcing her to look up at him. "Are you afraid of me, Evangeline?"

She shook her head, mutely. She felt his mouth, featherlight, touch her lips, and a deep, insistent longing built within her. She could not seem to focus on anything except how close he was, and the aching need she felt for him.

"Forgive the intrusion, your grace, but your tailor is here."

His hands dropped and he turned sharply to his valet, Bunyon, a frown on his brow. "You may tell the fellow to take himself to the devil."

"He has been waiting for over an hour, your grace."

Evangeline felt awash with embarrassment. Must he always make her behave like a wanton? She realized bleakly that he knew that she wanted him to. She said in an unnaturally high voice, "I have much to do, your grace! There is Edmund's geography lesson to prepare, and I must dress for her grace's card party! Please, see to your tailor!"

"It is most odd, Richard," the dowager duchess said as she sipped her tea. "Evangeline outright refused to attend Ranleagh's masquerade ball, because she claimed she did not own an appropriate costume. When I offered to procure her a mask and domino, she refused to hear of it. It was not my intention to shame her, of course! Her pride, in this instance, is misplaced. Will you speak to her? I am persuaded that she would enjoy herself. She is starting to worry me, Richard. Even

Grayson has mentioned that, as he put it, Madame appears downpin."

The duke frowned down at the glowing embers in the fireplace. It was true that Evangeline seemed more wan and withdrawn by the day. After Bunyon's interruption the day before, she had scarce given him the opportunity to speak to her. He had frightened her again. It seemed that he simply could not keep his hands to himself when he was alone with her. He wondered at himself. He was a gentleman and not a ravisher of woman.

"I am becoming a halfwit," he said aloud.

"No," the dowager duchess said gently. "You are merely uncertain about what you want. For you, my son, that is a new experience indeed."

"I am too old for new experiences," the duke said irritably, and kicked a dying ember with the toe of his boot. As the dowager duchess did not reply, he turned finally to face her. "I will speak to Evangeline. I wish her to go, and I do not see why she should refuse."

"You might try a little deception," the dowager duchess suggested, "instead of the *forceful* approach you seem so inclined to use with her. It is not to your best advantage, I have observed."

He shot her an harrassed look and said stiffly, "You might consider holding the reins less tightly yourself, Madam. Your subtlety is less than stunning."

As the duke expected, he found Evangeline with Edmund, in his room on the second floor of Clarendon House. They were sitting on the carpet in front of the fireplace, their heads together, pouring over drawings of Paris. "And that, love, is the Bastille, an infamous prison that was destroyed in 1789 by the *sans-culottes*, French revolutionaries."

The duke cleared his throat. "Excuse me, Evangeline, but her grace is expecting Edmund downstairs. Cook has made him some special cakes that she wishes him to try."

"Cook's plum cakes, Father?"

"Control your gluttony, Edmund. Something like plum cakes, I think."

Edmund gave Evangeline a look that sorely reminded her of a starving child. "Yes, do go have your treat. We can always look at the drawings of Paris. They, I daresay, won't spoil."

After Edmund had left them, extolling Cook's plum cakes to a footman outside the door, Evangeline said to the duke, "I hope you have not told your son an untruth, your grace."

"I beg your pardon, Evangeline? Let us just say that Cook is forever making the most outlandish pastries."

"Ah, so you won't be found out!"

"Exactly." He saw that she was beginning to look wary, and purposefully kept his distance from her. There were dark smudges beneath her expressive eyes. His concern for her made his voice unnaturally harsh. "I have come for a reckoning, Madame. How long have you been Edmund's governess?"

Evangeline smiled wryly. "I am not certain that I fill that role, your grace. I have not the talent, I fear."

"Nonsense. I would that you cease belittling yourself, Evangeline. In any case, according to my calculations, you have been with Edmund for over a month now. You have not as yet been paid for your services."

She looked at him, at sea. "I don't understand. Not only have you given me all of Marissa's gowns, but you have treated me like an honored guest. It is far more than I deserve, your grace."

"Nonetheless, it is what I wish." He drew a note from his waistcoat pocket. "I believe that fifty pounds is a fair amount for your services to date."

Evangeline rose slowly to her feet, too stunned by his words to speak. How could he offer to pay her, as he would any of his servants! Despite her protestations that she be treated as Edmund's governess, she would not have believed he thought of her in that way.

"I do not want any of your money!" she cried, cloaking her hurt with anger.

For the next few moments, he made a project of shaking out the ruffles over his wrists. He saw that she was flushed, but he simply did not understand her reaction. He said coolly, "The fifty pounds, as I have told you, is for your services to date, for your instruction and companionship to my son. You will accept it, graciously, if possible."

She gazed at him bleakly. Did he not even understand what he was doing?

"I have told you that I do not want your money!" she cried, backing away from him. "Why are you doing this? To make me come to understand what it is that you want of me? Dammit, is that what you pay your bloody mistresses?"

He was now quite as angry as she was at her spate of nonsensical accusations. "Hardly, Madame," he thundered at her. "I pay my mistresses for their beauty, charm, and skill. In my company, you have shown only the first of my three requirements. Let me make myself even clearer, Madame, for I can see that you're itching to yell at me for some further supposed slight. You will take the fifty pounds, or I swear to you, Evangeline, I will bare your bottom and thrash you!"

"Do not threaten me, your grace! Unlike your other servants, I will not be ordered about willy-nilly, and I am not so poor-spirited! You may take your insults and your money and go to the devil!"

He advanced toward her, and Evangeline found that her feet were scurrying back despite her show of bravado. He covered the distance between them in three long strides and grasped her shoulders in an iron grip, jerking her against him. "You are a rag-mannered witch, Madame. And I grow weary of your consigning me to Hades whenever I have the misfortune of ruffling your misbegotten pride!" His voice dropped. "For God's

sake, Evangeline, listen to me. I would be your friend,
if you will but let me."

She realized that he had not intended any insult. It
was simply that he did not understand. She whispered,
turning her face into his shoulder, "Forgive me for
ripping up at you. It is just that . . . you seemed to be
treating me as one of your . . . retainers."

He looked startled. "Good God, woman, how can
you so misunderstand me? I want you to have your own
money. That is all." He found that his hands moved of
their own accord to her back. He could feel her muscles, taut and knotted beneath his fingers, and he gently
began to stroke her. He said softly, "You unman me,
Evangeline, and make me feel the perfect bounder.
Will you not tell me what troubles you?" He waited
hopefully, willing her to tell him whatever it was that
was holding her back from him.

She knew in that moment that he truly cared for her,
and she felt a brief, yet terrible instant of temptation to
tell him the truth, to tell him that she loved him. But
she could not. She must never admit to her feeling for
him, for fate in the guise of Houchard and John Edgerton
would not allow it. She pulled away from him, her jaw
set. "There is nothing that troubles me, your grace! I
once told you that I—I did not like London. I do not
seem to be getting along well here."

"You may leave London whenever you like. You have
but to name the date."

The expression on her face was ludicrous in its dismay. She had no instruction from John Edgerton that
would allow her to leave London yet. She shook her
head and said in a strangled voice, "Yes, I will tell
you."

He cloaked his disappointment. Why would she not
trust him? "Since I am so obliging, then I think it only
just that you be likewise. I would like you to attend the
Ranleagh's masquerade ball with me this evening."

"But I do not have——" She broke off suddenly, realizing that he had duped her. "Ah, the fifty pounds. You have deceived me, your grace! Money of my own, indeed!"

"I am loathe to admit it, Madame, but in this case, deception was . . . necessary."

She found to her surprise that she was smiling despite herself. She had forced him to go to such lengths. She presented him with a low, mock curtsey. "Since you have gone to such great lengths, your grace, I suppose it would be petty of me to cavil! Very well, it shall be as you wish."

"A masquerade ball, unfortunately, gives license to behavior that is not always circumspect. I would prefer that you stay close to either my mother or myself."

The dowager duchess was thankful that the interior of the carriage was too dark for either Evangeline or the duke to see her face, for she was sorely tempted to laugh at her son's speech.

"I do not believe I merit an harangue from you, your grace, on how to conduct myself. I am not some witless chit with no notion of how to go on."

"Indeed, Richard, Evangeline does not appear at all *witless* to me," the dowager duchess said, throwing herself in the breach.

"Nonetheless," he continued, ignoring his mother's weak attempt at humor, "you will do as I bid you. I do not wish you to be placed in an awkward position because an overeager puppy has imbibed too much punch."

"You sound like the parson in his pulpit, your grace. Somehow, I have difficulty reconciling your righteous warning with your own touted proclivities."

The dowager duchess drew back. If Bunyon had dared to say such a thing to the duke, he would have had his ears soundly boxed. And if she herself had essayed such a rebuttal, he would have undoubtedly dashed her with one of his arrogant set-downs.

The duke's gloved hands itched to shake her, but since he had no wish to turn the carriage into a battleground, particularly with his mother present, he merely said on a mocking laugh, "It would seem to me that a warning coming from me, with all my touted proclivities, should make you more amenable to reason, Madame. Surely you have reached an age at which you do not willy-nilly scorn kindly meant advice."

The dowager duchess wished that some wise phrase would miraculously appear on her tongue. As it was, she found nothing to say when Evangeline gazed at her apologetically. "Now that you acknowledge my advanced years, your grace," Evangeline said with heavy sarcasm, "perhaps you will also be inclined to realize that I have no need to be prosed at as if I were some sort of empty-headed chit."

"Surely, Richard, you do not believe Evangeline to be an empty-headed chit!" the dowager duchess said, all innocence.

"I believe, Mother," the duke said, casting her a sardonic look, "that I usually accord Evangeline treatment that suits her behavior quite well."

He was beginning to sound at the end of his tether, and the dowager duchess was thankful that the carriage had turned onto the long, graveled drive that led to Ranleagh House.

"I am always struck by the beauty of all the lights," she said brightly, waving toward the mansion. "Is it not breath-taking, Evangeline? Lucille—Lady Ranleagh, you know—will be delighted. I vow there must be a hundred carriages! And wait until you see her servants—doubtless they will all be decked out in the costume of a bygone era."

"It is lovely, your grace," Evangeline said, gazing through the carriage window. She cast a drawing look toward the duke. "I much love to waltz. I hope there will be sufficient partners available."

He regarded her darkly, a black brow arched up-

ward. She gazed past him at the brightly lit windows of
Ranleagh House and heard the strains of a German
waltz. Tonight, she thought, she wanted to enjoy herself, to forget everything in the gaiety of the ball, and
the company of the duke.

As a footman hurried to let down the steps to their
carriage, she gazed at the duke through her lashes. His
face was set in stern lines. She vowed silently that for
the remainder of the evening she would not goad him
once.

"Your grace," came a portentous voice. Evangeline
looked up to see a butler, rendered less than dignified
in a bright red velvet doublet, stiff white ruff, and hose
of the sixteenth century. She smiled, relishing the
anonymity of her lavender mask, and the duke's arm
beneath her hand.

The butler led them up a wide staircase, past laughing guests gowned in the most outlandish fashion, and
ubiquitous footmen, attired as courtiers from Queen
Bess's court.

"I do want you to enjoy yourself this evening," the
dowager duchess said when the duke turned to greet
one of his cronies.

"There are so many people," Evangeline said, looking about her. "How can one possibly dance?"

"You will need an experienced partner," the duke said
as he again took her arm.

"Lucille!" the dowager duchess called toward a tall
lady dressed as a Roman matron.

"My dear, I would like you to meet a *very* good
friend of mine, Lady Ranleagh."

"So this is Madame de la Valette," said Lady Ranleagh
as she vigorously waved a violet feathered fan. "You
look enchanting, my dear. I vow I am fatigued at so
many young ladies attired in their so-boring shepherdess costumes! It was not like that when we were in our
salad days, Amelia!"

The dowager duchess laughed. "No, indeed, but then

we endured that wretched powdered hair and silk patches on our faces. The duke, of course," she continued, glancing at her son, "refused any costume save his black mask and domino."

"The duke, my dear Amelia, has no need for enchancements of any kind. I vow the ladies have been searching the doorway for the past half hour awaiting his entrance! Well, Richard, I trust you are prepared to calm the palpitating hearts."

"Of a certainty, Lucille. Am I not always cooperative with the ladies?"

"Rogue! I believe your compliance should begin with your cousin. Madame, allow me to present you a partner of some renown. Despite his ungainly size, he waltzes passably.

The duke smiled down at Evangeline. "Well, Madame? Will you accept me as your first partner?"

"It would be most small of me to turn you down, your grace, particularly after such a glowing introduction!"

Lady Ranleagh gazed at the dowager duchess quizzically, observing that her friend's eyes followed the couple. "She seems a charming girl," Lady Ranleagh said noncommittally.

"Oh yes, she is. She is certainly not one of our average insipid misses. Now, Lucille, will you likewise procure an elegant partner for me?"

The duke's hand tightened about Evangeline's waist as he guided her expertly through a crowded knot of dancers.

"You do dance beautifully, your grace," she said, already panting slightly from the vigorous exertion.

"As do you, my—cousin." How naturally *love* had come to his lips, with her in his arms and her hand upon his shoulder. He saw that her eyes were glowing behind her mask, and whirled her around the floor in wide circles. She laughed aloud, naturally and without reserve.

She smiled up at him when he slowed to a more

sedate pace. "I was certain that we were going to cannon into another couple! Is there anything you do not do well?"

He lowered his head and touched his chin for an instant against her hair. Her hair smelled faintly of roses. "There are several things I should wish to do better."

"For instance?"

"When you become too inquisitive, Evangeline, you lose your concentration. Already you have missed your step and nearly trod upon my foot. You would not wish us to appear clumsy on the dance floor, would you?"

"I am determined to keep peace with you tonight, your grace, and I simply shall not attend to your bothersome barbs."

"Perhaps then I can gain your attention with a compliment. You dance like an angel, Madame, and I find it a pleasure to dance with a lady who does not require me to become stoop-shouldered to hear her conversation."

"Why, your grace, I had not guessed that you could be so terribly amiable!"

The orchestra ended the waltz, and Evangeline knew more than a moment of disappointment. He did not move from her side, and she believed that he would engage her for the next dance. She looked questioningly up at him and saw that he was waving negligently toward Lady Jane Bellerman, clad, Evangeline saw with satisfaction, in a flowing shepherdess costume.

Out of pique, she said coldly, "I will not, of course, expect you to dance with me the *entire* evening. I imagine that many ladies are already itching to throw me off the balcony!"

"Possibly, but you may trust me to protect you. In any case, you do not want to dance with the same gentleman more than twice."

"Whyever not?" she asked, all innocence.

"It provides unnecessary gossip."

"Not even with you, your grace?" she asked in a silky voice.

"I have not asked you, Evangeline."

"You are a toad, your grace!"

"Really, Madame, I had thought that you could not be provoked this evening."

"Lady Jane is waving at you *again*, your grace," she said, a laughing challenge in her eyes.

"Ah yes, the virgin shepherdess."

"I did not know that shepherdesses were necessarily virgins."

"Ah, in England they are, you may be certain." He laughed softly. At her silence, he said, "Do I dare believe that this time I am to have the last word with you?"

She said finally, in a remarkably sweet voice, "Since you are my esteemed employer, I suppose it would be small of me not to occasionally allow you that privilege."

"You small?" He let his eyes flit down to her bosom. "Surely never that!"

"Is Sabrina also a tall lady?" she asked quickly, to forestall him from any further comments down that path.

"No, Sabrina is very slight. But, I have heard from my mother that she is breeding. That should, I would imagine, soon change her contours somewhat."

"Oh," Evangeline said only.

"I imagine your father never once took you over his knee to curb your wayward tongue."

"That, your grace, is none of your business!"

"But it is very much my business, Evangeline, particularly if you force me to rectify your sire's lapses."

The orchestra struck up another waltz and she was at once engaged by an Arthurian knight who appeared at her elbow. She gave the duke a saucy grin and melted into her partner's willing arms, all for his eyes, he knew. He grinned after her and returned to his mother, observed that she appeared well entertained by her aging Greek philosopher, Lord Harvey, and sauntered over to the waiting Lady Jane.

Evangeline had a difficult time not laughing at the flow of trite compliments that flowed from the very young and eager knight, anxious to impress her with his vast worldliness. She smiled and allowed herself to be amused, until he trod once, soundly, upon her toes.

Evangeline soon discovered, much to her delight, that even phlegmatic English gentlemen became most energetic at a masquerade ball. Between dances she had only enough time to catch her breath and an occasional glimpse of a nodding smile of approval from the dowager duchess. Her vanity was encouraged by a succession of outlandish compliments, and her only unanswered wish was to receive such attention from the duke. He did not again ask her to waltz, being much too occupied, she noticed with a tight-lipped grimace, with English shepherdesses. She supposed that he was punishing her for flinging his wretched Puritan advice out the carriage window. It came as a shock to her to be informed by a tipsy French chevalier of the last century that it was nearly midnight.

"Surely it is not that late," she exclaimed.

He chortled in a decidedly lecherous fashion. "Allow me to assist you to unmask. I am most adept at assisting ladies to remove most anything they require," he suggested, his hand tightening about her wrist.

"Oh my," Evangeline said in a high, breathless voice, "I do believe the Dowager Duchess of Portsmouth is waving to me! Pray excuse me, sir!" She slipped out of his grasp and made her way toward the long row of windows that gave onto the balcony. She drew in a deep breath of fresh air and walked through to the iron railing. She heard the laughter of servants from below and leaned her elbows on it to look down.

"Well, Madame de la Valette, you are a most sought-after young lady."

She whirled about at the softly-spoken words to face

a tall, slender man costumed in a scarlet domino and mask. There was something naggingly familiar about his voice, but she could not place it.

"I beg your pardon, sir. You know my name."

"It is midnight, you know." He raised his fingers to his mask and pulled the tie string loose.

Evangeline simply stared at him, at the mole on his cheek, at his eyes, resting sardonically upon her face. It was Conan DeWitt, the man she had met at the old Norman church in Chitterly.

9

"You!"

"Pray do not be so shocked. I am quite presentable in English society, as, I have gathered tonight, are you. I was unable to secure even a country dance with you."

"What are you doing here, Mr. DeWitt?"

"Actually, as the Lynx asked me to come here tonight, you might call me his emissary. I have a message for you, Eagle."

The smile she had worn for most of the evening faded from her face. She said in a taut voice, "Be quick about it, sir, for I must return to my party."

"Very well. You are to return to Chesleigh at once." He handed her a slender envelope. "Here are your instructions." He paused a moment, his eyes narrowed on her pale face as she quickly stuffed the envelope into her reticule. "I hear that you have had a crisis of conscience. It was always my belief, as I once told you, that women have fragile consciences, and are swayed by whatever happens to touch their tender hearts at the moment. I hope, for your sake, that you do not prove me correct."

She stiffened, but said only, "I wager there are

Englishmen who have had the misfortune to trust you, more's the pity!"

He withdrew an enamel snuffbox from his waistcoat pocket and flicked it open. As he inhaled a pinch of snuff, he said, "I do not care for your sharp tongue, Eagle. I do consider women occasionally useful, but my uses for them are somewhat different than the Frenchman Houchard's."

He stepped in front of her and grasped her upper arms in his hands.

"Let me go," she said in a voice of deadly calm. "You disgust me."

His eyes glittered with contempt. "Can it be that you are such an innocent? Or do you now compare all men to your duke? I wager that wealth and title would render me more palatable to you."

"The only thing that would make you acceptable to me is if you took your place in Newgate. Release me!"

"Evangeline!"

Conan DeWitt dropped his hands and took a lazy step back. Evangeline whirled about to see the duke step onto the balcony. She clasped her reticule tightly against her and said in a tight voice, "Your grace."

The duke tossed Conan DeWitt a curt nod. "DeWitt," he said, his voice tightly controlled. "I see that you have met my cousin."

My God, she thought, the duke knows him!

"Your grace." Conan DeWitt bowed, his voice all smooth deference. "Yes, your cousin has been kind enough to give me her opinion of England and Englishmen."

The duke eyed Evangeline, who stood rigid, staring dumbly at him. He had seen her wend her way toward the balcony and a man in scarlet domino purposefully follow her. That she would be foolish enough to come out onto the balcony alone angered him, but to see her held by Conan DeWitt made him want to shake her until her teeth rattled.

He turned to her and said in a formal tone, "It grows late, Evangeline. I trust you have had your fill of dancing and . . . conversation."

Evangeline nodded mutely. Without another glance at Conan DeWitt, she walked toward the duke and placed her hand upon his arm. "Yes, your grace, I have had my fill."

"A pleasure to have seen you again, your grace, Madame," she heard DeWitt say behind them.

Evangeline had to lengthen her stride to keep pace with the duke. At last, he said, without bothering to look at her, "What if I had not seen you go outside? You damned little fool! Conan DeWitt is a known womanizer and you obviously fascinated him. Does it please your vanity, Madame, to make men want you?"

"Please," she whispered, her eyes focused on the toes of her slippers, "let us just go."

The duke drew up abruptly, and she felt him stiffen. "Did he hurt you?" he barked.

She looked away from him for an instant, then resolutely shook her head. "No, 'twas nothing, your grace."

It did not require a piercing intellect, the dowager duchess thought, to realize that her delightful conversation on the carriage ride back to York Square was falling on deaf ears. She gave up the attempt, deciding that if she was *de trop*, it was better to be so quietly.

"Well my dears," the dowager duchess said firmly upon their arrival at Clarendon House, "a most enjoyable evening. Now, I will bid you both good night." She received an abstracted kiss on her cheek from the duke, and a quick hug from Evangeline.

The duke turned to Evangeline once the dowager duchess was no longer in their hearing.

"Do you have a moment? I wish to speak with you."

"Of course, your grace," she said, hesitating but an instant, and swept past him into the library. During their silent ride back to York Square, she knew that he had held his tongue only because the dowager duchess was present. It was inevitable, knowing his temper as she did, that he would want to cut up at her. She resolved to keep a tight rein on her own temper.

"Do you wish a fire built, your grace?"

"No, Grayson. You may take yourself to bed. I will douse the lights."

Evangeline walked to the cold fireplace and leaned her shoulders against the mantel. Although he no longer wore the black velvet mask, the domino swirled about his ankles as he approached her. He drew to a halt at her side, and his eyes—black pirate's eyes, she thought inconsequentially—seemed to rake at her.

"If you but had a cutlass, the image would be complete," she snapped, finally responding to his cold scrutiny.

"What image?"

"You look for all the world like a pirate."

"If I were, I might very well have flogged you by now." He frowned at himself for momentarily losing the calm he had regained on the carriage ride back to Clarendon House. He said after a flat pause, "I was very concerned about you when I saw you leave the ballroom, particularly with Conan DeWitt on your heels. Would you please tell me why you did something so ill-considered?"

She raised her chin. "I do not consider my actions at all ill-considered."

"Did you not realize that such an action could invite unpleasant gossip?"

"I have noticed, your grace, that gossip comes from the most ignorant and foolish of mouths! I do not care about such things."

He ground his teeth at her flippancy. "Dammit, Evangeline, I expected you to behave sensibly! Now, tell me, just why the devil did you go out onto the balcony, and with Conan DeWitt?"

"I would have you know, your grace, that I did not accompany Conan DeWitt. He followed me. My only fault was wishing to have a moment to myself and some fresh air! And I will tolerate no more unfounded accusations from you!"

She took a step away from him, only to find her shoulders clasped in an unyielding grip. "Unfounded! I see Conan DeWitt caressing you and you have the audacity to rant at me!"

Her cup was filled to brimming. Evangeline growled deep in her throat, drew back her arm, and drove her fisted hand into his stomach. He grunted, for she had caught him unawares. He stared down at her for a long moment.

"Perhaps," he said slowly, studying her flushed face, "I judged too quickly." He grinned suddenly and rubbed his hand over his stomach. "I begin to think that you would be a worthy opponent at Gentleman Jackson's boxing saloon."

"I am sorry for striking you," she said, raising her chin, "but, you were very provoking." She turned away from him for a moment, and said over her shoulder, "I wish to leave for Chesleigh tomorrow. I trust you recall your promise."

He was silent overlong. Finally, he said, "If it is your wish."

"It is, your grace."

"Very well."

She heard tension in his voice, and sought quickly to change the topic. "Who is that man, Conan DeWitt?"

The duke shrugged. "He is a gentleman newly arrived in London from somewhere in the Lake District, I believe. I met him but recently at White's. He is Lord Hampton's secretary, and much involved with his lordship in political matters."

He watched myriad expressions flit over her face, and wondered what she was thinking. He was taken aback when she asked, "What do you think will happen now that Napoleon is back in power?"

"My dear Evangeline, you have heard everyone say

that it must come to war again. I am of the same opinion. Unfortunately, our information is such that we never discover the truth of anything until weeks later. At least Wellington is in Brussels with the Prince of Orange."

"He is a competent commander, is he not?"

"Very competent. Although everyone is preaching doom, it is a fact that Napoleon decimated the experienced soldiers in his armies, particularly during 1812 on his march into Russia. What he has now are inexperienced boys and but a few tested generals. Wellington will crush him. It must happen."

"Yes," she said slowly, drawing a shaking breath, "it must happen. I am tired, your grace, and I must finish packing. Perhaps I will see you in the morning, before I leave."

He looked at her quizzically, but said only, "Good night, Evangeline. I trust you will sleep well."

The duke stood motionless for some time, staring across the expanse of the library toward the closed door. A crooked smile indented the corners of his mouth. He had begun by acting like a jealous fool, then finished with a singularly unromantic discussion of Napoleon. He turned and stared in amazement at himself in the gilt-edged mirror over the fireplace. For the first time in his life, he knew he was experiencing the rigors of an emotion he had always scoffed at.

By the time the duke reached his bedchamber, there was a rueful smile playing about his lips. She was a hellion—headstrong, willful, and altogether adorable. It now behooved him, he knew, to tred warily. He wondered, grinning at himself, how it was that he, a man who had never wanted to tie himself to one woman, had come to such a pass. Strangely enough, it disturbed him not one whit. Indeed, he thought, he could not now imagine Evangeline being out of his life. He knew that he wanted her, wanted her with him, wanted her as his wife.

He felt a shock of guilt the next morning when he saw her directing a footman with her several valises. There were dark smudges under her eyes, and she seemed pale and listless. She gave him a surprised, wary look after seeing his mountains of luggage piled high in the entrance hall.

"There is no need, your grace," she said, looking for all the world like a hunted creature, "for you to escort me back to Chesleigh."

"No, indeed. I am not simply escorting you, Evangeline, I plan to rusticate for a while. London in the height of the Season has lost its savor." The drawling indifference in his voice pleased him.

"I find that difficult to credit, your grace," she said sharply. "It is quite obvious to me that you find my . . . behavior wholly inexcusable."

"Perhaps so, Madame but I do feel the need to spend more time with my son." He supposed that a half truth was better than none. "Let us have our breakfast. I want to leave within the hour."

As he escorted her to the breakfast room, he said softly, "I have decided that you have need of my guiding hand. If you will but attend me closely, I think you can be rendered quite excusable."

She swallowed the retort, only to find that it would not remain unspoken. "You are being an abominable hypocrite! Your guiding hand indeed!"

"Not an encouraging beginning, Evangeline," he said with a wolfish grin.

When informed of the duke's and Evangeline's departure a short time later, the dowager duchess patted Evangeline's hand fondly. "Do not let Richard or my scapegrace grandson overtire you, my dear. Are you certain that you wish to leave London so soon?"

"Yes, your grace. I thank you for all your kindness to me."

"You must do, of course, what you think best, my

child. Now, if you would not mind, Evangeline, I would like to spend a few minutes alone with the duke."

When Evangeline had left the dowager duchess's bedchamber, she said to the duke, "As for you, my son, allow me to wish you luck. I have the distinct feeling that you will need it."

He gazed at her a moment. "Is there nothing you don't know, Mother?"

"I trust not, Richard," she said comfortably. "I am pleased that Edmund is so fond of her. I don't suppose that you plan to use your son as a . . . lever?"

"Now, Mother, you've always assured me that I am the most handsome, convincing gentleman of your acquaintance. Do you have so little faith in my abilities?"

"Perhaps, my love, you have grown overly confident. Evangeline, it appears to me, is a very independent young lady. I am inclined to believe that it is she who will set the terms." She paused a moment, gazing at the large portrait of the late duke, her husband, that hung over the fireplace. "It is a pity that she was but a child when your father decided that you would marry."

"Perhaps it is for the best. I fancy that a widower and a widow are well matched."

She laughed and he leaned down to kiss her cheek. "Do take care, Richard."

"You may be assured that I shall, as always, Mother," he drawled.

10

"So, Evangeline, you still refuse to tell me about your outing with Edmund at the cove?"

" 'Twas but a simple swimming excursion, your grace," she said, "something that I doubt you could possibly find at all interesting. And I, I must say, have little wish to think about it after such a large dinner."

"If you could, perhaps, paint me a picture of it, my dear, I vow that I would be much entertained."

She blushed at the image of his seeing her in her short muslin shift, clinging wet to her body. "You are being most . . . improper, your grace!"

"Alas, it is true. But as you see, Evangeline, I am all contrite."

"Ha!" she said, laughing. She peered suspiciously at him from beneath her lashes.

He leaned his shoulders negligently against the mantelpiece, a glass of sherry in his hand, and looked thoughtful a moment. He said abruptly, "I like to see you gay and carefree. You have been too infrequently such since your arrival at Chesleigh."

She shifted uncomfortably in her chair. "I suppose I am a . . . serious person, your grace," she said finally, dropping her eyes upon her own sherry glass.

"Well, my very serious Evangeline, I fear it will be too chilly tomorrow for your swimming lesson with Edmund. Perhaps you would like to come with me to Southhampton. We could sail to the Isle of Wight. If it pleased you, we could remain at my house in Ventnor for several days."

Her fingers tightened about the crystal glass stem. The instruction given to her by Conan DeWitt was that she meet one of Houchard's men the following evening at the cove. "No!" she said quickly. "That is," she amended, seeing one of his black brows wing upward, "I am not a good sailor, your grace, and I have a fear of yachts! I know it is stupid, but I cannot seem to help it."

"A good swimmer but afraid of the water," he said dryly. "Really, Evangeline, you do not have to lie to keep yourself out of my company. Is it that you fear I will try to seduce you? I promise you that I have no ulterior motive."

She lowered her head, unable to meet his eyes. She wished her lie had not sounded so lame. "Please forgive me, your grace," she said at last, knowing she had to say something, "but I do not wish to leave Chesleigh."

"Why the devil not?"

She winced at the harshness in his voice. "I—I simply do not want to."

He pushed his broad sholders away from the mantelpiece, snapped down his glass, and strode over to her. He knew that he wasn't being particularly gentle with her, but it was all he could do not to glower at her. His invitation to her to sail to Ventnor on his yacht was an idea he was loathe to give up. Since their return to Chesleigh three days before, she had done her best to avoid him. Only yesterday, he had asked her to go riding with him. She had fidgeted for a moment, then insisted in a too bright voice that Edmund would also enjoy such a treat. He eyed her now with growing frustration.

"There is no reason for you to continue playing games with me, Evangeline. No, please do not interrupt with yet more of your protestations. If you find my company distasteful, you have but to tell me. I assure you that I never assault helpless virgins or widows—unless, that is, they wish it." He drew to a halt when she raised her white face. He remembered her eager passion when he had held her, how she had moaned softly into his mouth. "My God, it is not me you fear, is it?"

She gazed up at him, and saw that his dark eyes had fallen from her face to her breasts. To her confusion, he laughed softly. "So it is yourself you fear. I thank you for the compliment, Madame."

Her face flamed with color. She did fear herself and him for the feelings he aroused in her. Her words of denial would not say themselves. She became aware that he was studying her, a curious expression in his eyes.

"Evangeline?"

She started at the tenderness in his voice.

"Will you do me the honor of becoming my wife?"

Her head whipped up and she stared up at him, open-mouthed, not willing to believe his words. "You do not know what you're saying, your grace!"

He stood over her, and she felt the power of him even before he touched her. "Of course I do, little fool."

"No!" she cried. "It is not—possible! You cannot mean it!" She rose quickly and walked behind the chair, so stunned that she did nothing but clutch feverishly at its stiff brocaded back.

He did not approach her again, thinking that he had frightened her. He wondered at himself. How the devil could he have allowed himself to rush his fences so abruptly?

He drew a deep breath and said calmly, "I would only mock you during one of our colorful arguments, Evangeline. Marriage is a serious business. Believe me that I would not joke about how I wish to spend my life."

She felt her heart turn wildly in her bosom. For one joyous moment she wanted to say yes, she wanted to pour out her heart to him. But she could not. He would either hate her or she would lead him to betray everything he loved. To allow him to wed a traitor to his country would leave him without a shred of honor. She felt tears sting the back of her eyes, tears of rage at her helplessness.

She turned away from him and said in a faraway, wintry voice, "I thank you, your grace, but my answer to your gracious offer must be no. I am sorry if it distresses you——"

"How many times have you used that stilted phrase?"

She heard harsh, incredulous anger in his voice and forced herself to ignore it. She turned back to him. "It is an English lady whom you must wed, your grace, not some half French nobody without a dowry who has already been once married."

"No, my dear. I have no wish for an English lady. It is a lady who is half French, enchantingly stubborn, proud, and quite beautiful I want to wed. You must know that a dowry or lack thereof means nothing. As to your having already been married, it makes no matter. How could you ever think that it would?"

Her fingers fretted mercilessly with the brocade. "I cannot," she whispered. "Please, do not press me further."

"I am not a blind man, Evangeline. You care for me, and I have seen your affection for Edmund. I will press you, my love. Come, why do you feel that you cannot wed me? I promise most faithfully I shall not beat you."

"I will not try to deny my feelings for you, your grace——"

"Richard."

"But . . . Richard, I have no wish to wed any man, ever. Please, leave go."

"No, Evangeline, I will not leave go. Will you not answer me truthfully? Do you distrust me for some reason?"

"You said that you had never loved, that you believed yourself incapable of such an emotion. Even Marissa."

The tension left his face and he smiled. "That is quite true. Perhaps I am in my dotage. Give me three or four decades and then we will discuss my obvious weakness for you again."

She felt like she was drowning, and he was offering her life once again. For an instant, the truth hovered on her lips, but her father's face rose in her mind, and she knew it could not be. She repeated over and over to herself that she was an enemy to all he loved. She could not tell him that, and he would despise her if she wed him and he discovered her for what she was, as he most assuredly would. She could not bear the hatred he would feel for her. She knew she must leave Chesleigh, and him, before he discovered the truth.

She drew a deep, convulsive breath. "I do not love you, your grace. You have mistaken my feelings."

He had told her he was not a blind man. He had watched a myriad of pained shadows cross her expressive face. He sought to understand her. "Then what are your feelings that I have so misunderstood?

She had thought he would leave her in anger, but she saw he would not be willing to leave go. She raised her eyes to his face, knowing that she must hurt him, and herself. She remembered Lady Jane Bellerman's taunts, and prayed she could play the role in which that lady had cast her.

"You do not have to offer me marriage, your grace. You asked me what my feelings for you are. I find you a very desirable man, as I suspect most women do. That is all." She forced herself to shrug her shoulders indifferently. "After all, as Lady Jane said, Englishmen do not wed ladies who have known the married state. You may admit it to me, your grace, it is my body you wish, not interminable years in my company."

For a long moment the duke was so taken aback that he could think of nothing to say. It did not make sense, until he saw that she was standing rigidly stiff, her shoulders squared defiantly. He knew her well enough to recognize that she was acting, her flippant, carelessly spoken words a sham.

"I do not understand you, Evangeline," he said only, studying her face.

Again, she shrugged with Gaelic indifference. "I assure you, your grace, there is nothing to understand. If I were entirely English and a young unmarried lady, no doubt I should be deliriously happy to have such a wealthy, titled nobleman offer me marriage. However, I am half French and have already experienced all the supposed rewards promised by the married state. My . . . morals and . . . aspirations are quite different." She hoped to see fury in his eyes, but his expression remained impassive.

"I find you most perplexing, Madame," he said finally, his voice so dispassionate that she wondered if he had even heeded her words. "It appears to me that you now have but one use for men. Did your first husband treat you so badly?"

She forced a metallic laugh. "Of course not! Indeed, Henri was vastly amusing and a lover of some prowess. I suppose that I simply prefer my widowed state, and the freedom to do precisely as I wish. And I would never say, your grace, that men are so limited in their uses."

At last she saw anger building in his dark eyes. He made no move toward her, but allowed his gaze to flit over her, thoroughly and insultingly, from her chestnut curls down to her lemon slippers. "That is what you wish, Evangeline? It is, as you well know, but the beginning."

He walked purposely toward her, and she found she

did not want to draw away from him. He closed his
hands about her shoulders and jerked her savagely against
him. Out of surprise, she tried to twist out of his grasp,
but he easily tightened his hold. He captured her chin
in his hand and forced her face upward. He lowered his
head, slowly and deliberately, and kissed her, not gently, but with savage anger.

"Let me go!" she cried, her words muted by his
mouth.

He drew back from her, and again to her surprise, he
laughed. "There is no further need for playacting,
Evangeline."

"No, your grace, please, you don't understand. . . !"

He paid her no heed, and drew her once again into
the circle of his arms. She felt his fingers tangle about
her hair, pulling out the confining pins, until her thick
tresses rippled freely down her back.

"Do you remember when I told you your hair is
exquisite?" he asked, his voice suddenly husky.

"Yes," she whispered, "I remember, but it is not——"
She did not know what it was that she would have said.
His mouth covered hers and his tongue was insistent
against her lips. His hands roved over her hips, caressing and pressing her upward against him.

She cried out softly, and parted her lips to him. She
arched her body against him, and wrapped her fingers
in his thick black hair, reveling in the sheer sensation of
him. She felt helpless to stop him, or herself. He released her mouth and she felt his lips pressing against
her temples, her cheeks, the hollow of her throat. He
drew back, his hands still cupping her hips, and gazed
down into her face.

"What are you feeling, Evangeline?"

She did not think it an odd question, for she had no
experience with men. She opened her eyes, and for a
long moment, found herself unable to say anything.
There was no longer anger in his dark eyes, only
tenderness.

"I—I would give my life for you," she whispered.

He stared at her, then gave a shaky laugh. He felt a tightening in his throat. "Will you always surprise me with the unexpected?"

"I—I do not know."

"Would you tell me why a woman who merely has a wish for a lover would feel so strongly about her lover's well-being?"

He heard her breath catch, and could feel her struggling with herself. "I love you, Evangline. Are the words so hard for you to speak?"

He felt her hands tighten about his arms. She pressed her face inward against his shoulder, and shook her head.

He eased his frustration by giving free rein to his desire; he crushed her against him, and captured her mouth. He felt her tremble and a soft moan broke from her lips. "Do you want me, Evangeline? Do you desire me as I desire you?"

She was held by his dark eyes. "Yes," she whispered, and mutely raised her lips to him again.

"Will you come with me now? Will you make love with me?"

She felt his hands lightly caressing her back, felt his hard body against her. She suddenly could not bear the thought that soon she would have to leave him, and never know the love and passion they could share. Surely it could not be so terribly wrong to show him the love she could not admit to. She did not want to deny him, or herself. She nodded slowly. "Yes," she murmured against his shoulder, "I wish to spend tonight with you."

"Then come, my love."

As she walked beside him up the stairs, she wrapped his arm about her and leaned close against him, wanting her senses to memorize the feel of him.

"After you, Evangeline."

She surprised them both by hesitating, her eyes wide

and confused upon his face. He smiled at her, gently shoved her inside, and closed the door.

She found her lips dry. "I think . . . that is, I am not certain that . . ."

He ignored her pitiful protest and drew her into his arms. "Part your lips, Evangeline. It will, as you well know, heighten your pleasure."

She started to speak, but his mouth closed over hers, and he pressed himself hard against her belly. The knowledge that he would enter her, just as his tongue was possessing her mouth, brought a moan from her throat. She returned his kisses with clumsy, innocent passion, and she clutched at him, wanting to somehow become a part of him.

"What do you feel now?" he whispered into her mouth.

"As if I will shatter if you leave me," she said breathlessly, without thought. "I did not know that one could feel so . . . incomplete."

The image of her faceless husband rose in his mind. How could any man have cheated himself of her passion?

"I grow tired of your gown." He pulled her hard against him and prodded the tiny buttons at the back of her dress. They parted easily under his practiced fingers, and the gown slipped free from her shoulders. It fell softly to the carpet.

"I must tell you, your grace," she panted. "You must believe me, for I mean it. It is only your . . . body that I wish. I will not wed you."

He appeared to consider her words quite dispassionately for a moment, though he had difficulty suppressing a grin. So insistent she was even now. Well, they would both know soon what was to be. "As you will, my lady," he said only.

He eased away the lace straps of her chemise and watched the soft muslin fall away from her full breasts to her belly. He tugged at it again and it fell from her hips, leaving the delicate triangle of soft chestnut curls naked to his eyes. For a moment, he did not allow himself to touch her, for fear that he would lose himself in her. She gazed at him, her eyes uncertain and questioning. She wanted to ask him why he was staring at her. "I am naked," she whispered foolishly.

He gave a shaking laugh and tore his eyes away from her. "Yes, you are. To see you thus and know that I will soon possess you gives me great delight."

"What do you wish me to do to please you?"

There was maidenly innocence in her voice. He frowned, for her tone seemed to him nonsensical, almost as if they were anywhere but in his bedchamber. "I recall speaking with you once, long ago, about a man's needs. Surely I am not so hard to understand."

"Of course I understand," she said. A discordant note sounded in his mind, and she saw it written on his face. She stood before him, knowing that she should grab her gown and flee. But his hands were upon her again, gentle upon her breasts, and she could not bear for him to stop. She wrapped her arms about his neck, and pulled him down to her. His hands swept down her back until they again cupped her hips and pressed her belly against him. An insistent ache built within her that left her breathless when he finally released her.

He swept her up into his arms and laid her gently upon his bed, then straightened above her to strip off his clothes. He cursed as he pulled off his recalcitrant boots. When he stood before her, naked, she gasped.

"Is my lady pleased?"

Evangeline pressed her thighs together at the sight of his swelled member, and looked away from him.

"You must know that I will not hurt you," he said, a black brow arched upward questioningly. "I am, after all, made for your pleasure." He leaned over her, his tongue lightly trailing over her breast, and pressed his body against her. She gasped aloud when his fingers caressed the softness of her thighs. He raised his head and grinned sardonically at her.

"You are no longer the tease, I see."

She looked up into his face, dark and harshly beautiful. She felt a delicious warmth invading her, and she
knew that she wanted more than anything to belong to
him, to let herself forget for at least one night that she
must leave him. A half sob broke from her throat and
she reared up, burying her face against his chest.

Although he did not understand her, he set himself
to soothe her. His gentle caressing had quite another
effect, and Evangeline clung to him, her hands soon
moving feverishly over his chest and back, as if to
memorize the feel of him. It was she who sought out his
mouth.

He studied her face, drawn into the vague, smoky
sheen in her eyes. His hand caressed her belly and he
felt the taut muscles tense beneath his fingers. Her
flesh was smooth, like soft silk.

She tried to move upward against him, but he pressed
her back. "No, Evangeline. Lie still." His fingers touched
the soft curls between her thighs, and gently probed
until they found her.

She gasped, her eyes widened in surprise. But her
embarrassment at this intimacy gave way to the waves
of exquisite pleasure his probing fingers sent upward.
She felt her legs go slack and opened herself to him.
His fingers gently parted her and he lifted himself
above her. She drew in her breath when she felt him
pressing against her.

She was warm and moist, but he could feel her
stretching to hold him. Suddenly, he drew up, his eyes
flying to her face. It was her maidenhead he felt! Her
eyes were wide upon his face as he stared at her. It
came to him with a shock that she did not even realize
he would be able to tell that she was a virgin. He
looked at her eyes once again, and let his questions
remain unasked.

"Forgive me, Evangeline, but I must hurt you, just
for a moment."

She cried out and stiffened in pain when he pushed suddenly into her. He felt her fingernails dig into his arms, and forced himself to calm, for he did not want to hurt her more.

"Lie still," he said softly, as he carefully balanced himself on his elbows above her.

Evangeline felt startled that he had hurt her. She felt him deep inside her, filling her, and as her pain subsided, she felt strangely suspended, uncertain of what she should do.

"I am sorry," she whispered uncertainly into his mouth. "I wanted so to give you pleasure. Will you always hurt me?"

He cut off her words with deep, gentle kisses, uncertain how to answer her. He felt himself throbbing deep within her, and he sought to distract himself. "You are being a goose, Evangeline. You are giving me great pleasure. As, of course, you must know," he added mendaciously. She blinked at him, but said nothing. "No, my love, I'll never hurt you again."

She closed her eyes a moment. "I feel so close to you . . . we are so intimate, as if I were a part of you."

"You are." He felt her lips soft against his chin, her hands clutching tightly about his back. He felt his control close to breaking, and he began to move within her.

"Am I hurting you?"

She shook her head, masses of rich chestnut hair framing her face. "No, Richard. Don't stop."

She felt him thrusting deep within her, his fingers rhythmically caressing her. She moved against him, her mouth eager and soft against his, and she gave herself to him freely and naturally, moaning her cries of pleasure into his mouth. Her passion broke his control, and he gave himself over to her and to his own pleasure.

For several moments, she lay languidly beneath him, aware only of the incredible moments that had bound them together. She felt replete and absurdly happy. "I love you," she said, unable to keep the words unspoken.

He raised his head, balancing himself above her. "I know." He smiled down at her, knowing that now he would never let her leave him. He waited hopefully for her to continue.

He saw her bite her lower lip, and her eyes became suddenly hooded. "I did not mean . . . that is . . ." She was fleeing from him again, behind a barrier of deception that he could not fathom.

He wanted to shake her. "What do you not mean?"

She flinched at his harshness, but shook her head, obdurately silent.

"I do not wish to crush you," he said, and pulled her onto her side against him. She nestled against him, pressing her face into his shoulder. "I think you would like to crush me. I do not mean to make you so angry."

"You only make me angry when you refuse to trust me. I believe, Evangeline, that there is much that you should tell me. It is time for you to begin."

She wanted to yell at him to leave well enough alone. Why could he not simply accept her and the moment instead of forcing her away from him? "Please . . . I cannot. Do not force me to say any more tonight, your grace."

"Your grace? For God's sake, woman, we have just made love—cannot you bring yourself to call me by my name?"

"Forgive me . . . Richard."

"What is it a matter of, then?"

Another lie, Evangeline. You must lie to him again. It is over. Her voice was muffled, for she could not bring herself to look at him. "I do not love you. It is merely that you are an excellent lover. Indeed, you are the most exciting gentleman of my acquaintance. I thank you for the pleasure you gave me, which is all that I sought." She tried to pull away from him, when to her chagrin he burst out laughing and held her fast.

"I see no reason for such amusement, your grace! I have told you the truth, just as you requested."

"So I am the most skilled of all of your lovers?"

"Yes," she said, raising her chin.

"Even though I hurt you?"

"You are very . . . large."

"Then I am also the best endowed of all your lovers?"

She felt the rumbling laughter deep in his chest. She arched back against his arms and hit him with her fist. "Damn you! You will cease to taunt me!"

He grabbed her hands, and easily rolled her onto her back, jerking her arms above her head. She struggled briefly against his hold, then lay rigid beneath him.

"I should beat you, you know." His voice was a soft caress.

She sought only to escape him now. "Let me go! I wish to go back to my room."

He looked down at her pale face, his eyes mocking. "Oh no, my little tease. As your most skilled lover, I would not dream of letting you leave my bed in anger. I will ensure that I leave a . . . lasting impression." He lowered his face and kissed her.

She fought him and herself, willing herself not to succumb to him. "Let me go!" she gasped when finally he left her mouth. "I do not want you!"

His lips caressed the wildly fluttering pulse at the base of her throat, and his hands glided possessively over her body, his fingers teasing her, pushing her to respond to him. He moved sensuously over her and his huge manhood pressed hard against her belly.

"Oh, damn you!" she cried, unable to deny him, and pressed her body frantically against him.

When he finally entered her, she held her breath, waiting for the pain, but there was only pulsing warmth. Her belly suddenly seemed to explode with the pleasure, and she shuddered uncontrollably, nearly consumed by her climax.

"Tell me again that you do not love me."

She raised wild eyes to his face, unspeaking, and burst into wrenching sobs.

He stroked her tumbled hair, and lightly kissed her forehead, her temples, and the salty tears on her cheeks. "I had not believed that you would be such a weeping woman, my love. Cannot I even speak to you without you dissolving into tears?"

She tightened her hold about his back, and shook her head against his shoulder. She sniffed down her tears, and to her chagrin, she began to hiccup.

He grinned down at her. "I see that we cannot have further conversation until I have relieved you of your ailment. Let me go for a moment, Evangeline, and I'll fetch you a glass of water."

She let him go, albeit unwillingly.

"You may be quite certain that I will come back to you," he said. When he handed her a glass of water, he said dryly, "I have also brought you a handkerchief."

She frowned up at him but wiped her nose.

"There, that is much better," he said easily. He glanced only briefly at the small splotches of blood on her thighs. "You look like a desirable woman again." She said nothing, and he walked away from her toward the armoire. He returned with a basin of water and a washcloth.

"What is that for?" she asked warily, struggling up on her elbows.

"Hush and lie back."

"But why?"

"I am going to bathe you."

Her cheeks flamed. "Of course you will not! That is certainly something I shall do for myself!"

"It is always the lover who performs that task," he said with exquisite calm. "I assume that Frenchmen are no different from Englishmen in that regard."

Her eyes fell. "No, of course not."

She lay on her back, her eyes tightly closed, while the damp washcloth traveled between her thighs.

"Evangeline."

She opened her eyes to see him sitting beside her. "It seems, my love, that you are expressive only in my arms. Perhaps I can assist you to be more . . . open to me in other situations. To begin with, my dear, I know that you are—were a virgin."

"That is not true!" she gasped, shaking her head violently back and forth. "You are mistaken, your grace! I have told you——"

"You are very innocent, my love, and excessively foolish."

She gaped at him. "But, how could you . . . that is, I——"

"Suffice it to say that I do know. That is why I hurt you. It leads me to one of two conclusions, Evangeline. I believe that I shall choose the second. You were never married, were you?"

Her eyes were nearly black in the dim light. Fool! she screamed silently to herself. She shook her head, knowing that he was implacable, at least in this.

"No. I have never been married."

"Then why did you come to Chesleigh as Madame de la Valette?"

A kaleidoscope of faces whirled through her mind. Houchard, grim and unwavering in his mission. Edgerton—the Lynx—ruthless, a murderer. And Mrs. Needle, lifeless and cold in the dull morning light. She ran her tongue over her dry lips. "I cannot—I will not tell you anything. Please, Richard, leave go!"

He rose and tossed the washcloth into the basin. It was a simple, physical movement that calmed his anger. "As odd as it may seem," he said in a flat voice, "I know that you love me. Your offering of yourself to me to-night was proof of that. No, do not interrupt me yet with more lies, Evangeline. You will never have the wherewithall to play the harlot; it was foolish of you to attempt it, particularly with me. What I cannot understand—and believe me, I have tried—is why you came

here in the first place. You must believe that I would
provide you any assistance in my power. You have but
to tell me what it is that troubles you."

Her eyes held a desperate gleam. She looked vulnerable and bewildered, like a small child caught in the
throes of a nightmare.

When she finally spoke, the words seemed wrenched
out of her. "It is true that I love you. I did not want to,
but I could not seem to help myself. And you are right.
Since I could not have you for my husband, I wanted to
give you all that I could. As to the rest . . ." She bit
her lip and resolutely shook her head. "I do not ask you
to trust me. I have treated you too illy to expect that."

"Then what do you expect me to do with you?"

"I must—that is, I wish to remain at Chesleigh."

"Why? Why must you remain at Chesleigh?"

Her eyes fell from his set face. She could not bear his
questions. She squirmed out of the covers and dashed
past him, bending down to retrieve her discarded gown.

"No!" she shouted at him as he rose to stop her. She
pulled the gown over her head, and thrust her arms
through the sleeves. Like a graceful panther, he strode
soundlessly toward her.

"Please," she cried, thrusting her hands in front of
her to ward him off, "let me go!" She whirled about and
twisted frantically at the ivory knob. He could hear her
feverish breathing, but it was the wild, pleading look in
her eyes that held him still as she slipped through the
door.

11

"Mrs. Dickinson tells me that you haven't breakfasted yet, Evangeline. Would you like to join me?"

Evangeline started. How could it be he? She had dawdled purposefully in her room until Emma assured her she had seen the duke go off to the stables. "I—I did not expect you to be here, your grace."

He smiled at her, and offered her his arm. "I was waiting for you, of course. I thought that you would likely try to avoid me this morning, and thus decided that a little subterfuge was in order. We must talk, you know."

As there was nothing for it, she nodded, accepted his arm, and walked stiffly beside him into the morning room. He proffered her a chair most solicitously, and elaborately served her coffee himself. She did her best to ignore him, gazing with great interest out the window onto the west lawn, and nibbled perfunctorily on a flakey *croissant*.

"You did not sleep well."

She raised wary eyes to his face, and shook her head.

He said matter-of-factly, "Please don't look so alarmed, Evangeline. I have no intention of throwing you over my shoulder and hauling you to my bed."

She answered with an embarrassed flush.

"Indeed, I have decided that I do not want you in my bed again until you have agreed to become my wife. I take it from your downcast face that you have not reconsidered?"

"I have considered many things, your grace," she said, "but I do not believe that I wish to answer your question."

"You would prefer to be my mistress?"

She delighted him by whipping her head about, aghast. "So at last I have Mademoiselle Evangeline de Beauchamps before me, and not a harlot or a widow. Would you care to tell me about her now, my love?"

She gazed at him stonily.

"Is it so hard to deny you love me, Evangeline?"

She turned her face away from him, and whispered, "No, I will never again deny that." She faltered a moment, then seemed to collect herself. She turned back to him, her eyes pleading. "If you love me, you will grant me time—time to think about what it is I wish to do. Is it too much to ask of you, your grace?"

He smiled at her, thinking she had made quite a concession. At last he was making progress. "I suppose it is not too much to ask. You see before you the most patient of men. Only on condition, though, that you promise to cease hiding from me. It won't do, you know, to have you tiptoeing about trying to avoid me."

He grinned at the disbelieving look on her face. "To show good faith, would you like to come riding with me? I promise you that even my horse will keep his distance."

There was only a sliver of moon that evening, and the whitecaps that tipped the waves rolling into the cove reflected tiny points of light in the dark night. Evangeline pulled her dark cloak closely about her, gathered the hood about her face against the cold night air, and walked swiftly toward the dock to meet the longboat cutting through the waves toward her. She heard hushed whispers among the men as the boat scraped against the dock. One of them sprang out and spoke quietly to the two men remaining in the boat, then pushed it with his boot away from the dock.

He walked softly toward her, his boots noiseless on the wooden planks.

"You are the Eagle?" She heard incredulous surprise in his voice that she was a woman.

"Yes," she said. "And you are Paul Treyson?"

He smiled wryly. "Yes. I did not expect the Eagle to be a woman." He handed her a thick envelope. "Here are my instructions. I was told that I am to give you time to read them."

Instead of returning to the cave, Evangeline knelt down on the beach, lighted a match, and quickly read through his letters of introduction. He was to become an assistant to the powerful Rothchild in London.

She dropped the burned match, quickly wrote her initials on the bottom of the paper, and rose. "Very well, Monsieur. It grows late, you must hurry."

"You work quickly, Eagle. Here are your papers."

He handed her two envelopes. One she recognized as her next instructions from Houchard, the other was a letter from her father.

"It will not be long now," the man said softly, "before your position takes on new and special meaning. The Emperor will engage the Allies and their English Iron Duke within the month. You will be more valuable than ever to us."

Evangeline's hand fisted about the envelopes. It would be weeks at least before Houchard would free her and her father. He had promised, damn him, he had promised it would be soon!

"You must go now," she said, and retreated back toward the cave. She pictured the duke, his dark eyes resting gently on her face, telling her that he would give her time to think. There had been nothing else she could have told him, and saying those words, knowing that she waited only for word that she was free to join her father in Paris, had made her feel despicable. She would find a way to speak to Edgerton, make him realize that it was impossible to continue.

Evangeline started abruptly as a loud staccato of gunfire and a man's cry of pain broke the silence. She whirled about. She heard shouts from the cliff. For an instant, she froze, unable to move or to think. They had been discovered!

She crouched low and dashed to the cave, her eyes straining to see in the darkness. In the distance, she heard the tramping of heavy boots, and loud, excited voices. She turned and saw black-cloaked men rushing down the cliff path to the beach, cutting off her escape.

She heard a cultured gentleman's voice ring above the others. "Search the beach, men! The other man must be nearby. Don't let him escape!" She was almost certain that it was Lord Pettigrew who spoke.

Evangeline ran to the back of the cave, her mind clogged with fear. She would be killed, or worse, captured. She thought of her father, that he would die with her because she had failed. And the duke . . . Richard. Surely, no one would believe him guilty of being a traitor to England!

She sat huddled into a small ball at the back of the cave, waiting for them to discover her. She heard the muted splashing of water, and men's voices drawing closer. Her eyes rested helplessly on the cave entrance.

"God's bones!" she heard one man growl. "We can't get past this point. The tide's coming in."

"There's naught here anyway," another man called. "The cliff meets the water just beyond. The scoundrel could not escape that way, 'tis too sheer."

She heard them pause, then splash their way back up the beach.

They did not know of the cave! A surge of hope filled her, as she realized that the rising tide offered her her chance of escape. The water lapped at her ankles, and Evangeline slowly splashed forward, listening desperately for them, but there was only the sound of the sea.

She forced herself to wait for what seemed an eternity, until the rising water licked about her thighs. Her legs felt numb with cold, and harsh tears stung the back of her eyes. She brushed them angrily away, and pushed forward. Just a few more feet, she chanted to herself, and she would be able to swim outward. A wave crashed unexpectedly upon her, throwing her off her feet, and the vicious tide sucked her under, thrashing her uncontrolled against the rocks at the mouth of the cave. She felt a sharp pain in her ribs, and for an instant, she could not breathe. She grabbed frantically at an outjutting rock, struggling against her heavy, sodden clothing, and pulled herself, rock by rock, to the far side of the cave. She dashed the salty water from her eyes and stared upward at the sheer cliff above her. There was no choice.

She drew a deep breath and swam outward, fighting the waves with all her strength. When she could struggle against the tide no longer, she fell forward in the water, and let the sea wash her back to shore. When she felt coarse sand and sharp stones tear at her body, she felt no pain, only a tremendous sense of relief.

She lay face down on the beach, and retched salty water hoarsely into the wet sand, too tired to rise. When she could, she pulled herself to her feet, and stumbled, hunched over, toward the cliff. She heard muted voices up the beach, near the cliff path. She pulled herself upward, reaching frantically for roots. The ground gave way beneath her numb feet, and loose rock and rubble tumbled down below her. She froze, for it sounded like an avalanche in her ears. She saw the edge of the cliff above her, and finally pulled herself up.

She rolled atop the even ground, and lay still a

moment to regain her breath. Slowly, she rose, not daring to stand upright.

She saw Chesleigh in the distance, proud and ageless, its lighted windows pinpoints of white in the dark night. She ran toward it, crouched over, her wet cloak slapping at her legs.

She heard a shout in the distance. "I see him! Stop!"

Evangeline hurtled forward, as fast as she could. She heard a shot and then another, but they seemed to come from a great distance. She ran to the line of lime trees bordering the graveled drive that circled around to the north face of Chesleigh, and pulled up against an oak tree, hugging its rough bark. She cursed her raspy breath, for it dinned loudly in her ears, and stuffed her fist against her mouth.

From a great distance, she heard a man's shout, "This way, men! I saw the bloody bastard over there, near the road!" Lord Pettigrew's voice answered, stern in command. "Do not kill him. I want him quite alive."

She closed her eyes tightly and pressed her cheek against the rough bark of the tree. She heard their heavy booted steps moving off, back toward the road. She forced herself to remain still, waiting as long as she dared.

She crawled through the thick hedges that bordered the drive, and rose to her feet only when she faced the north wing. She drew the key from her pocket, drew a deep breath, and ran, bowed over, to the castle. The looming stone walls shadowed her as her numbed fingers fought to insert the key. "Open, damn you," she whispered fiercely as she twisted the key in the lock.

The lock finally clicked into place, and she pushed the door open only wide enough to slip through. When she stood safely inside, she leaned heavily against the thick door, then quickly turned to lock it. Only her heavy breathing broke the silence of the castle as she made her way to her room, even the most owlish of the servants abed.

She lit a candle in her room and turned to stare numbly at the bedraggled shadowy figure in her mirror, at her tangled hair, plastered against her face, her sodden, torn cloak. She was trembling uncontrollably from cold. She quickly stripped off her wet clothes, ignoring the pain from bruises and cuts that seemed to cover her, and drew her nightgown over her head.

Though her body gradually warmed as she huddled under the covers in her bed, she could not seem to stop her trembling, nor could she manage to think coherently. She could still hear the shouts of Lord Pettigrew's men when they believed they had seen her. Even now she wondered if they would burst into her room. In a frenzy of anxiety, she bounded from her bed and hastily stuffed her wet clothes under the armoire. She stumbled back into her bed and forced herself to close her eyes. There was nothing more she could do.

Early morning shafts of sunlight fell on Evangeline's face and pulled her from a short, fitful sleep. She lay quietly, thankful that it was morning and she was safe in her room. She ignored the nagging twists of pain that drew at her senses, and forced herself to think.

Paul Treyson was doubtless dead, shot by Lord Pettigrew's men. They would still be scouring the area for his accomplice, but at least they searched for a man. She guessed that Lord Pettigrew's men may have already come to Chesleigh, and she realized that she could not remain in bed, pleading some illness. Richard might guess. She thought of her father, and whimpered softly in impotent fear. If she were to save him, she must first save herself.

Evangeline pulled herself upright and threw back the covers. She looked toward the clock on her night table and saw to her surprise that it was but six o'clock in the morning. She felt her hair, stiff and sticky from the salt water, clinging about her face. For the first time she examined her body. An ugly purple bruise spread over her ribs and angry scratches covered her arms and legs. She drew her nightgown over herself and pulled a shawl about her hair to hide it from Emma's inquisitive eyes.

If Emma was surprised at such an early call from her mistress, she gave no sign of it, merely looked at Evangeline with a worried frown.

"You look very tired, Madame. Are you certain that you wish me to bring your bath water so early?"

Evangeline responded to her maid's hesitant question with a bright, unconcerned voice, careful to keep her hands hidden in the folds of her nightgown. "Yes, his grace has an outing planned this morning and I want to wash my hair."

"Yes, Madame," Emma replied dubiously. She walked slowly from the room, as if expecting Evangeline to call her back. Once the copper tub was filled with hot water and the footmen dismissed, she found herself again abruptly dismissed.

"You are certain that you do not wish me to assist you, Madame?"

"No, Emma," Evangeline said firmly, "I have a fancy to see to myself this morning."

When Emma had once again reluctantly left the bed-chamber, Evangeline eyed the hot water and the smarting cuts, and lowered herself slowly into the tub. She bit her lip as she scrubbed herself, careful to avoid her aching ribs.

Two hours had passed before she finished drying and curling her hair. She chose a very feminine, frivolous gown, one that fit snugly over her breasts and flaired out to a ruffled hem. If ever she needed to appear the epitome of helpless, fragile womanhood, today was the day. She looked down at her hands and hastily donned a pair of white mittens.

She was thankful she did not see the duke when she reached the entrance hall. She was on the point of retreating into the breakfast room when she heard carriage wheels in the graveled drive. She walked quickly into the drawing room and drew back the heavy curtain to see Lord Pettigrew climb out of his carriage. His face looked coldly stern and she closed her eyes, biting her lips against fear.

She heard Bassick's voice, bidding him welcome. It was some minutes more before she heard the duke's voice.

"Drew! Have you had success?"

"In a manner of speaking, Richard," she heard him say in a low voice. "Let us speak privately."

Evangeline pressed close to the drawing room door until their footsteps receded down the corridor. She forced herself to wait some minutes longer before she followed them.

If Bassick thought it odd that she should suddenly appear, he gave no sign of it, merely bowed and bade her a good morning. She forced herself to greet him brightly before turning away to walk to the duke's library. She drew a deep breath before the closed doors, then drew them open and walked in, forcing a smile to her lips.

Lord Pettigrew had only just begun telling the duke of the events of the previous evening when Evangeline entered the library. He suppressed the impatient frown that was threatening to furrow his brow. She looked lovely, her face alight with carefree laughter. He thought of Felicia and smiled back at her.

"I bid you good morning, Madame," he said, rising from his chair.

"I hope I am not disturbing you, my lord. It is such a lovely morning. I thought perhaps his grace would care to take a stroll with me and Edmund."

The duke was standing against his desk, his arms crossed over his chest. His eyes were upon her thick chestnut hair, piled in careless curls atop her head with soft tendrils falling over her forehead. She looked like a exquisite model of the fashionable lady, complete to her white mittens. But when she spoke, he felt himself stiffen, for her tone was somehow unnatural, too light and flirtatious.

"Well, actually, Madame . . ." Lord Pettigrew began, and threw an uncertain glance in the duke's direction.

"Good morning, Evangeline," the duke interposed calmly. He strode to her and raised a mittened hand to his lips. He looked at her closely and saw a haunted expression in her eyes, and something else that he could not fathom.

"I think it appropriate that you join us now, Evangeline. I believe it only fair that you hear what we have done."

"What do you mean, your grace?" she asked, as he helped her to a chair. "You sound most mysterious!"

He frowned again at her manner, but said calmly, "I did not tell you sooner because I did not wish you upset further. After Mrs. Needle's murder, I hired a former Bow Street Runner to investigate for me whilst we were in London. I was informed before we left London that he had seen, as he termed it, strange goings-on at the cove—a lantern light as a signal and bloody mysterious chaps rowing to the dock. He thought they were French. I spoke to Drew and he believed it worthwhile to investigate the matter himself. How many evenings have you and your men spent at the cove, Drew?"

"Three nights, including last evening. As I was telling you, Richard, your Bow Street Runner was quite right."

Evangeline clapped a hand over her breast. "Good heavens! You cannot mean it, my lord!"

Lord Pettigrew shot the duke an harrassed look, but Richard merely regarded him blandly. "Please continue, Drew."

"One of my fellows spotted two cloaked men at the dock. Unfortunately, when one of them gained the cliff path and we confronted him, he lost his head and ran, and we were forced to shoot. I do not know how the other man, the one who brought him in, managed to escape us. You know, Richard, how treacherous the cliffs are. But somehow, he must have scaled the rocks without our seeing him."

"Oh my dear sir, you mean the scoundrel eluded you? You have proof that he was French?"

"Yes, Madame. There was a packet on the dead man, some kind of instructions in code, with initials scrawled in the corner. Also, before he died, he whispered something in French. All I could make out was the word *l'Aigle*, and *traître*. It seems likely that he thought the other man had betrayed him." He continued toward the duke, "We searched the entire area last night. I am here to ask for your help."

"Of course, Drew. Do you have reason to believe that the other man—the Eagle—is a local?"

"It seems likely. He must have known the area quite well to escape our net. As fantastic as it seems, it does appear that Chesleigh has been used as an entry point for Bonaparte's henchmen. As we thought, Richard, Mrs. Needle's murder must somehow be connected. I would like your permission to question your servants. It is possible that one of them could have seen something."

The duke did not answer for several moments. He looked at Evangeline, who was gazing with innocent horror at Drew.

"You may do whatever you think necessary, Drew," he said finally. "Evangeline, is there anything you can tell Lord Pettigrew?"

"I? It seems all so fantastic, my lord!"

To the duke's relief, Lord Pettigrew rose impatiently. "My men will not hold your servants long, Richard. I will keep you informed. It is doubtful that the Eagle will again use your beach, but I will, of course, have several of my men continue to watch."

Evangeline rose. "I hope that you find him, my lord. I vow that I will not sleep tonight. If you gentlemen do not mind, I shall see to Edmund now. Good-bye, my lord."

Lord Pettigrew bowed over her hand. "You will be safe, I promise you, Madame."

She gave him a brilliant smile and left the library. The duke stared after her, his lips drawn in a thin line.

"Would you like to stay at Chesleigh tonight, Drew?"

"No, I thank you, Richard. I will remain at the Raven Inn today, but I must leave for London this evening. My latest intelligence is that Napoleon will start for Belgium within the next few days. Wellington is waiting for him."

"You will keep me informed, Drew?" the duke asked as he walked Lord Pettigrew to his carriage.

"You may be certain of it, Richard. I can imagine how it must make you feel—a French spy using your private beach."

"The idea is beginning to seem less fantastic."

The duke gave Bassick instructions, nodded briefly toward the two men Lord Pettigrew had left behind, and headed for the nursery. He did not find her there. He entered her bedchamber, saw that the room was empty, and turned, only to stop at the door.

Some ten minutes later, he found her in a small, sunny parlor on the second floor. She was standing near the window, staring over the Channel, her back to him. He closed the door firmly behind him, and leaned against it.

"Your performance was exquisite. Drew was either admiring your beauty or cursing your stupid woman's prattle. Did you believe that you could fool me?"

Evangeline closed her eyes at his furious tone. She shook her head, not turning. "I do not know what you are talking about, your grace."

"Ah, my beautiful virgin—former virgin I should say— let me be more specific. You are also a man—the Eagle, and a spy for Napoleon."

She turned slowly to face him, and said with desperate calm, "You are weaving a fantasy, your grace. How could I possibly be a man?" She laughed dryly. "Really, I pray that you but look at me."

"Perhaps I should, Evangeline." He strode over to her. "How odd it is that you are wearing gloves." He grasped her hands in his and jerked the mittens from them. His voice was bleakly harsh. "I trust that you did not suffer these unfeminine scratches during our love-making. Don't bother to lie to me, Evangeline, unless you would also care to explain the damp and torn clothes I found stuffed beneath your armoire. Damn you, Evangeline, you will tell me the truth!"

His face was pale with fury, and she wrenched her hands from his grasp. She licked her dry lips. He knew and there was no hope for it. "Very well," she whispered, "what you have said is true."

He grasped her shoulders in an iron grip. "God, that I could have been so blind! An indigent relation, a beautiful woman who needed my help! You damned little liar!"

"I have done only what I had to do."

"And I have danced finely to your tune, have I not? What decided you to come to my bed, Evangeline? Did you think that I would be less likely to betray you if I discovered the truth?"

"I am sorry," she said, her voice breaking. "I never wanted to hurt you . . . I would rather have died than have you discover what I am, and hate me. I have hated myself, but there was no choice."

She weaved where she stood. Her legs went limp and she fell forward against him.

He caught her about her waist before she fell, and hauled her roughly into his arms. His anger hung impotently, for she could not hear him. He carried her to his bedchamber, past a gaping maid and two footmen, and laid her on his bed, jerking loose the high muslin collar about her throat. Several angry scratches slashed downward to her shoulder. He quickly stripped off her clothing, furious with her, for she could be seriously hurt. He gazed down at the ugly bruise over her ribs, at the many scratches, and drew a deep, steadying breath. It struck him with blinding force that she could easily have been killed.

Evangeline slowly opened her eyes to see the duke staring down at her, his brow furrowed.

"I did not mean to faint," she said, absurdly. She realized vaguely that she was naked beneath the cover, and gazed up at him in consternation.

"Please, Richard," she said, her voice catching, "let me go. I will receive my punishment, never fear. Do not give me over to Lord Pettigrew."

"So you would disappear from me just as suddenly as you arrived. No, Evangeline, I will not let you go, until I myself wish it." He paused a moment, and whipped back the cover, letting his eyes rove insultingly over her body. He said harshly, "I must admit to admiration for your skill . . . in so many areas."

She flinched at his harshness, and clutched at the cover, pulling it over herself. "Please, do not . . ." Her voice was suspended. She whispered finally, "What will you do?"

"First I will ensure that you have done yourself no lasting injury." She saw that he would not be gainsaid, closed her eyes tightly, and turned her face away from him on the pillow. She felt his fingers lightly probing at her ribs.

"Your ribs are not broken," he said coolly, and covered her. "No, do not move. You are a mass of scratches and cuts and must be attended to."

She lay quietly, watching him stride to a dresser at the far side of the bedchamber. His movements were swift and abrupt, and when he returned to the bedside, his face was harshly set. She tried to rise to her elbows.

"For God's sake, hold still."

She felt his fingers lightly massaging an ointment into

the worst of the scratches. He realized that this hands were shaking. He stared down at her averted face.

As if she sensed that he was gazing at her, Evangeline slowly turned her eyes to his face. There was a bitter, helpless smile on her lips. "Do not let me hurt you," she whispered. "You must protect yourself and your family."

"For the moment, you will keep your opinions to yourself," he said. He thought of the previous night when he had lain comfortably in his bed and she had been struggling back to Chesleigh, her life in the balance. He found himself marveling at her force of will. If Lord Pettigrew had somehow come to suspect her, her performance would have convinced him of her innocence. Drew doubtless believed her a foolish, quite frivolous woman now.

"There, it is done," he said inconsequentially. The physical action had calmed his anger. He drew a chair to her bedside and sat down, formed his fingers into a steeple, and tapped them thoughtfully together.

He said in a cold, even voice, "Certain things are now clear to me, Mademoiselle. Your unexpected arrival at Chesleigh, your indigent status, and your unremitting insistence on remaining at Chesleigh. Even your claimed widowhood. Had you arrived as a supposed innocent young lady, the proprieties would have demanded that I provide at the very least a chaperone—that, or not allow you to remain." He paused for a moment, recalling Evangeline's grief at the death of the old woman.

"I am also certain that you were innocent of Mrs. Needle's murder. But you know who killed her, don't you, Evangeline? If I had not taken matters into my own hands, would you still be bringing spies into England?"

She closed her eyes and whispered, "Yes."

He suddenly remembered her insistence upon visiting Drew at the Ministry. "And tell me, why did you

wish to visit the Ministry? Surely, yours was not a
foolish request."

"No, I was ordered to leave an envelope in Lord
Pettigrew's office. I do not know what its contents are."

"I believe it is time for you to tell me everything,
Evangeline."

He saw silent anguish in her eyes, and uncertainty,
but she shook her head.

"You would still have me believe that you are naught
but a cold-blooded spy who has,, in the most calculat-
ing manner, deceived me and my entire family."

"No!" she cried, rearing up. "It is not like that! I had
no choice!"

He was held by her words. He gentled his voice. "I
have asked you before to trust me, Evangeline. Surely
it is not asking too much . . . now."

"You are an English gentleman, your grace, not a
traitor."

He said more softly still, hearing growing hesitance
in her voice, "You said that you did not want to hurt
me, Evangeline. If you do not tell me the truth now,
soon Drew will be sending his men to arrest two trai-
tors to England."

She turned wild eyes to his face. "Why cannot you
save yourself? Surely no one would seriously believe
you guilty!"

"Perhaps. But it will be none of your doing." He rose
abruptly and stood over her. "If I am to see someone I
love go to the gallows, Evangeline, is it not fair that you
at least tell me why? If I could but understand you,
perhaps all is not yet lost, regardless of what you have
done." He gazed down at her, studying her face, wondering if at last he had convinced her to speak.

She looked away from him for she thought that he
was wrong, that all was lost. Indeed, she thought bleakly, it hardly mattered now what she told him, except to
him, and to her.

"Very well," she said slowly, her fingers knotting

about the bed cover. "My father is not dead. He is being held prisoner by a man named Houchard in Paris."

The duke felt a surge of relief. "Tell me all of it, Evangeline."

She told him in a halting voice of the night Biron and Villiers had come to their home, of the journey to Paris, her meeting with Houchard. "He knew all about my family and yours. You were to be my dupe, my cat's paw, else he would have my father killed as a traitor. Only the Lynx would know the truth."

"The Lynx?"

She nodded and for a moment could not speak. "John Edgerton is the Lynx."

The duke started back in appalled surprise. "The devil!"

"Yes, 'twas one of his men who murdered poor Mrs. Needle. He is ruthless, Napoleon's man. He would kill anyone to ensure Bonaparte's success."

"So you are not loyal to Bonaparte?"

She looked as if he had struck her. "If it were in my power, I would kill him."

Her eyes were filled with rage, and he could not disbelieve her. "Very well. But why Mrs. Needle? Why would Edgerton want Mrs. Needle killed?"

He saw her eyes dim with pain, and his hand moved to cover hers. "Come, you must tell me about it."

"It was my fault!" she cried. " "God, if only I had not told him about her! Mrs. Needle sensed that I was unhappy, that I was disturbed about something. I mentioned her name to him only to show him that I was not good at acting my role, that others might well come to suspect me. I hoped that he and Houchard would set me free." Her voice became fiercely bitter. "She was dead within the month."

The duke thought about the vagaries of fate that had brought her to him in the first place. "Why did you not tell me the truth after Mrs. Needle's death? You must have guessed, even then, that I would have done what I could to help you."

She raised tortured eyes to his face. "There were so many reasons! I feared for my father's life, for I knew that Houchard would have killed him just as easily as John Edgerton gave the order to kill Mrs. Needle. And I could not endanger your life. When you asked me to wed you, I wanted to flee from England, for I knew that I would bring you nothing but disgrace. I was not worthy of your affection. I did not know that I would betray myself when you first . . . made love to me."

He allowed a slight smile to soften his face. "I cannot recall ever having been so taken aback in my life. May I assume that you offered yourself to me because you saw no future for us?"

"Yes. I suppose it was not a terribly proper thing for a young lady to do, but I could not help myself."

She had lifted his sense of betrayal from his shoulders, and he smiled at her crookedly. "If you so much as ever keep the flimsiest secret from me again, I will beat you."

She said quietly, "Could I do aught else? Even now, my father could be dead, murdered because of my failure." As soon as the words passed her lips, she broke into rasping sobs.

He swiftly sat down beside her, gathered her gently into his arms, and stroked her hair. "Hush, Evangeline. There will be no failure, my love, not if I can help it."

She pulled back in his arms. "What am I to do now, Richard? God, what am I to do?"

"It is no longer a question of just you, Evangeline. It is now both of us."

Every chance word, every detail was recalled and discussed to the duke's satisfaction. A black brow arched upward when she told him of Conan DeWitt.

"Good God!" he exclaimed. "No wonder you were furious at me when I accused you of flirting with him!"

A fleeting smile touched her lips. "He is a dangerous man, quite without feeling, I think, and he has a very low regard for women."

She was held silent, reckoning with what she saw as the inevitable. "Richard, when John Edgerton realizes that Paul Treyson is missing, he will quickly discover that he is dead and that I failed him. There is no choice. I must return to France, to plead with Houchard! It was not, after all, my fault. There is no reason for him to kill my father when he learns the truth of the matter."

"Rubbish," the duke said, his voice abstracted.

"It is not rubbish to——"

He reached out his hand and lightly touched his fingertips to her lips.

"Dear one, listen to me for a moment. I believe I've hit upon a way that will extricate not only you from this mess, but also your father. But it requires that I move quickly. I must seek out Drew immediately."

She gazed at him fearfully. "Richard, what is it you are planning to do?"

He pulled her possessively against him. "Evangeline," he murmured against her ear, "do you remember our first night together—it was all of two nights ago."

He felt her lips curve into a smile against his cheek. "How could I not?"

"You trusted me then. I only ask the same from you now."

Her breath caught, and she buried her face against his neck.

"Now, my love," he said firmly, pushing her back onto the bed, "I must go. I will return soon, you may depend on it."

12

The duke returned to Chesleigh late in the afternoon to find Evangeline ferociously pacing the library. He said from the doorway as he flung his driving cloak onto a settee, "What is this, Evangeline? I thought to find you snug in your bed, not wearing out my carpet."

"Your grace!" She started forward, then stopped, her face strained and hesitant. "You are smiling! Tell me, what have you done? What did Lord Pettigrew say?"

"I have but a few moments, my love. If you will cease wringing your hands and come here, I will tell you exactly what is to happen."

He waited patiently for her to sit in the chair he held for her. He smiled down at her and lightly touched his fingertips to her lips to silence her questions. "As I told you, Evangeline, I had an idea, but it needed both Drew's approval and refinement. I made it clear to him that you, my dear, the unwilling Eagle, possess a good deal of information that would be his if he were amenable to forgetting your past . . . transgressions. When he recovered from his shock that the flighty, seemingly helpless lady he had seen just this morning was none other than the Eagle, he helped himself to a liberal glass of sherry. His real shock came when he learned

John Edgerton is a Bonapartist. Once I had told him all
the facts, he became like a man possessed. In short, my
dear, one of Drew's men will pose as the dead spy, Paul
Treyson, and seek out Edgerton in London. Once
Edgerton makes it clear to his esteemed audience that
he knows the code, we will have him."

Evangeline tensed. "Who is to be this esteemed audience, your grace? I cannot imagine that John Edgerton
would give himself away in front of anyone."

"Why Drew and I, of course, and Lord Melberry,
one of the highest ranking members of the Ministry.
And, of course, he will not know we are there. No,
don't protest, Evangeline. For once, you will remain
here at Chesleigh, quite safe. Once we have Edgerton,
Drew is certain that the Ministry will agree to exchange
him for your father, and for all the information you will
freely provide to them."

For several moments, she simply stared at him. "It
cannot be so simple, your grace! What if Napoleon will
not accept the trade? What if the gentlemen in the
Ministry refuse to allow——"

The duke held up a staying hand. "Evangeline. I
have always understood, and Drew agrees, that Napoleon, if he has few other admirable traits, does recognize the men who are loyal to him. As to the gentlemen
in the Ministry—" he smiled wryly—"I would that you
believe that I as well as Drew do exercise some power."
He grew brisk once more. "Now, my love, I must leave
you. We must move quickly, before Edgerton realizes
that something is amiss."

She rose and clutched at his sleeves. "I—I do not
want you to feel that you must, that is, that you owe me
loyalty or assistance, or——"

"Is that what you believe my motives to be?" he
asked, his eyes steady upon her upturned face.

"No," she whispered, turning her face into his shoulder. "I am afraid, Richard."

It was on the tip of his tongue to tell her that he too

was afraid, but he wanted to spare her his doubts. He said, his voice light with unconcern, "Contrive to have faith in me, Madame, and also, a bit in Lord Pettigrew. If you must fret whilst I am gone, let it be about how you will soon have no other concern than pleasing your husband." He tweaked the tip of her nose and lightly kissed her pale lips. "All will go well, Evangeline, you will see. Now, I must go."

"Can I not come with you?"

"On no account!" he said, his voice suddenly harsh. "You will promise me to remain here. Drew and I will return as soon as this business is concluded in London."

She gnawed at her lower lip, then sighed deeply. "Very well, I promise." She suddenly caught his sleeve. "Oh my God, I nearly forgot! Richard, you remember the letter I told you about that I left in Lord Pettigrew's office? I fear its contents. I cannot imagine what it contains except information that could in some way implicate Lord Pettigrew. It must be destroyed." She quickly told him of the letter's hiding place amid the dusty tomes on the bookshelf.

"I trust, my love, that if you have left any documents in *my* library, you will duly remove them by the time I return!"

The duke kissed her once again, flung his driving cloak over his shoulder, and left her standing, an uncertain smile on her lips, in the middle of the library.

He paused by the front door and spoke in a low voice to Bassick. "I will return by tomorrow afternoon I trust, Bassick. Ensure by all means that Madame de la Valette remains at Chesleigh. She is not, at present, in the best of health, and I do not want her venturing forth until I return."

He shrugged into his driving cloak and stepped into the afternoon sun, his stride brisk. He leaped into his curricle and urged his matched bays toward the London road.

*   *   *

Evangeline sat in a window seat in the nursery, her chin cupped in her hands, staring out over the Channel. She vaguely heard Edmund explaining meticulously to a rapt Ellen the correct proportions of flour and salt they needed to make a map of England.

She had passed most of the day wandering about Chesleigh, unable to keep herself still, or to keep her thoughts from swinging from bleak despair to tantalizing hope. To be sitting idle, ignorant of what was happening, was almost unbearable. She should have insisted upon accompanying the duke to London, instead of allowing him to play the knight errant, regardless of his reasons.

She bounded to her feet, surprising Edmund from his discourse. She brushed a distraught hand across her forehead, oblivious of his wide eyes resting upon her face.

"Where did Papa go, Cousin Eve? Why didn't he say good-bye to me?"

Evangeline forced herself to calm. "He was much occupied by a . . . business matter, Edmund. He will be back soon. Indeed, I expect him momentarily."

Edmund's eyes darkened in quick suspicion. "He did not go to fight Napoleon, did he?"

She gave a shaky laugh, and sank down to her knees beside him. "Oh no, my love, never that!" She hugged him, and tugged on the shock of hair that hung over his forehead. "But that is what you would like to do, isn't it, Edmund?"

At his enthusiastic nod, she said brightly, "Well, since you cannot as yet leave me, why do we not put the flour and salt to good use?"

They were interrupted by a footman standing in the open doorway. "There is a gentleman downstairs, Madame, sent by the duke to see you."

Evangeline forced herself to say calmly, "Ellen will help you now, Edmund. I will be back soon."

It was all she could do to walk sedately down the stairway and allow the footman to open the drawing room door for her. She walked nervously toward a gentleman who stood with his back to her, facing the fireplace.

"Yes?" she asked, her voice breathless with anxiety.

Conan DeWitt turned, holding a small pistol, and aimed it directly at her.

"Close the door, Madame Eagle," he said softly, "and do not cry out. You may rest assured that I would kill anyone who happened to come in, including that old gray-bearded butler."

"The duke?" she whispered. Her fingers were clutching the back of a chair so tightly that the knuckles showed white.

"Close the door," he repeated harshly.

"Answer me, damn you," she cried, once she had done his bidding.

He laughed. "I would like to tell you that he is dead, shot through his black heart, but a few moments of thinking on your part would convince you otherwise. Have you no concern for John Edgerton, Eagle? It is because of him that I am here, as you know."

Evangeline felt such a flood of relief that she was unable for a moment to understand the import of his words. She gazed toward him, a new fear clutching at her. "John Edgerton sent you here?"

"Oh no, you little bitch," he snarled at her. "That part of your plan served you well. One of his servants came to me, to warn me that he was lost. I told John not to trust you! You conniving little whore, did you part your thighs for your powerful duke so that he would help you?"

His insults did not touch her, her only coherent thought that Edgerton had been taken.

Evangeline suddenly smiled at him. "Yes, Mr. DeWitt, all is lost, and there is naught you can do about it! My father will now be saved and you . . ." She shrugged her shoulders. "I suggest that you take your leave back to your beloved Bonaparte."

He strode toward her until he towered over her, and she could hear his angry breath.

"Oh yes, I will go back, but I will not go back alone. Do you think that I would leave you here with your duke, to tell the English everything you know? No, Eagle, you will come with me, for I am certain that both Edgerton and Houchard will want to thank you personally for what you have done. Edgerton, fool that he is, had a fondness for you. You will soon know what he is like when he is betrayed. Do not do anything foolish, for you are worth very little more to me alive than dead."

Evangeline stared at him mutely, her bravado broken in her fear. For a moment she wanted to laugh at the irony of what was happening, but the sound that finally emerged from her throat was a soft moan.

The duke jumped wearily down from his curricle and waved expectantly toward Lord Pettigrew, whose carriage was rumbling up the drive behind him. He shoved open the great front doors, threw back his head, and shouted her name.

"Your grace."

"Where is Madame, Bassick?" he demanded, still expecting to see her at any moment rushing down the stairs.

"She is in the drawing room, your grace, with the gentleman you sent to see her. I shall inform her of your return."

"What gentleman?" the duke roared. He did not wait for Bassick to reply. He rushed through the entrance hall and flung the drawing room doors open. He saw a heavy brocade curtain lifting slightly in the breeze through an open window. The room was empty.

He strode back into the corridor, a knot of fear twisting in his belly, and nearly collided with Bassick.

"Who was the gentleman?" the duke shouted, grasping his butler by his narrow shoulders.

Bassick knew something was terribly wrong, and for an instant his mind refused to work. "He said his name was Ferguson, your grace."

"What did he look like?" At Bassick's fumbling silence, the duke forced himself to calm his voice. "Quickly, Bassick. Can you remember anything at all about him?"

"He was young, your grace, not above thirty. A pleasant gentleman, he seemed, and a large man. A mole, your grace . . . there was a large mole on his cheek."

"Richard? What the devil is going on here?"

The duke whipped about at the sound of Lord Pettigrew's voice. "It is Conan DeWitt, he has taken Evangeline." He ignored Drew's aghast expression and quickly rapped out orders to Bassick.

"Get all the able-bodied men, Bassick, and arm them." He paused a moment. "What kind of conveyance did he have?"

"A—a horse, your grace! There was no carriage, I am certain of it."

Without a backward glance at either his butler or Lord Pettigrew, the duke strode out of the castle, and broke into a run toward the stables. DeWitt had come either to kill her or to take her with him to France. He could not very well expect to get far if he held Evangeline before him on his horse.

Trevlin was sitting on his haunches at the stable entrance, mending a bridle.

"Trevlin," the duke shouted, still some feet away from him, "have you seen Evan—Madame?"

"Yes, your grace," Trevlin said, pausing a moment to scratch his left ear. "She was with a gentleman, walking yon toward the cliffs."

The duke heard Drew panting to a halt behind him. "The cliffs!" the duke shouted, his voice hoarse in his fear. He bounded away from the stables, over the rutted path, Drew at his heels, trying to keep up with him. He was some fifty yards distant from the cliffs when he heard Evangeline's terrified scream, and then a thin, wailing yell.

"Oh my God," Lord Pettigrew panted, momentarily frozen in his tracks.

But the duke didn't stop. Blood pounded at his temples and his raspy breath sounded like thunder in his ears. He was afraid to think of what that scream meant. The rocky terrain sloped upward to the cliff edge and he saw a splash of light blue on the outjutting promontory, hovering at the very edge of the cliff.

"Evangeline!" he shouted in his mind, but his voice was only a thready whisper. He raced toward the promontory, and saw her on her hands and knees, her muslin gown spread about her, her face buried in her hands. He leaned over to clasp her shoulders with trembling hands, so filled with relief that for the moment he could not speak.

"Evangeline," he repeated softly, his fingers gripping her so tightly that she winced.

She slowly raised her face, and he saw that her pupils were nearly black, and wide with terror. "You have come," she said. "I—I realized that he was going to kill me, not take me to France with him. He kept pushing me closer and closer to the cliff edge." She raised wild eyes to the duke. "I did not want to die . . . I did not want to leave you!"

"Nay, love," he said, and dropped to his haunches to pull her against him.

"I fell," she whispered, pressing her face against his chest, "and when he leaned over to shove me, I grabbed his legs and he—he tripped over me." Her lips moved, but no more words emerged. Mutely, she pointed toward the cliff.

The duke rose and strode to the cliff edge. Sprawled

upon the jagged rocks below lay Conan DeWitt, the crashing waves washing over his body.

"He is dead?" he heard her whisper.

"Yes, Evangeline," he said gently, turning back to her, "he is quite dead."

13

"The French have agreed to the exchange, Madame. Your father will be with you in London by tomorrow night."

"Thank you, Drew," the duke said, his hand tightening on Evangeline's shoulder. "Now, I can concentrate on turning my Eagle into a dove."

"And I think, my lord," Evangeline said, a sparkling smile in her eyes, "that you now know me well enough to call me by my given name."

Lord Pettigrew smiled. "I believe . . . Evangeline, that you are quite right. After seeing the contents of that letter, I trust you will understand if I do not invite you to my offices in the future." He paused a moment, then said wryly, "After this adventure, I am glad to find myself looking forward to thinking about nothing more than the outlandish bills I will doubtless receive shortly from Felicia's dressmaker."

"So you have decided to take the plunge, sir," Evangeline said, smiling shyly toward the duke.

"Yes, but not until Wellington has beaten the Emperor. I have no intention of spending my honeymoon in London. It cannot be long now, as I keep telling Felicia."

For the moment, the duke cared not one whit about either Wellington or Napoleon. He gazed possessively at Evangeline, her thick hair pulled back from her face, with loose soft curls falling over her forehead.

Lord Pettigrew guffawed at the duke's abstraction. "I assume, Richard, that I also have the honor of wishing you happy."

The duke pulled his eyes from Evangeline's face. "Since she cannot seem to live without me, I suppose that as a man of honor, I must succumb to her blandishments. I will endeavor to keep her so occupied that she will have no more time to indulge in anything more dangerous than keeping up with my son. I am certain the English Ministry will be delighted to hear that."

"Wretched man! I will tell you, my lord, it is my belief that he wishes to wed me merely because he is too tight to continue paying a governess's wages."

"As I recall, my love, the one time I managed to pay you wages, you abused me most unjustly for what you perceived, in your weak, feminine mind, as an insult."

"You were full of trickery, your grace, and well you know it!"

"I believe your mother will be pleased, Richard," Lord Pettigrew said, somewhat disconcerted by their banter. He discovered that he was somewhat disapproving of a lady's expressing herself so freely to her lord.

"Evangeline and I will travel to London tomorrow," the duke said. "I hope to induce my mother to receive her. Unlike you, Drew, we intend to wed as quickly as possible. We await only Monsieur de Beauchamps. You will support me, I trust?"

"Indeed I will, with pleasure! Just as you will, I trust, do the same for me. Now I must return to London, else I'll be in Felicia's black books. Good day, Evangeline."

"My lord," Evangeline replied. "Do say hello to Miss Storleigh for me."

Once Lord Pettigrew had left, the duke turned to

Evangeline and said in his most peremptory voice, "Come here, my dove, I have wanted to kiss you for the past hour."

"How you already begin to play the tyrant and order me about," she complained, but her feet carried her quickly across the room to him.

He caught her against him, and for a long moment, simply held her, his face buried in her hair. "I have decided to keep you," he murmured, "even if you are half French."

"Miserable man," she said without heat, as her fingers traced the line of his jaw, "I am convinced that it is my French half that desires you beyond reason."

"Then I must bring your English half into line, I see." He let his hand trail to her breast, and lightly caressed its softness. She parted her lips to him, and his mouth closed over hers.

He felt a shock of pleasure when her hand stroked lightly down his chest to his belly. Her busy fingers fluttered and stilled. "Tell me what to do," she whispered into his neck. "I am very ignorant, but I much want to please you."

"If you please me much more, I dread to think of the look on Bassick's face were he to interrupt us." He pulled her more tightly against him, trapping her hand between them. She felt his pulsing hardness through her gown and petticoat, and let her exploring fingers splay downward.

"Evangeline, for God's sake," he gasped, pulling her hand away, albeit unwillingly. "I have no wish to be seduced in the drawing room!"

She smiled up at him, her lips parted, and gazed wistfully at him. "I wish always to be with you, Richard," she said softly, and tightened her hands about his neck to draw him closer.

He said on a mock sigh, "It is a fate I suppose I must now endure. When I think of all the ladies who will be distraught now that I am no longer free to . . ."

She eyed him severely, and tapped her fingertips on his shoulder. He answered by lazily caressing his hands down her back, and her eyes took on a sleepy look. She said softly, "I rpomise to keep you so exhausted, your grace, that you will not have the strength or inclination to look elsewhere."

"Then I shall not overly repine."

She suddenly clasped him to her. "Thank you, Richard. Were it not for you, I would have never seen my father again."

He grinned ruefully. "I do hope he gives his approval, and will be willing to speak to me in the bargain."

"Why would he not? Ah, the famous rift between our families. But surely you will tell me now what happened."

"I do suppose you have that right. Actually, love, it all had to do with Marissa's dowry, a large part of which was supposedly valuable jewels. They turned out to be paste. Your uncle refused to hear of it, accusing my father of stealing the jewels to wring more money out of him. I thought my father would expire from apoplexy. He severed the ties between the Clarendons and all the Beauchamps from that day onward."

"You know, Mrs. Needle mentioned the split between our families, but she refused to tell me anything. I had been imagining all sorts of awful things."

"It seems quite silly now," he said, shaking his head. "Your father, of course, took his brother's side, which is why I never saw that terribly serious half French girl again."

"I fear, your grace," she said demurely, "that you will have to be in her company a great deal of the time now. As for my father, I think he will be so relieved that we are both safe that he will forgive your father's impertinence. It will probably bother him more that you are a prosing, boring Englishman."

"And not at all like your very exciting French husband, who, according to all accounts, was an excellent lover, and a man of great sensitivity, and——"

"I would that you be quiet, your grace!" she said, caught between embarrassment and amusement.

"That is only one way to ensure my silence, Madame," he said, and allowed her to kiss him.

Bassick stood in the doorway, a look of consternation on his face. He turned abruptly to remove Lord Edmund when that young gentleman slipped under his arm and dashed into the room.

"Papa! Why are you nuzzling Cousin Eve . . . and kissing her!"

"Forgive me, your grace," Bassick began, his face rumpling in embarrassment.

The duke slowly released her and turned to his butler and to his small son, who was staring up at him, his hands on his hips.

"Do not distress yourself, Bassick. You will please inform the staff that they will soon have a new mistress."

Bassick bowed formally toward Evangeline. "Everyone will be most pleased, your grace, most pleased."

Bassick bowed himself out of the door, and the duke looked down at his son. "Well, Edmund?"

"You were kissing her, Papa!"

The duke dropped down on his haunches. "I have no choice in the matter, son. You see, when a lady convinces a gentleman to wed her, he must do . . . certain things, else she'll feel insulted."

"Richard, you are abominable!" Evangeline dropped down to her knees and took Edmund's hand in hers. "Do you mind, Edmund? There will be few changes, you will see. And you will no longer have to suffer me as a governess."

"Actually, scamp," the duke interposed, "you'll have a mother, which is far more amusing than having a cousin or a governess."

"And we'll always be together, Edmund, just the three of us."

The duke cast her a wicked look. "She is not being

entirely honest, Edmund. Actually, I plan to give you brothers and sisters to bully."

Evangeline felt a flush of red rush to her cheeks. She wondered suddenly if she were already carrying one of Edmund's future siblings.

"When?" Edmund asked baldly.

"Just as quickly as I can manage it, son. What do you say, shall we allow her to stay?"

Edmund appeared to give his father's question weighty consideration. He at last conceded, his small fingers squeezing Evangeline's, "She never teases me, Papa, and she does swim well."

The duke grinned. "And she is full of pluck. As to her swimming, I must observe her myself in order to form an accurate judgment."

"She can swim with us if she is my new mama?"

"Most assuredly. Even without clothes."

"Very well," Edmund said in a prim voice. "But you must promise not to take her away, Papa, and leave me behind."

The duke thought of the extended wedding trip he was planning and made a swift adjustment. He shot a rueful grin toward Evangeline, who nodded enthusiastically. "I promise. You must tell Ellen now to pack your trunks. We all leave for London on the morrow."

Edmund gave a shout of pleasure and ran as fast as he could from the drawing room, yelling Ellen's name at the top of his lungs.

"You do not mind?" the duke asked. "I promise you we will be alone at night."

"Of course I do not mind. But, Richard, only at night?"

A black brow winged upward. "You shock me, Evangeline! But since you are not, after all, an innocent virgin, I suppose your show of enthusiasm is not too improper."

"As well you should know your grace!" she said, pummeling her fists lightly against his chest. She drew

up short and stammered in a suddenly shy voice, "I—
that is, I do not wish to shock you, or have you believe . . ."

"Silly wench," he said, and closed off further comment by kissing her soundly. "You will always have me
most willingly at your beck and call, whenever the need
. . arises."

She giggled, and pressed herself tightly against him.
She cupped his face between her hands, rose on her
tiptoes, and kissed him full on the mouth.

"Do you know, my love," he murmured in her ear,
"it is a glorious day, and I know of a charming spot that
would be ideal for an afternoon visit."

"It will be as you wish, your grace," she said, smiling
roguishly up at him. "If you are to be at my beck and
call, it would be most unjust of me to cavil."

About the Author

Catherine Coulter was born and raised on a ranch in Texas and educated at the University of Texas and Boston College, a background which has left her equally fond of horseback riding, Baroque music, and European history. She has traveled widely and settled for a time in England and France, where she developed a special interest in Regency England and the Napoleonic era.

Today, Catherine Coulter is both a writer and a businesswoman, living in San Francisco. She is also the author of several other Regency Romances—THE AUTUMN COUNTESS, THE REBEL BRIDE, LORD DEVERILL'S HEIR, THE GENEROUS EARL, LORD HARRY'S FOLLY, AN HONORABLE OFFER—as well as an historical romance, THE DEVIL'S EMBRACE—available in Signet editions.

A new realm of romance and passion—
in Signet's Super Regency novels . . .

The GAME of LOVE

EDITH LAYTON

author of the award-winning *Love in Disguise*
*A fiery beauty dares to yield to her passion for a
handsome stranger with a shadowy past . . .*

Beautiful Francesca Wyndham was taking a
gamble when she fell in love with Arden Lyons,
a gentleman who was clearly anything but a
gentleman when it came to winning what he
wanted: a hand of cards, a test of strength, or a
lady's favors. Though Francesca knew nothing
about this man . . . though his past was a dark
mystery . . . she dared to pit her innocence
against his expertise. It was definitely a game
where passion took all. . . .